Pretty Remedy

By S.E. Hall

© S.E.Hall 2015

S.E. Hall

 dedication

Remedy- n. something that corrects or counteracts

v. to solve, correct, or improve (something)

Everyone has that one person who is their remedy—your number one fan who doesn't need to know how many other runners were in the race, the part where you messed up, or the other person's side of the story. To them, you always win.

Your remedy is the first person you want to tell when it's funny or sad, the good news and the bad because you know their answer will be exactly what you need to hear. Their words may not hold a lesson; they may tell a bold-faced lie that sounds like bull even to you, but they'll say it, because it's what you need to hear. That's why you called them.

In return, these people should be revered. You're not too busy to answer when they call, listen when they talk, serve when they need. Cherish them. For they are few.

This book is dedicated to the remedies.

S.E. Hall

table of contents

Chapter 1 7

Chapter 2 19

Chapter 3 28

Chapter 4 38

Chapter 5 52

Chapter 6 66

Chapter 7 78

Chapter 8 97

Chapter 9 109

Chapter 10 122

Chapter 11 136

Chapter 12 151

Chapter 13 164

Chapter 14 175

Chapter 15 187

Chapter 16 200

Chapter 17 210

Chapter 18 224

Chapter 19 233

Chapter 20 244

Chapter 21 253

Chapter 22 265

Chapter 23 278

Chapter 24 290

Chapter 25 300

Chapter 26 309

Chapter 27 318

Chapter 28 329

About the Author 340

Other Books by S.E. Hall 342

Playlist...344

Acknowledgements 345

Sneak Peek of Matched 350

S.E. Hall

CHAPTER *one*

Rhett

There's nothing better than getting lost in a woman—greedy lips molded around me or warm pussy smothering my dick—either one. Take now for instance; I just finished burying myself in some pretty pink heat as she screeched and moaned my name 'til the guests in the next room felt as if they knew me personally. Then she begged to lick her essence off me and get me hard again for round two.

But we're done here. Rule #1, written in blood *and* stone: never, *ever* double dip. If they're coming back for more physically, they're coming back for more of the other stuff too… more talking, more feelings, and most definitely more expectations.

None of which I do.

"Where ya going?" Her manipulative mewl slithers down my spine like stage-five clinger fingernails on a chalkboard.

"Things to do," I answer, void of any emotion except desire—for escape. I keep my back to her as I speed-dress, slowing only at my zipper... for obvious reasons.

"But his game will last all night." I swear her voice didn't sound near as nasally downstairs. "Come back to bed, baby."

"Sorry, can't." *And I'm far from your baby.* "It'd be a real good idea for you to mosey back to Sugar Daddy or your own suite before he notices you're gone."

"W-well, when will I see you again?" The bed squeaks.

Please don't let her be getting up to come after me. All buttoned and zipped, shoes on, I turn to offer a contrived but warm parting grin and damn near knock her over. Wrapped in a sheet, she's standing an inch from me.

"You might not." I patronizingly stroke her arm. "But you already knew that, so why ask?" I'm about to call her by name, until I realize I can't remember it. *Coco's not right. Chanel maybe?* "Listen, *you.*" I nauseate myself with the syrupy condescension I'm slathering on thick. "We both had fun, and we talked about this beforehand. Besides, have you seen you?" I let my eyes travel the length of her and back up for convincing emphasis. "Women who look like you should *never* have to ask for more. It's my loss."

"Bu—"

"Sshh," I hush her, one finger on her lips. "Tell me good-bye nicely, and let me walk away. Don't make this any harder than it already is, please."

For one fleeting moment, that telltale "I got this" sparkle returns to her eyes, and the corners of her mouth lift in a knowing grin.

She *doesn't* know. Nor does she "got" anything.

She rises to her tiptoes, curls her arms around my neck, and kisses the hell out of me, putting her all into it.

For the briefest moment I allow it, and then I pull away. Another grin tugs at my lips— this one not as contrived since I'm about to make my escape—and I walk backward to the door. "Take care of yourself, beautiful." Ignoring her further, desperate attempts to convince me to stay, I soundlessly close the door to the Arabian Nights penthouse and rush down the hall, praying for the veil of anonymity.

It always happens the same way. Every. Damn. Time. The second I finish coming, the blip of exhilaration dissipates, and I'm left feeling vapid and angry. I turn my back on my latest conquest and, blocking out the images of insincere, physical satiation, scurry off like a criminal.

Maybe I should quit fucking them.

Or maybe I shouldn't.

The tête-à-têtes and unrequited clinginess are as much their fault as mine—more so in fact, if everyone's being honest with themselves. I tell them straight up, in plain English, no "code" or sidestepping what I'm *really*

9

saying, that it's *one* fuck. I offer absolutely nothing more, and they accept. But women have a specific order and purpose to everything they do. It shouldn't eat at *me* when another woman discovers her plan didn't work, and— *surprise!*—she isn't the one "different" enough to change me.

You want to be the *lady* worthy of a call the next day, flowers, *a ring*? Then don't ride the dick until you get at least one of them. And if you do jump on—gyrating and grinding in what you're just certain is some mystical, "he's never had it so good before" kind of way—and it doesn't work, don't blame anyone but yourself. Who was really trying to manipulate whom?

The walk from the penthouse to the club on the other side of the building takes less than ten minutes, and my bullshit rationalizing fades with the pulsing beat as I make my way up to the bar.

"'Bout time," JC yells over the music and slides a cold bottle of Bud my way. "Down that, then get your ass out there. Shawn'll start crying if he doesn't get help soon."

I don't give a shit about Shawn. I might actually enjoy watching him lose it, but I told Thatcher I'd help, so I drain the beer and head outside to bounce the entrance. The line's about thirty bodies too deep when I get there. Check ID, pull back rope… how hard can it be?

"Dude, where you been?" Shawn asks.

"Your mom's," I bite out, waving half his line over to mine.

"That supposed to be funny?" He bows up and quickly cowers right the fuck back down when I step to him.

I raise my brows in challenge, begging him to throw. I'm never short on pent-up aggression that could stand an excuse to escape. "Not supposed to be anything," I bite out. "You want help, or you want your ass beat? You can either fear me or respect me. I don't give a fuck which one you pick."

"Called this shit." JC's behind us, shoving Shawn in the shoulder. "Shawn, Rhett'll wipe the parking lot with you right before Thatch fires your punk ass. Shut the hell up and be grateful for the help, man. Give us a minute." JC jerks his chin, silently asking me to step aside with him, causing everyone who just moved into my line to collectively groan.

When we're out of earshot, he asks, "W'sup, Casanova? Bad night?"

If only he knew. Casanova may *seem* an appropriate nickname, and in way of random and numerous liaisons, it is. But anyone with more than a cliché knowledge of Giacomo Casanova knows he prided himself on his mastery of attentiveness, small favors, and verbal communication. He enjoyed softening a woman's heart rather than mere easy conquests. Nothing like me.

But even if I educated JC, he wouldn't "get" it, so I simply shrug. "Eh."

"Eh?" he parrots. "What the fuck is *eh*? She not any good?"

"Good enough," I answer, as curious as ever why he always finds an excuse to ask me. There aren't that many variations of pussy: really tight, tight, not tight, or *really not tight*; wet or sloppy; etc. What descriptive narrative he's always fishing for beats the hell outta me.

"Thatcher said her man was down about ten grand and possibly in lung failure from all those Cubans he tokes." JC laughs.

Her man of whom he speaks is actually *someone else's* man—another woman's husband to be precise. He's at least twenty-five years her senior, one liver spot away from officially being declared a block of head cheese, and I'm guessing at least one of his kids graduated high school around the same time as his arm-minx. Thatcher knows everything about his high rollers, and he shares their chronicles of adultery and gold-digging with me. I think venting his disgust helps absolve him of misplaced guilt. Of which he should have absolutely none. Thatcher's more straightforward with his trysts than even I am. To each their own though. It's none of my business. And since loyalty's obviously running scarce instead of rampant, I *am* able to forgive myself. At least for as long as it takes to give it to some high-rollers' girl... the way she likes it. The way she'll take it and beg for it *without* me draping her in diamonds first.

The wealthy men are cheaters who get cheated on... cry me a river of hypocrisy.

But my justifications usually stop making sense in less time than I spend fucking. *Damn conscience.* Pain in my ass.

"So how good is good enough?" JC asks, disturbing my circling thoughts.

The man needs to get laid yesterday. Guys notice very little specifics of the sex *they're actually having*, let alone ask another dude for every sordid detail of theirs. Any bragging—which isn't my style—that I've ever heard consisted of about ten words and two high-fives, tops. But JC? This kid wants a damn PowerPoint. I humor him though, because he, along with Thatcher and myself, have quite the sweet setup, and it takes all of us to keep our covert operations running smoothly.

"Are we still talking about this? Jesus, I don't know. She had all the right parts and didn't lay there like a china doll, afraid of breaking a nail or messing up her hair. That mouth of hers could siphon mud through a coffee stirrer, so like I said… good enough. Could've lived without the overdone moans and dramatized departure, but far from a waste of time."

"Nice," he drawls with a slow, impressed whistle.

"If you say so. Anyway, I'm here to work the door. How 'bout I go do that?"

"Hey, Happy, sometime today?" the chick in front of me snipes, tapping her foot impatiently, license shoved in my face. "Why would they put the *un*welcome wagon at the front door?" she asks someone behind her.

"That loud mouth of yours, I swear. Knock it off," her friend—whom I still can't see— chastises.

"Well, damn, what sense does it make to put the grumpiest motherfucker in the building at the front door?" she continues, not lacking a valid point. "Do they *want* people to turn around and leave?"

Now she's just talking out her ass. No one leaves because of me. Keep telling yourself that though, sweetheart. You and I both know I could hit it if I wanted to.

"Move." The friend gently pushes her aside and steps up.

Explains why I couldn't see her—she's the tiniest little sprite in the forest.

"I'm sorry about my friend," she says softly while pulling out her license. "She's not always so bitchy. She does sleep sometimes."

And funny... what do we have here?

I chuckle but concentrate on her laminated stats.

Reece N. Kelly

Turned twenty-one just a few days ago.

Green eyes

5'3"—my ass. Must be some of that new Common Core figuring.

Lives in Connecticut?

"Happy late birthday, Reece. This your club initiation?" I ask.

"Wh-what?" Her head pops up as she blushes beautifully, vibrant even in the dusk.

"Long way from home for some clubbing. Don't they have any of these in Connecticut?"

Mouth agape, her head turns left, right, then back at me. "How do you know all that?"

She asks so quietly, I find myself leaning in to hear her. To reply, my head dips until my mouth softly brushes her ear. "I'm holding your driver's license, small fry."

"Dear God," she groans, squeezing her eyes shut. "I can't believe I asked that." Still refusing to open her eyes, she blindly holds out the hand not rubbing her forehead. "Just hand it back to me and pretend I'm not the biggest moron alive, please."

"I'll say," her friend interrupts, grabbing Reece's arm. "Let's get all that *suave* you're workin' inside. I'm kinda in a hurry."

"Ignore her," I whisper in her ear that I've yet to leave. "She's got nothing on you." I place Reece's license back in her hand and curl her fingers around it for her, then turn her hand over. I lean back and yell, "Shawn, you got that marker?"

"Bu-but I'm twenty-one now. You saw," she argues in her miniature voice, eyes now open wide.

Laughing, I nod. "I know. Show the waitress this." I write a black twelve on the back of her hand. "Have a great time, Reece."

She looks as though she wants to question me but doesn't, silent as her friend drags her away.

I casually glance over my left shoulder, and my lips twist into a half-smile. Despite the incessant tugging on her arm, her curious eyes are pinned right on me.

CHAPTER two

Reece

Time to shove my thoughts of the hot, captivating doorman aside. My best friend needs to slow her roll before she does something she may forever regret.

"Landry." I grab her elbow, stopping her just inside the door. "Maybe—I could be wrong, but *just maybe*—you should rethink this. Do you love Stephen?" I asked that louder than I'm sure she'd like her problems announced, but even just shy of "the thick of things," the music's overbearing.

"Yes," she snaps, ripping her arm from my hold. "What kind of question is that?"

"And you want to marry him? Spend the rest of your *entire* life with *only* him?"

"Say what you have to say! We're wasting time standing here philosophizing!" she yells back.

17

To and fro, order and anarchy—that's Landry and me in an antonymous nutshell. We've been friends since before I even knew the word antonymous, and our relationship is the same push/pull today as it was way back then. Our lives are as different as we are. Landry's always apartment, city, and men bouncing, working whatever minimum wage job doesn't "bore" her that week—no, thank you. Her patented brand of "life by the seat of your panties" would send my OCD into maximum overdrive.

But I do envy her in so many other ways.

"Honey, I love you and support you no matter what, but…" I take a deep breath, deciding it needs said. "I think leaving your bachelorette party to come spy on your fiancé might be a sign that your relationship's a *tad shy* of marriage material."

There, I put it out there. What kind of best friend and maid of honor would I be if I didn't? Call me crazy, but if you don't trust him enough to leave him be at his bachelor party… does the red flag need to sing and dance too?

"Ladies." A scantily clad waitress with shiny blond hair and legs up to her neck approaches us. "Can I show you to a table?"

As tucked in the corner as I could get us, our impromptu *Lifetime* moment is still kind of blocking the walkway.

"Please." I smile at her, once again holding Landry's arm.

"Oh." The waitress's eyes grow big. "You get that twelve on your hand here?"

"I, um…" I pull my hand back and duck my face, heated with my blush. "It's nothing."

"Oh, it's something." She snorts. "You have no idea. Follow me."

"Come on," I hiss at Landry and tug her along. "We're here because of you. Feel free to take the lead anytime now."

"You stopped me, remember? I'm not here to sit at a table. I'm here to find my fiancé!"

"Let's stick together, please. What if someone—"

"They won't, or they would've already. Geez, wanna check the ego?" She shakes her head and rolls her eyes. "Seriously, chill out and attempt to have some fun!"

Before I can get a grip on her, she storms off into the massive swarm of bodies, flashing lights and deafening music—I'm not sure I'm a fan of clubs. This night won't end well. I can almost guarantee when we're reunited, I'll be picking up a once-again broken Landry and trying to piece her back together. If her gut says he's here and doing something wrong, then he is. Landry's instincts are, more often than not, spot on. She just hasn't quite mastered applying her uncanny gift to her *own* decisions yet.

She wears me out, truly, but she knows and accepts everything about me and *sometimes* gets me to have a little fun. Like tonight was supposed to be. I just turned twenty-one, which brings all kinds of freedoms I've never enjoyed.

Since she's supposedly stopped her man-hopping to get married, she talked me into coming out to Vegas for not only her bachelorette party but a much-needed break. A "let go before you really start grinding the ax" break, if you will. Her last hoorah before matrimony was the perfect reason to get me to live a little, feel my age.

Or so I thought.

But neither of us are having the time of our lives, and now, we're not even doing it together. Once the waitress leads me through the maze of sinuous mayhem to table twelve, she takes my order and saunters away, leaving me to sit, stiff and awkward, alone. I'm not exactly terrified—I'm not a prude, and there're no signs of immediate danger—just unfamiliar with the atmosphere.

Nor am I a shut-in, far from it, but meeting my life goals dominates my time and attention. Thus, my wavering level of comfort and lack of social "moves" at the door. Could I have possibly made a bigger ass of myself with the gorgeous bouncer? For crying in the night—the guy was holding my driver's license and I actually asked, *out loud*, how he knew those few things about me—like my name and birthday—often found on driver's licenses. That's not novice; that's blatant idiocy. My humiliation causes my body and face to flush, so I lift my heavy blond mane off my neck and lean back to get some fresh air... since oddly enough, this club has some weird lack-of-outside-walls thing going on.

The only things between my back and downtown Vegas right now are sheer dark red drapes and the night air. No windows, bricks, nothing. It's different, creating a sexy, exposed ambience, all while making it very easy for someone to sneak up behind you and rip you out of your seat.

Forget waiting for my drink. I rise from my seat quickly, straighten my skirt, and decide to go find Landry. I immediately realize that won't be as easy as it sounds. Bodies everywhere are tangling and sweating against each other with the shameless intimacy only alcohol can provide. Before I know it, I'm swept up into the mob.

I struggle to weave through the swarm, ignoring the far too many hands sampling a feel of my body. But I'm forced to walk backward, deeper into the mosh pit, by an obviously drunk and menacingly large man moving all up in my "I don't want to dance" space. I'm not panicked per se—surely *someone* will notice and save me if he gets too out of line—but I'm certainly uneasy.

My back hits a wall. Under any other circumstances, this would be when I'd kick, scream… something. But I instantly, instinctively, recognize this wall. The signature scent and baritone chuckle that snared my senses at the door greet me again now. My body goes lax with a security that should alarm me, and the creepy guy stops his advance, his eyes bugging out before he spins and all but runs away.

With an absurd familiarity, my hips are now being moved for me, his large, purposeful hands gripping them from behind. His rigid physique and unmistakable desire are pressed flush against my back, and all I feel is… noticed, pursued, *desired.* Some version of myself I've never met lifts her hair, hotter now than ever, and moves

21

with him. The hard but supple rocking of his hips and dig of his fingers overcome my every inhibition. It's above and beyond the sexiest, most liberated I've ever felt, swaying to the rhythm of his heartbeat, the command of his frame. One hand stays at my hip, guiding our synchronized union, while his other holds up my hair for me.

He blows up and down my neck, completely defeating any cooling purpose. "Better?" His voice is low and breathy in my ear, his head bent and lips hinting at my slightly ticklish flesh.

I nod and keep dancing, fearful what speaking aloud, which would need to be either very loud or whispered just for him, would reveal. My voice could betray me and tell him exactly what his feral proximity is doing to me. That would be bad...very bad. I don't do hookups or one-night stands; I don't even date regularly. So while I'm all too eager to surrender to this mysterious, intoxicating bubble for a few songs, that'll have to be it.

I'll give Landry time to sort out her possible catastrophe. Yeah, this is me being a helpful friend.

"Red Nose" plays, and his suggestive swagger behind me changes, not to a raunchy grind but a slower, closer—I didn't think that was possible—seduction. He releases his hold on my hair to skim his fingertips down both my arms and entrap my hands. He pulls our entwined fingers up and wraps my arms behind his neck, rendering me defenseless against the demanding instruction of his pelvis and chest— to which I submit seamlessly. He's so much larger than me, so "things" don't exactly line up how I'm sure he'd like, but our bodies still allow for his total domination. I let my eyes shut, and my head fall back, as I writhe harder against his body, lost in the moment.

"Hated this song until right now." His deep, devastatingly masculine words waft along my neck. "Now I love it. Love the way you move to it even more."

An unnamable sound, something between a squeak and a gasp, gets away from me. I'm shocked at how inviting I find his boldness. I clasp down on our joined hands, embracing the wave of sexuality washing over me. Should I say thank you? *No, definitely not.*

"You always dance with strange men like this?" he murmurs, tugging me impossibly closer to him.

I shake my head and inhale sharply as his hands move down, teasing my thighs and the hem of my skirt. *God, what am I doing?* His rough fingertips and gentle strokes have stolen any semblance of my composure.

"I believe you. Aren't you going to ask my name then?" he taunts in my ear.

I shake my head again, which he seems to thrive on, judging by his low hum.

"Leave your arms up," he growls, running his hands achingly slow up and down my sides, learning every curve of my body. They trail across my stomach, exploring. "No, huh? I'm gonna tell you anyway, tiny dancer. It's Rhett, Rhett Foster. So the man you recognized the minute he slid up behind you—which I liked very much by the way—now has a name."

Why does that name... where have I... no, I'm hearing things, or romanticizing in my head. I want to associate this moment with other things so badly that I've subconsciously done just that. He probably actually said his name was Fred Jones, right? Right. Or... lots of people have the same name. Why, I bet there's at least five-hundred Fred Joneses in the world. It's impossible, too convenient, or inconvenient depending on how you look at it, to even fathom. Then again... Vegas is a strange place.

Unable to resist another second, I glance over my shoulder at the man controlling my movements and heart rate. A tremor only believable in novels vibrates along my limbs. His eyes—which are, my best guess in this lighting, a dark blue—are clearly smoldering, and the nostrils of his strong, Romanesque nose are flared. His confidence is palpable, whereas I'm emerging from my fog and surely look like the frightened, helpless baby bunny I now feel. *I see the weed-eater coming toward my grassy hideout—yet I don't move.* Well, I move, just not away from him.

"Tell me how you knew." He smiles down at me, tracing a fingertip along my jawline, never stopping the taunt of his hips.

"Kn-knew what?" My already meek stutter fades with each syllable.

A cocky grin transforms his face from mesmerizing to indescribable. "That it was me behind you. Immediately, you knew me. How?"

Often the way a person asks you something—their inflections, how hard and fast they swallow, the desperate longing for validation in their eyes—tells you how important your answer is to them. In spite of the noise and dim lighting, somehow I'm certain that what I say next is vital to him. I'm just not sure why or how to answer. He's inviting honesty, or I'm over-thinking it and about to embarrass myself.

I open my mouth to reply, but needing a cloak, I close my eyes and bow my head.

But he won't allow that. He tilts my head back up with a finger under my chin. "No way, Teaspoon." With one powerful maneuvering of my hips, he turns my body to face him. "Tell me. Open those eyes, look at me, and say it. Make me wanna write a love song."

Damn. He's got an excellent start to one right there.

"Your laugh. I heard it outside too. But mostly… your smell," I mumble, trying to step back, my heavy breaths propelling my ample breasts against his chest. His arm snakes around my waist and hauls me back to him. "Outside, on the breeze, I-I smelled you." *Oh, sweet floor, open and swallow me whole, now or never.*

"Nuh uh, Reece, get 'em on me."

I assume he means my once-again shut eyes, so I comply. "I recognized your smell when you walked up behind me. Yes, I scented you like a pervy headcase." I bulge out my eyes and huff, exasperated and exposed. "There, happy?"

His laugh is hearty and deep, a melodic noise for which he owes God money… or maybe I do? I stare at him, speechless—which isn't unusual for me. The way the sound permeates my chest and tickles whatever parts make you happy to be alive—that's a bit unnerving.

"I need a drink," I blurt, overwhelmed by my inexplicable draw to him, and spin to march away. The tinge of liquid calm will round off my edges, but I'm stopped by an authoritative hand at my elbow.

Ominous, smoky words rumble at me from behind. "Drink, fine. Prancing away, alone, through a bar? Not happening. Let's go." He moves in front of me to pilot, interlacing our fingers. "I wrote that number on your hand for a reason. I wanna know where you are. You're quite the wanderer."

Yes, yes, I should scream and be completely freaked out by my bossy stranger… yet I'm only beguiled and tingly. "Do all your table twelve girls just do what you say?" I yell over the music.

He turns toward me with the wickedest of grins. "Do you want to hear you're the first girl I've ever marked?"

"Not if it isn't true."

"Then let's go get you that drink."

That was my cue to rip my hand from his, tear my eyes away from his tight ass, and storm away, insulted. Guess I should brush up on taking cues, 'cause I'm still following him.

The bartender serves us immediately—I assume because Rhett works here—and I order a Long Island iced tea. *Go big, Reece. You're gonna puke from nerves soon anyway.*

"There you are!" Landry's shriek pierces through all the noise I'd blocked out, brutally interrupting the Rhett-induced fog I wasn't ready to leave. "He's here, fucking with some redheaded waitress. I knew it!"

CHAPTER three

Rhett

I'd long since decided I don't like the friend and should ignore her, but On Tap only employs one waitress with red hair, so I have no choice but to eavesdrop on her blathering. JC evidently overheard as well. He leans over the bar, zoned in and shooting me an apprehensive look.

"What was your name again?" I ask her, my hand on Reece's hip. I'm ready for this chick to get gone so I can slide my hand around other places.

"Landry. You need to know that why?" she sneers.

I feel Reece tense under my touch.

"Hey," Reece says far too sweetly, rubbing her friend's arm, "it's not his fault, be nice. What'd you see, Lan? You want to leave?"

Also not happening. I dig my fingers into her luscious curve and pull her body into mine. The only place Reece is going tonight is underneath me.

"Hell no, I don't wanna leave," Landry says. "I'm gonna confront them both. I just have to wait 'til she gets a break or whatever and they actually hook up, so I can bust 'em in the act."

"Are you sure he's not just drunk and flirting a little too much?" Reece reasons, as I grow increasingly impatient.

"Well, let's see. Last week, when I searched his phone, the lovely snatch sext I found was from a ginger. And whadda ya know, the waitress who tongue-fucked his ear while his hand was up her skirt is...also a ginger! You tell me!"

Now it's officially my business.

"Jarrett's here tonight, man," JC mutters. "Up in VIP."

"Landry," I snarl, "*who* is this *he* with his hand up skirts?"

"What's with this guy?" she asks Reece, jerking a thumb my way.

"I, uh..." Reece's eyes flit between Landry and me as she searches for words, so I rescue her.

"The *one* redheaded waitress who works here just so happens to be my brother's girlfriend," I say. "So I'm interested in why *you're* interested in tracking Jarrett's hand, or I'm more than a little puzzled as to who the fuck's hand you're actually tracking. Feel me?"

Reece gasps, and her eyes fill with a sympathy that makes my skin crawl.

"My fiancé!" Landry screams, tears following.

"Fuckkk," JC drones, sweeping a hand down his face. "Some bachelor party booked Vanessa's section. That's why Jarrett's perched in VIP. Eagle-eye view."

"Now wait," Reece blusters, squirming out of my hold to lay a hand on mine and Landry's shoulders. "Let's not jump to any conclusions. Landry, show us."

"Fuck that. Grab your drink and follow me," I demand, pulling Reece toward the stairs to the VIP section. There'll be no vigilante, crazy-female bullshit breaking my brother's heart until I've surveyed the situation. Guys get drunk, and Ness plays friendly to make tips. Doesn't mean anything more than that… yet.

Reece talks to Landry as we approach the stairs. "M-maybe it was a different girl's hoo-ha in the picture, which p.s., is reason enough to have already canceled the wedding. And maybe this Jarred—"

"Jarrett," I correct. "Up, both of you."

I gesture for Landry to take the steps ahead of us, then guide Reece with a hand at the small of her back. I follow them, distracted as all hell. Despite possessing the certainty of a newborn fawn, the way Reece climbs stairs is lethal to any other thoughts. From the small amount of information I've gathered thus far, I've got a crisp hundo that says Landry dressed her tonight. So far, that's the *only* point in Landry's favor.

No way did my shy teeny-meeny paint that skirt over her ripe peach of an ass of her own accord. Nor did she decide the top that droops just low enough in both the front and back to lure me in was a good idea. The propped-up sandal things on her feet though? *Those* she picked—hoping amongst hopes to appear the bullshit 5'3" she claims on her license—and they're doing crazy nice things for her toned calves and thighs. No question, Reece is white-flame fucking hot in the most fascinatingly fun-sized kind of way.

I did not just think *spinner*.

When we reach the top, my private screening of *"This* is how to climb stairs, ladies" over, I return my palm to the dip of her back and lead her to the corner booth. Jarrett sits nearby, his eyes trained on something that's causing lines of worry to case them.

"Brother?" I clap him on the shoulder, but he doesn't even notice. "Jarrett, can I get a second? Slide in," I prompt Reece, who clamps on to Landry's hand and drags her into the booth beside her. "Jar—"

"What?" He turns toward me, deep creases in his brow, hair sticking up, bulbous blood vessels looking about to pop. "What the fuck do you need right this goddamn minute?"

"Your girl stepping out?" I ask calmly, more than willing to bear the brunt of his anger.

"I'm not airing my shit in front of tonight's pussy platter. Jesus, Rhett, not cool. Gimme a shout when you're done and we'll talk."

"First of all, watch your mouth," I scold him like the lil' shit he's acting. He knows better than to call me out or disrespect a woman, regardless of what he *thinks* he knows about her. "Apologize to Reece"—I indicate her with a tip of my head—"and might wanna do the same to her friend. Thinkin' you two are about to have a lot to discuss."

"Seriously, bro? I'm a little fucking busy for this shit. Nessy's messing with some needledick motherfucker down there!"

"Hey!" Landry screeches, slamming both hands flat on the table. "He's *not* a needledick! If he was, I wouldn't care that he's messin' around with *your whore*! And I'm not his pussy"—she stabs a finger in my direction—"and Reece isn't ever *anybody's* pussy, so shut it, prick! You're not the only one with problems!"

And then there's that. I may have seriously misjudged Landry; she's up to two points. I want to fix the crimson shade of mortification on Reece's cheeks though. "Get up, come sit over here," I grate at Landry and pull out the chair closest to me.

"What? I'm not moving. Didn't you hear me? Reece doesn't—"

"Landry, quit talking and move your ass," Reece snaps, looking at the table of course, but still pretty forceful and hot as hell.

Landry's slow to rise, her skeptical eyes boring into me, and she *hip checks* me as she crosses in front of me. There's definitely something about her growing on me. She flounces down in the chair beside Jarrett as I slide in with Reece and lay my hand on her trembling knee.

"Hey." I give her leg a squeeze. "Why are you shaking?"

She turns her face slightly toward my own, her head dipped so that her golden hair falls over us. "Landry's, well…" She sighs, lifting her eyes to mine. "A loose cannon. If the miraculous bout of stability her engagement brought on turns out to be a hoax, her fallout will be considerable."

"Jarrett'll be crushed too," I empathize, unashamedly staring at her tiny but plump lips. They're so temptingly close, I could trace them with my tongue without even moving.

"No, you don't understand. Landry won't get sad. She'll get crazy, self-destructive."

"Hmm." I'm unsure what to say. Another thing of which I'm positive—having known Reece for a minute— Landry's problems will be made Reece's. "Let's worry when we have to, huh?" I smile and squeeze her knee again, some of the worry sliding off her face as she agrees. "What'd you two figure out over there?" I say louder, to get Fred and Velma's attention.

"Reece, is it?" Jarrett asks her, civility reinstated. She nods and he continues. "I apologize for my crude, unfair behavior. Won't happen again."

"Apology accepted, thank you," she rushes out, diving into her drink.

"Vanessa's break's in ten minutes. So we'll see. She doesn't know I'm here. Didn't get the chance to mention it before I walked up on her eating some dude's ear. Left the way I came, been sitting here watching ever since." He sighs, and I want to kill all responsible for the agonized look on his face. "Only one place to hide and play here, so if she takes him to the closet beside the game room, you're bailing me out tonight."

"*That's* your move?" I ask. "This guy may not even know you exist, and *he's* damn sure not the one who owes you any loyalty or explanation. You're going straight for him?"

"Well Rhett, I can't exactly hit her, now can I?"

"You could talk to her first, rather than spend a night in jail and leave her wide open to spend it with him. Unless he knew. Then, by all means, whip his ass. But you're only gonna figure that out by talking to Ness."

"Or"—Landry sits up straighter, holding up a finger—"we could act like we know nothing and fuck around on them right back!"

"Told you," Reece whispers to me, and I can't help but laugh. Then she goes right back to draining her seven-liquor tea.

"That might work." My brother drops his voice and his eyes, working the latter up and down Landry. "I could so get with that plan."

It seems his bereavement period may be speedier than I thought.

"Alright then." She giggles and stands, giving him her hand. "Let's go gather our 'reason we fuck now' evidence, shall we?"

"We shall." Jarrett grins, the first genuine one since we arrived, and accepts her hand. "Be back," he says to me and heads off on his mission.

"Jar," I holler and he looks back. "Don't start shit in here, man. Respect for Thatcher at least, yes?"

His head jerks in agreement and they're gone, leaving me to Reece. *Or Reece to me.*

"Finally," I exhale. "I could use a little R&R."

"I bet. After all this, I'm thinking about some rest and relaxation myself."

"That sounds good too, but I meant Rhett and Reece." I give her a wink; fuck it, works for other guys, and I'm in unfamiliar territory here. I never "talk," but this girl demands it… without ever demanding it.

"So you work here?" she asks timidly, eyes once again aimed at the table.

"If we're gonna talk," I tease with a lighthearted laugh as I slide out of the booth and back in across from her, "let's do it like this, where you're more prone to actually look at me. Wh—" My mouth gapes as I wipe my face. "Did you just flick your drink on me?"

"That I did." She giggles, her face lighting up with a smile that disparages the sun.

"You done?" I challenge her. "If so, I'll answer your question. No, I don't work here." Elbows propped on the table, I steeple my fingers and rest my chin on them, eyeing her pointedly.

"Then why were you at the door?" She goes in for a last, desperate slurp from her empty glass.

I wave to grab JC's attention and point at her, then mouth "beer for me," to which he nods. "The bartender you sorta met earlier? That's my friend JC, and my other buddy Thatcher manages this place. So when someone calls in or whatever, I help them out. They return the favor when I need it."

"What favors do you need?" She looks up and to the side, where Kelsey's approaching with our order.

I toss a quick glare at JC, who's watching and laughing his ass off. *Prick.*

"Hey, Rhett." Kelsey lets the words drip out her mouth as she leans over twice as far as needed to set down my beer, her tits threatening to fall out her shirt. "Is this all you need? I can help with anything"—she offers Reece a snarky grin—"again."

"I don't care if you've slept with him." Reece shrugs. "I just met him. So less snarky and more *my drinky* would be great."

Oh, fuck me! My head falls back, my laugh a pleasantly surprised and very impressed howl that takes me minutes from which to recover. When I do, I lock eyes with Kelsey and growl. "Watch that shit, or you'll be gone, understand?"

"Whatever." She slams Reece's glass down in front of her and stomps off.

"That was pretty kickass, Teaspoon. You're just full of surprises." I tip back my bottle, watching her over the end of it.

"You really can go chase her or make plans to, uh, whatever. You aren't obligated to watch over me until Landry gets back."

"I appreciate that"—my lip twitches in amusement—"but I'll pass. Even if you weren't here, she'd still be a no." I reach across the table for her hand and brush my thumb on the underside of her wrist. "You, however, are very much a yes."

CHAPTER *four*

Reece

The most illicit, mysterious night of my life... nothing more than mundane solicitation. "I wouldn't mind hanging out with you a little bit longer, but then I need to find Landry and head home. *With her.*"

His eyes narrow as he rubs his jaw in silent consideration. He wants me. Admittedly, I am madly attracted to him, but even if I'd known him longer than say, five minutes, I can't and won't do a thing about it.

"Alright." His eyes, which are indeed an indefinite shade of blue, and posture defrost. "Let's talk." His expression glazes over with wolfish assuredness, marring what I'd almost been sure was the most handsome face I'd ever seen.

Why do I get the feeling he thinks he's doing me a favor, confident that he's simply postponing the inevitable?

He should stick to doors and dance floors, because his charm elsewhere is severely lacking.

"You know what? Never mind, I'm ready to go. Let's see if we can find Landry and your brother."

"So soon?" He tilts a brow.

"You're not interested in talking to me. You're interesting in patronizing me out of my panties."

"Patronizing isn't the right word, and surprisingly, I'm interested in both your conversation and your panties."

"I had fun. The dance was *something*." I stand and he sighs as he does the same. "But it's time for me to go."

He says nothing, those dictatorial hands of his once again leading me back to the bar and JC, which I tolerate. Tolerate isn't the right word either; I absorb it, despite my disappointment in the predictable turn of events.

"You seen Jarrett?" he asks JC when he's able to snare his attention.

"Uh yeah, about that. He didn't tell you?"

"Tell me what?" Rhett snaps.

"Vanessa clocked out and they all left. Your friend too." He nods my way with a worried frown.

"That can't be right," I squawk, retrieving my phone from my cleavage as discreetly as possible. "She can't just leave me. I..." Her voicemail drones in my ear. I press Call a second time, my frustration and panic soaring to threatening levels so suddenly I think I may vomit.

"Voicemail!" I inform… possibly *everyone* in the bar. "She can't! I don't live in this town, or have my purse, or—"

Rhett stops me just short of hyperventilation with a soothing smile and stroke of his hand on my cheek. "Stay with me. You were going to anyway."

"No, I wasn't," I huff, tempted to slap the predatory smirk off his face. "Let me try again."

I cower from his touch and turn away, stabbing at Call so hard my fingernail bends. Voicemail. I feel tears building in my eyes as I sniffle, typing out a text.

Me: Where r u? I have no purse, car or your address! Come get me!

I wait, watching my phone as though the answer to all of life's riddles will flash across the screen at any second. After at least five minutes, I suck back the tears and turn to face defeat… and him. "What am I supposed to do now?"

He scrubs a hand over his face and blows out a grumpy, annoyed breath. "Again, more than welcome to stay the night with me." I'm already shaking my head no before he's finished. "Okay then. JC?" Rhett leans across the bar, the two of them having a quick conversation I can't hear, then Rhett looks back at me. "You're all set. JC's gonna help ya out."

"What? Where are you going?" I cringe at the sound of my vulnerability.

"I got something I need to take care of, but you're in good hands, I swear." He gives me a soft chin knock. "It was nice meeting you, Reece. Sorry your friend did this to you."

And then he's walking away. I watch, absolutely dumfounded. I'm sure he thinks he's far enough into the crowd to blend in, which he's isn't, when his arm slides around his new, curvy companion. I bristle with contempt at... myself. *To think*, I was feeling guilty, without *concrete evidence even,* actually considering risking it all to be candid with the alluring... cold-hearted, single-minded stranger!

"Reece?" JC touches my shoulder, gentleman enough to taper the pity in his voice.

I spin to face him, stranded and pathetic, never feeling more helpless in my life.

"Listen, our friend Thatcher's the pit boss at the casino on the other side of this place. Let's walk over and he'll comp you a room for the night. You can track down your friend in the morning. Rhett'll meet us there."

I have no other real options. Could I call home for a rescue? Out. Of. The. Question. I'm so not in the mood for an "I told ya so" or an actual full-throttle rescue, which Ozzie's would be. If I chance finding my own hotel for the night, the clerk there or cabbie on the ride over may be far worse than the jerk who just abandoned me for his guaranteed piece of ass. And oh yeah, I don't have my purse to pay for either anyway!

"No, he won't. I saw her," I mumble, trudging along behind JC. *Well, not her face, but her body was phenomenal enough, even from afar, that I don't really blame him.*

"I got you the Garden of Eden suite. Sixth floor, elevator's right over there." JC points. "You want me to take you up?"

He's being gallant, genuinely asking with no hidden agenda—unlike his friend.

"No, I'll be fine. And thank you, JC. I really appreciate it. As soon as I have my stuff, I'll pay you back."

"It's no problem. My pleasure, in fact. Don't worry about paying back anything that didn't cost anyone a thing. Have a good night." He smiles, gives my shoulder a quick, jovial rub, and hustles away. He's probably not supposed to leave the bar.

I ignore the elevator, head for the door marked Stairs, and start the daunting climb up six flights. That gives me just enough time to stew on Landry's bitch move and Rhett's dick one. I can't decide who I'm more disappointed in, as unsettling as that is shocking. He seemed... kind and charming in a perfectly balanced broody, sexy way. Well, to hell with his phony, presumptuous ass! And Landry? This is way beyond her usual scope of flaky.

When I reach the sixth floor, I walk the hall without hurry, more engrossed in the titles on each door than my weariness and aching feet. All these rooms are themed, and I can't help but wonder what lies within each. Eh, except that one—Dungeons and Dragons—I'd rather not know.

I almost miss the fact that I've arrived at my room because I'm caught up in the music coming from one suite over—"Hawaiian Delight." It's that version of "Somewhere Over The Rainbow" sung by the guy with an "I something K something" name no one can pronounce, and I tap my foot with a bona fide smile. Even after all the unpleasant curveballs thrown at me tonight, I did manage to inadvertently upgrade my vacation from Landry's couch to a free night in a lush Vegas hotel. No one telling me I can't do something or breathing down my neck with self-serving advisement.

Not that I'm letting Landry off the hook by any means. For all she knows, I could be bedding down tonight in a dumpster, beaten and/or dead.

But enough with the unhappy thoughts. The Garden of Eden's gonna be awesome, and I enter slowly, breath held in anticipation. I flip on the light and shut the door, gasping in enchantment. It's amazing! The walls perfectly depict a garden, an inset whirlpool tub fills a corner right out in the open, and a humongous bed dressed in black and red is in the center. There's even a single bottle of champagne on chill- a special touch I suspect JC knew I'd appreciate after the night I've had. I love the room and totally get it—temptation the obvious message.

A noise that I never make escapes me. *No, not me at all.* My head jerks to the right as I hear it again. The music ends, and the sounds of feminine pleasure coming from next door are unmistakable. Already trying all kinds of uncharacteristic things tonight, I tiptoe—which is ludicrous, since I'm pretty sure I could River Dance in army boots and they wouldn't notice—over to the wall and plant my ear against it. When in the room of temptation and tempted…

I'm no expert, not even close, but I'm still calling bullshit on this chick. No one *actually* gets it like that… outside of a Kindle anyway.

"Harder!" she yelps.

Harder? The floor under *me* is shaking! Not that I'm counting, but three headboard bangs and artificial squeals later, I hear *him*. His carnal grunts in primal bass have my body flushing and panties damp. It's the most uninhibited, hypnotizing sound that's ever teased my ears, and I'd give anything to one day have a sweaty beast of a man making it for me.

Forget my premature astonishment. The Garden of Eden's about as divine as plucking out my nose hairs with tweezers! I took a hot bubble bath as she begged for round two, and as far as I could decipher, he placated her by graciously "allowing" her to give him a blowjob. I even tried to play music in my room while she begged for "that big cock." Again, he refused her, but the pan-flute nonsense just made me feel worse.

Curiouser and curiouser... he won't take off his shirt, and she's offered up everything but the cherry—I'm guessing she lost a *longggggg* time ago—on top or her firstborn to make it happen. If she blubbers about it one more time, I'm gonna go toss my own damn shirt in her face.

He probably has backne. Such a shame, 'cause the indecently sensual noises he makes when he gets off are not ones I'd pin on a guy whose back is covered in boils. Has to be it though. Why else would it be such a big deal when he obviously has no problem dropping his pants like they're hot?

I'm *almost* feeling sorry for him, his shrew refusing to be tamed, but at her pouty, "My ass doesn't count as twice, do me in my ass," I. AM. DONE. No sympathy and no more tolerance! If my gluttonous room service order hadn't just arrived, I'd be marching over there and giving those Hawaiian tourists an earful.

As aggravated as I am horny and jealous, I snag the robe off its hook, jam my arms in the sleeves, tie it around my waist tight enough to risk loss of airflow, and storm to the door. Jerking it open, I offer the delivery guy a forced smile, indicating with my arm for him to wheel in the tray. I thank him and tip with the five dollars I have left on my person, fully planning to make Landry pay for the food I charged to the room if and when she gets here. I'm *seconds*

S.E. Hall

from closing the door behind him and gorging until I fall asleep when their "door of debauchery" opens.

Out comes one petulant, swelled-lipped Penny Parsons, and she stomps down the hall. If my jaw wasn't on the floor, I'd laugh, a vindicating gut release filled with love for Karma. You can't walk by a newsstand or magazine rack, turn on the TV, or get on the internet without being force-fed Madame Perfect Pants... and I just had house seats to her ass—where he wouldn't "do her"— being patronized then dismissed! The infamous Penny Parsons *thwarted*... oh, if my mood didn't just perk right the hell up!

Red and yellow, black and white, we are all precious in his sight! Jesus loves average girls who haven't been tucked, stuffed and fluffed, and every once in a while, when he's afraid we might actually drown in our tubs of ice cream—he reminds us of such! I'm feeling rather happy with the balance of the world, a huge smile of restored faith on my face, when out *he* steps.

Rhett.

Still working on zipping up his fly no less!

I should move—duck back into the safety of my room, blend in with the door, *or something*—yet I don't move. I'm literally frozen in place.

The guy I deep down wanted to have sex with but wouldn't have sex with—I feel as if I just had sex with. Well, I feel as dirty and used, more so perhaps, as I would've if I'd actually slept with him. He's vastly different from who I hoped, and was still holding out some silver of optimism, he was. Every groan, every deliciously rumbled command he gave her, suddenly feel even more up close… and acutely intimate.

"What are *you* doing here?" he snarls, barging into my space, his dark blue eyes blazing.

Too bad. When he's not grumbling loathsomely at me, or disturbing the tranquility of Eden with his undignified "one time only" antics, he's actually quite dazzling. His hair's tousled, tan skin dewy from exertion, and I can smell the sex on him. It's as sickening as it is primal and dizzying.

"JC gave me this room." I cross my arms and shift my weight to one side, hip jutting out in insolence. "I realize you spent some brain cells in there"—my eyes cut to his door—"but Landry and your brother took off, *right before you did*, and I'm kind of stranded. Ringing any bells?"

He continues to exhale hotly through his nose, jaw muscle twitching as he tries to grind his teeth to dust, and says nothing.

So I go on. "Syphilis—that's the one that affects your mind the worst. *Please* tell me you have a punch card at the free clinic?"

"Jealous?" He leans into me, challenge rolling off him in torrential waves.

"Of *one* shot at an STD? Is that a real question?" *Who am I right now?* It's like I have rabies, cruel, none-of-my-business cut-downs frothing out my mouth. He was charismatic and helpful *most* of the night and certainly had no obligations to babysit me any longer than he did. Granted, his tone could've been a little less abrasive when he spotted me standing here, but my level of spiteful antagonism still feels a bit over the top.

Wait, *why* am I defending him?

"No, no question. I'm positive I already know the answer. I assume most women *are* jealous of Kim though," he jabs back.

"Her name is Penny, you jackass. Hope your *skills* are better than your memory." *See? I'm begging for a fight, and I'm not a very good fighter.*

One arm shoots up, hand braced on the wall beside my head, caging me in before I can move, let alone bob and weave. "How dare you judge me, you uptight, needin' fucked lil' priss."

I suck in a huge, appalled breath and bite the inside of my cheek, silently warning my eyes that I'll poke them out myself if they dare water.

"These suites are five hundred dollars a night. JC should've given you a third-floor room or something." He rolls those eyes I no longer think are striking as one corner of his mouth coils in disgust. "Great." He runs a hand backward through his short, raven-colored hair. "Thatch'll love this."

I would normally crumble into a blubbery mess once the door was closed behind me, but not tonight. No, tonight, my defenses are beyond up, and I'm committed to the verbal spar; no backing down now. I've endured being abandoned in an unfamiliar city by my best friend, made to suffer through the acoustic play-by-play of his tactless sexcapades, and apparently been offered a room too good for me. Not to mention I'd not only had a few drinks downstairs, but since helped myself to some of the champagne in said room—shit, remind me to make Landry pay for that too—so I've got liquid courage flowing through my bloodstream.

Indignation blooms fast and furious in my chest, and my mouth once again runs amuck. "Ya know what, *Don Juan*? I appreciate the room, but having said that…" I gulp, searching my non-existent reservoir of scathing words, having already spewed more than I knew I knew. "Well, fuck you very much! My boobs are as real as my brain *and* my morals. A *real* man would know that makes me *seventh*-floor worthy! I belong on the low-rent third floor with the blue light specials about as much as you belong in, in a fairytale!" My chest heaves up and down when I fall silent, at a loss. I've never given a staggeringly handsome man a tongue lashing before. Do I storm away? Say more? I'm unsure of the protocol.

"And then there's that." He laughs softly, his bemused stare transfixed on what I'm sure is my enflamed face.

"There's what?" I ask, baffled. One second we're dancing, then holding what I thought was an amicable conversation, next we're screaming and insulting each other for reasons unknown, and for the grand finale, he's back to flirting! I don't pretend to know the ins and outs of courtship, but I'd venture to say… this isn't how it's done.

"Intelligible wit and substance, two things I haven't encountered in way too long. You're this big." He squints one eye and holds up a small gap with his thumb and index finger. "Very deceiving wrapping for so much content."

I shrug, unsure if he's speaking rhetorically... or what the appropriate response is if he's not.

"Then again"—his head tilts, as though he's deliberating—"few things have the insides to justify their shiny outsides, so add 'standing corrected' to the list."

Not the worst thing he's said...

"So, um"—I fidget, subtly backing through my open door—"can I stay here, or do I need to move to the third floor?" I hold up a hand when his mouth opens. "I'm extremely grateful for any room you can spare, and I'm sorry for what I said earlier. I'm sure there're some very lovely women down there. Not what I meant at all."

"Not what I meant at all either. Nor would I be apologizing to people who didn't even hear me." He smirks then takes me completely aback—to the point I flinch—by tapping the end of my nose. "Stay true to yourself, and quit judging me, spouting off things you don't mean and will berate yourself for saying later." Eyes back to their stunning shade of blue with an extra twinkle thrown in, he leans farther into me. "And in the interest of staying true, admit it—you listened the whole time, wondering how I'd feel on you, in you, what dirty things I'd make you do." With one cocked brow, he goads me to argue or deny it, as sure of my inner thoughts as he is accurate. "I'd be grumpy too. Enjoy the room, Teaspoon."

Just like that, he turns and leaves, mumbling what I think sounded like, "Maybe I should quit fucking them." I shake off my wonderment and retreat into my free garden. As I lie in the wasted, beautifully provocative bed and stare at the ceiling, I think of anything and everything I can…besides this weird-as-hell night.

I guess what they say about Vegas is more than some catchy slogan—anything can happen.

CHAPTER *five*

Rhett

When the scalding shower's all but burned off my top layer of skin and doused any remnants of inane, desolate sex off me, I collapse on my bed and will my brain to turn off long enough to allow my body some rest. Any time I try to sleep, no matter how physically exhausted I am, my mind insists on reeling and fighting against me.

I detest "victims" who hobble around on mental crutches their whole life, yet here I lay, haunted and bitter. Every single reason I have to be a cynical asshole, I wear like my very own heavy wooden cross to bear.

I'm a replica of that which I loathe.

And I've never been good at alone. Leads to thinking. Which is exactly why, when Reece made it clear I'd be spending the night without her, I ensured that didn't equate to *alone*.

The minute Reece turned her back to make a phone call and what's-her-name sidled by, I knew I'd make the wrong decision, the "Rhett" decision—pussy over propriety. I might've stood a chance if she'd been *anyone* else, but I'd had my eye on that particular prize for the last few weeks, ever since she started coming around, shooting a... I don't care—in Vegas. A centerfold three times running, her pictures keep boys and grown men alike, the world over, from being able to sleep on their stomachs. And the guy most often at her side—young, single and a renowned "Most Eligible Bachelor"—turned the *real* challenge into theft, which appealed to my baser competitiveness even more than simply getting my dick in her.

"You as bored as I am?" she asks in throaty, feminine invitation.

"I could get that way. Why do you ask?" I shoot her a look of interest from the corner of my eye.

"You've had more than one eye on me for a while now. Wanna find out?" Her hand brushes my ass while her saucy eyes reel me in.

"And your bachelor?" I ask, purely for vexing foreplay. I'm unconcerned with the answer.

She holds up her pinkie finger and wiggles it, a faux pout on her lips. "Not even worth slipping off both pant legs. But you—"

"Give me fifteen minutes." I slide the card from my pocket and slip it into her hand while making a show of an

obligatory hug and kiss to each cheek for a high-profile patron. "Hawaiian Delight Suite, sixth floor."

"I don't get kept waiting." She walks backward. "I'm going now, and if I turn around and you're not right behind me, don't ever bothering looking again."

You know what I chose, portraying the role of vapid puppet impeccably.

What it all boils down to is bitterness. Envy is a silent, cold-blooded killer, extinguishing a little more life from me every day. I *envy* Liz, my once best friend and only girl I've ever paid prose to. We grew up as neighbors, inseparable, and not too long ago, I thought we were each other's everything. Both from affluent families with money to blow and the mutual burning desire to flee our town of misery as fast as possible, we spent years on the road together in our semi-serious band, See You Next Tuesday. But one new *male* guitarist later, she finally found her "where I'm supposed to be," and well... I'm not on the road in a band anymore, now am I?

I'm jealous as hell of my brother, Jarrett. *Also* while in the band, he met Vanessa—and immediately took to walking on air. Even now, with that seemingly serious romance burnt to ashes, he's already giving off vibes of an expeditious comeback. A perpetual "happy-go-lucky fucker," the cruel wrath of what our father "knew best" never quite penetrated or tainted Jarrett's internal makeup. As it did mine.

I'm resentful of every band and its every member booked at the casino; they're on stage, doing what they love. Hell, even on the nights I too take the stage, they're happier—trust me. Life is making a fool of me, and one thing I'd like to think I'm not, is a fool.

Yet before the thought's complete, *foolishly*, I cave, roll to my side, and open the nightstand drawer. Letting the sleeping pill dissolve under my tongue, immune now to the metallic taste (much like sucking on pennies), I close my eyes and try to erase the many different images of Reece that play on the backs of my lids. The sultry version, her complete abandon as she submitted, mind and body, to our dance; her playful smile when we talked; the look of fear and disappointment as I "offloaded" her onto JC to pursue a meaningless fuck, and my personal favorite—her sassy mouth and jealous-as-all-hell scowl in the hall.

Which reminds me—JC thinks he's a funny man, putting Reece in the room right beside the one he knew damn good and well I'd be using. Or perhaps that was his clever way of earning her favor? He'd best think the fuck again; Reece isn't an option for him. She apparently isn't an option for me either. Fine, but that means we're *all* a no.

I'm backpedaling, getting myself worked up over a chick? One I barely know and whose tricks aren't that original—be the girl who stands out among the masses by shooting me down, making me chase it—but they worked, didn't they? I'm lying here thinking about her instead of the one I just banged. Obviously I need rest, so I try to dismiss all thoughts and regrets and conjure up some new song lyrics until sleep takes mercy upon me.

In what I'd swear is only minutes after I'd finally fallen asleep, the repetitive trill of my phone—more specifically the annoying "Your brother's calling" ringtone Jarrett found and programmed in—wakes me. Groggier than normal, I grapple around blindly and hear the damn thing hit the floor.

"Fuck!" I sit up, scrubbing my hands over my face in hopes of moderate coherency, and stretch to reach the— once more for shits and giggles—*ringing* phone.

"What?" I yell in his ear, falling back on my pillow. Wasted movement, because there's not a doubt in my mind that this call, no matter how it begins, will end with me leaving my apartment.

"Bro, I've had enough screaming for, well, ever. Listen, I need your help."

"With what? Shit, what time is it? Where are you?"

"Quit yelling. My head's about to split open, okay?"

"Okay, buttercup," I reply in sarcastic, but hushed, mockery. "Can you please enlighten me as to your location?"

"I'm outside the police station, in Landry's car."

Well, I'm up now. I have a newfound clarity in spite of the sleeping aid. "Explain to me your route from Point A to Point Pokey. What the hell, Jarrett?"

"Vanessa called the cops, said she felt threatened while she was at my place packing her shit. I *was* buzzing, and a picture of us *may* have flown across the room and accidentally hit the wall." He heaves out a sigh, more dejection than anger. "So they hauled me in. Landry posted bail and talked to her dickhead. He's gonna make himself scarce for a while, let Landry get her stuff out of their place in peace. I mean, he got Ness, so of course he's happy and cooperative."

"Hey!" Landry protests in the background, accompanied by what I'm pretty sure is a slap on his arm.

"I didn't mean it like that," he coddles her in some voice I don't ever want to hear again.

"So, go get her stuff. Why am I awake?"

"She's got big furniture. *She* can't lift it, and I'm pretty sure Dickwrinkle won't help me. Come on, Rhett. If it was pussy, you'd already be there. Oh, and Landry wants you to bring the smokin' hot midget with you. By the way, I get the whole spinner thing, but no way you'll be able to sixty—ow! The fuck, woman?" He got slapped again.

"Bring Reece!" Landry yells and Jarrett winces, shushing her volume. "I need her!"

"Don't say shit like that about her again, or you'll *wish* it was Landry hitting you, yes?"

"My bad, I meant little person."

"Yeah, 'cause *that's* the part I was worried about." I shake my head.

"Sorry, geez, you could probably make sixty-nine work," he grumbles.

"Just stop, you're gonna sprain something. And watch it, I'm not kidding."

He doesn't need to respond further; he already knows.

"And Reece isn't with me. She's in a suite at Goldsbury and I'm at home," I grit through a clenched jaw, especially aggravated because… you tell me, and we'll both know.

"She's what?" The struggle for the phone's audible, then Landry's squawking in my ear. "I trusted you with her and you left her *alone* in a hotel in Vegas? What the fuck is wrong with you? Reece's not, she doesn't—"

"*Me*? You don't even know me, and I was trusted? Last time I checked, Reece is a grown woman who not once asked for a sitter." Quite the opposite in fact. She made it amply clear that her night with me ended… right when it ended. "Just calm down. I'll go get her and we'll meet you there. Text me the address. And maybe look around for a mirror there, *best friend.* She trusted *you* not to leave her at all!"

"Who is it?" her sleepy voice finally calls out after I've been lightly knocking for at least five minutes.

"It's Rhett," I whisper into the door seam. I don't need all of floor six to wake up and witness this.

"Are you *high* or *lost*?" she asks haughtily. "No way am I opening this door to you."

I turn my head at the chuckle behind me. There's Thatcher in his black boss suit, looking sharp, unlike me, and making his way over with a patronizing grin. "Problem? Saw ya on the monitor. You know, if we need to revisit what DL means, I can make time for that." He claps me on the shoulder with one hand, straightening his tie with the other.

"Who's out there with you?" Reece hisses. "A gang bang is more likely to be had next door, if you can wrangle up another supermodel."

Thatcher's eyebrows shoot halfway up his forehead as he bites in his laugh. "You need help?"

"No." I bang my head against the door and leave it there. "Tea, open up. The boss is out here and I can't have this scene in the hallway. Landry needs you. She sent me to come get you."

"She knows my number. Why didn't she call me herself?"

"I. Don't. Know. Now open the door, or I'm coming in my own way." Which would definitely ruin the "no scene" plan.

I hear the chain drop, the lock turn over, then two green eyes and a button nose peek through a miniscule crack. "Is she all right?" Her small voice trembles.

"Yeah." I nod and exhale. "Please let us in."

She backs up, allowing a wide berth between herself and our entry. She clutches the front of her robe in a white-knuckle grip, her huge, trepid eyes glued on Thatcher.

He notices and steps forward with his hand extended. "Thatcher King. Nice to meet you..."

"Reece Kelly." She juts her chin up proudly and shakes his hand with gusto. "And to what do I owe *your* visit, may I ask?" she requests with calm warrant, no bite.

His shoulders bounce with his silent laughter. "You may. I'm the boss here and saw Rhett's little dilemma on the monitors. Thought I'd come see if I could be of assistance. JC might have also mentioned a problem in the club last night and that he comp'd a lovely lady a room on six. My job is to make sure all is well and to your satisfaction." He lifts her hand and kisses her knuckles. "Do I know you?"

A sweet flush, the likes of which *I've* caused before, warms the apples of her cheeks. "No!" she answers too quickly, too defensively. "I mean, no, not that I'm aware of."

"Hmmm..." He considers her.

"No way, man. So far from your type it isn't even funny." I step between them, dislodging her hand from his claws, and turn her by the shoulders. "Get dressed and let's go help your friend. I'm tired, and we only have a little time that her ex is gonna cooperate."

"Fine. Should I wear the robe for extra warmth?"

"What?"

She swivels back to me and reaches up to tug on my beanie. "I just thought maybe I missed a cold snap in the zany, unpredictable weather of Las Vegas. I don't have anything with me besides the robe to protect me from the harsh elements." She wraps her arms around herself and shivers like a lil' smartass.

"Why, thank you Tea." I wink at her.

Her little face twists in confusion. "For?"

"For the compliment. You did just say 'dayummm, Rhett, your sexy ass beanie's turning me on.'" I grin.

"No, not what I said and not what's happening."

"You noticed enough to mention it. You sure 'bout that?" I slant a brow in taunting question.

"Positive." She rolls her eyes and turns to walk away, glancing over her shoulder to give Thatch a finger wave and gorgeous smile—a.k.a. fucking with me. "Nice to meet you, Thatcher King, boss man." Then she closes the door to the bathroom.

"Don't ask," I warn him, walking to the door and opening it in unsubtle invitation to leave.

"I'll go, but you had Penny Parsons last night if rumor serves me right?"

"Doesn't matter. This girl's never even heard of the shit you're into, trust me. And she lives halfway across the country, only here for a visit. So get it out of your head, now."

"Methinks thou doth protest too much." He chuckles.

"You're right, I do. Now go. I'm in a hurry to help out Jarrett."

"You're also a chump." He bro-slaps my face twice with a tsk. "Later."

"Reece, let's roll!" I urge her just as she emerges from the bathroom, back in last night's outfit, her shiny blond hair pulled up.

She smirks infectiously, brushing by me. "Lead the way."

I take her out the back way, avoiding another run-in with Thatcher, JC or any other hard-on who wants a turn at the "Reece Welcome Committee." Barely out the door, I stay well in her peripheral as I cautiously approach her. *Always advance on the tiny creature in an unaggressive and calming manner, or they'll dart off. Remember, they're more scared of you than you are of them.*

"That one." I touch her elbow and steer her left, pointing at the cherry red '69 Shelby Mustang I splurged on. *My baby.*

I open her door and help her in, then round the hood. As I do, her immediate movement catches my eye and sparks a fond memory that plays so vividly; I swear if I reopened my eyes, the brilliant, eccentric old fart would be standing right in front of me. My late grandfather, my favorite person in the world, just crept his way into my morning.

"Two things, boy, that'll tell ya all you need to know. First one is, make sure your door is locked when you get her settled in the car. If she reaches over and unlocks it for you on her own, she cares—thoughtful and giving by nature. That's the girl you hold hands with, work for that first kiss, then keep working until she thinks you're worthy of her forever. And when you finally convince her, use every damn day to make sure she never changes her mind."

The minute I'd shut her door and taken one, maybe two, steps toward my side, Reece was stretched as far as her tiny body would allow, pulling up the manual lock on mine.

"Buckle up," I grunt, the sound of uncomfortable discovery and meaningful advice long buried revealing itself. I know the next steps here are put in key, turn on ignition, drive... so why I'm choosing to sit frozen and gawk at her baffles me.

"You lost your keys, didn't you?" she asks with a teasing grin.

No, just my mind. I shake my head back and forth in slow motion.

"You forgot something inside?" she guesses.

I take my time with another head shake.

"Rhett, I'm starting to feel panicky. Why aren't you talking? Are you having a stroke? This is the universal sign for choking," She wraps both hands around her throat.

63

"How many fingers am I holding up?" *Two.* "You're freaking me out. SPEAK!"

"You ever been in this old of a car?" I'm finally able to articulate, in a curious, almost fascinated tone I haven't had reason to use in a while. *Since the last time this girl had me using it.*

"I don't know." She sits up straighter and answers with a hint of defiance. "How old of a car is it?"

"Sixty-nine." Yes, I coat it in convenient innuendo and throw in a grin.

"Did you pick that year just so you could use that cheesy line on women in your car?" She rolls her eyes.

"Nope, but you're blushing, so it worked out nicely."

"It really didn't."

Yes, it did. The corner of her mouth is twitching and she's struggling to keep her eyes averted.

"But no," she adds, "I guess I haven't ever ridden in a classic. Why?"

"You pulled up the door lock for me. What made you do that?" I speak lower and lean toward her in a comforting way, since I sense she's anything but.

"Well, there's no automatic button"—she points at her door panel—"and the stick thing was pushed down, so I brilliantly deduced"—an impish smirk and tap to her temple—"to. Pull. Up."

Before I realize it, I'm laughing softly and running the back of my hand down her cheek. "So you've never done that before?"

"No." Her brow wrinkles in utter confusion. "And another first—this conversation. Well beyond the strangest and most in-depth one I've ever had about door locks. Seriously, you mind telling me why we've been sitting here for a good five minutes examining this? What are we even talking about?" Her tiny hands flutter up and out in question.

"Nothing." I run my tongue along my teeth leisurely, giving my skepticism versus captivation time to debate.

"*Nothing?* You're a man, let me ask you. Are you guys aware you have your own language? Coded, cryptic meanderings about random, non-substantial things, like door locks for example, yet you mumble 'nothing' when asked a direct question? I swear, talking to guys is like trying to work Sudoku with a Sharpie... while blindfolded. Do you do it just to aggravate us, or is it truly a chromosomal thing?"

"A little of both." I laugh. "But this, *hear*. Thank you." I slide my hand farther down her velvety cheek, then along her jawline at the same speed those little puffs of air slip past her parted lips. "For getting my door for me. Very thoughtful, Teaspoon."

"You're welcome," she whispers, clearly puzzled as to why it's momentous...but shivering because she knows it is.

CHAPTER
six

Reece

When I said I wouldn't scrutinize all that Vegas has offered so far, I lied. I spent all night tossing and turning, my mind a swirling vortex of analysis—focusing on one particular facet. I ran the entire mental gamut of possible "takes" on Rhett—from he's an asshole and I'm better off, to he owed me nothing, I'm certainly not perfect, to I'd been justified in insulting him. The only reason I'm revisiting it now is because of the intangible shift that joined him behind the wheel.

And the beanie.

Nothing not to like about a beanie.

But in all seriousness, whatever he stopped and pondered, eyes closed and head tilted back as though hungry for the sun's heat, it was significant. As is the weight of his affectionate gaze, currently cast on me.

No, I'm being ridiculous, sleep deprived, and a hopeless romantic. I turn toward him a smidge. "So, what am I gonna do about Landry?" I ask of he who knows nothing about my friend or her "history," purely in the interest of tension filling conversation.

He laughs, appropriate considering. "How should I know? She got her own apartment to move back into?" He pulls his gaze from me and starts the car.

"Nope," I pop.

"Job?"

"Quit last week."

"Family? Savings? Any remnants of a life or independence before this guy?"

"She's not super close with her family and savings is a definite no. Landry's, um…" I mull it over, deciding on the most respectful way to say it. "Landry's a very spontaneous person. I'm never sure what her plans are, and just when I think I do, they change the next day."

He doesn't respond. The normally quiet click of the blinker booms through our silence.

"It'll all be over soon" is the mantra in my head, enabling me to remain cool and collected. I live hundreds of miles away and will be returning there before you know it, while they'll all be left to gallivant free and crazy in Vegas.

I'm almost positive I'm jealous.

"We're here."

His icy, bored tone draws my thoughts back to now, as well as his second mood swing of the morning. I climb out, as does he, to find what I assume is Jarrett's truck backed up to the open front door of Landry's cute, albeit small, white house. I wonder if he parked both left tires on what was once a flower bed, which I'm certain Landry didn't plant, on purpose?

"Yo!" Rhett yells inside.

"In here," Jarrett hollers back. "Grab the dolly outta my truck on your way."

Rhett grumbles something under his breath then jumps up in the bed and unloads the dolly. When both his feet are back on the ground, he reaches behind his head and yanks his shirt over and off in one tug.

Several things all register at once, the foremost of which is—I thought he had "a thing" about taking off his shirt? Secondly, *Penny Parsons* couldn't get the job done. Third, and hands down the most mesmerizing, is my introduction to every sculpted part of his finely cared for upper body.

"Okay for me to head inside now, or you need me to knock out a couple pirouettes, maybe come a little closer so you can get a better look?" He teases when he catches me...*surveying.*

My traitorous eyes amble up his glorious length, coming to rest on his antagonizing blue ones that give his wry smirk extra zing. Damn my stupid blush, blazing up my neck and face. "Ease up on the ego, boy toy. I was simply wondering a couple things."

"Which were?" One brow lifts.

"How do you know what a pirouette is?"

"*Black Swan*, forced to watch it. Turned out all right though—Natalie Portman's a cutie. Next?"

"To what does the moving party owe the coveted award of you shedding your shirt? You know, the one thing even the magnificent, newsworthy Penny Parsons couldn't accomplish?" I cross my arms and purse my lips, damn proud of the intelligible verbiage I'm managing, despite my flustered brain.

"No chance of something *impersonal* being made *personal* here. If I could figure out how to fuck 'em through my pants, I'd leave them on too. Women tend to get all sappy, asking questions that are none of their fucking business and conjuring up deeper meanings. A lot like you're doing now, actually." He scowls.

Oh, there's deeper meaning behind it all right. *Taking off your shirt's more personal than having sex with someone?* Um, no, and he doesn't believe that for a second. It's another of his nonsensical idiosyncrasies I've yet to unravel... kinda like the door locks. But I'll be damned if I act as if I care now that I've been compared to his hussies. He thinks he's a mystery, but I've seen more of him than what his shirt keeps covered.

"Penny Parsons? *The* Penny Parsons?" Jarrett chooses now to come barreling through the front door. "Damn, bro, you really upped your game. Gimme some." He lifts his hand for a congratulatory high-five that Rhett doesn't reciprocate.

Instead, Rhett pins me with a "go to hell" look and scoots past Jarrett to storm inside.

Jarrett turns to me. "What the hell was that all about?"

I shrug and plaster on a tight grin. "Nothing much. Your brother ditched me 'cause my legs didn't fly open fast enough and he landed himself right between the *very* accommodating pair of Ms. Parsons. But don't worry, I got to hear the whole thing. It was"—I place my hand over my heart and sigh dreamily—"magical."

"Yeah, whatever you say. Um, Landry needs your help packing."

I nod, suddenly embarrassed by my childish theatrics, and slink past him to go find Landry. She's on the floor of the bedroom, crying and throwing things in boxes with the finesse of Godzilla. My original plan of chewing her a new ass vanishes with the lost, angry look in her eyes.

"Landry, honey, why don't you let me do this? If it's worth packing, it's worth keeping in one piece, right?" I say calmly, while carefully extracting a figurine from her death grip.

"I'm taking our bed." She sniffles. "He's not fucking her in it!"

"I'd say that's reasonable. I'll ask them to load it next. Now what about your clothes, bathroom, electronics? We need to hurry. I don't want Stephen coming back and causing a scene."

"You're right." She wipes her nose and jumps up, determination anew. "I'll do the closet. You get what's in that dresser." She points.

Once everything that will fit is packed in the truck or crammed in Landry and Rhett's small cars, we all come to the same sudden epiphany. Looking back and forth at one another, I pray someone has an answer… or at least a good idea.

"Where are we taking all this? And the two of you?" Rhett finally asks.

The million-dollar question, which I defer to Landry, silently asking her the same with wide, imploring eyes.

"Reece, you got any money?" Her tears spring free as she mouses out the question.

"A little. Why?"

"No, I mean *money*, like to loan me for a place."

I do, but if I make a noticeable withdrawal, it'll get noticed. I'll worry about that later though—this is Landry. My oldest, *only really*, friend. My human, who frustrates me almost as often as she reminds me why I adore her. "Yes, of course. Whatever you need."

"Hold up," Jarrett busts in, waving his arms. "Nobody get all crazy. Listen." He holds Landry's shoulders, dipping his face even to hers. "If Ness is moving into *your* pad, move into hers! I've got two bedrooms and I owe you big for posting bail for me. You took a huge leap of faith. Let me return the favor."

S.E. Hall

"Oh no, I couldn't." She clutches her chest, which is so unlike her, and tugs her bottom lip in her teeth. "Unless, you're sure?" *There* she is, fluttering eyelashes, insta-Southern belle twang and all.

She's Connecticut born and raised. Just sayin'.

"Why not?" Jarrett laughs, and as my hand slowly raises to answer, Rhett lowers it for me with a soft chuckle. "It'll be fun. Hell, I spent years on a bus with the most uptight female on the planet. This'll be a breeze."

I look at Rhett, who's standing rigidly, his arms crossed over his once-again covered chest, stoic mask on his face. I nudge him and use my expression to try and plead with him to do something, but he denies me with a brisk shake of his head.

"It's settled then. Let's get going!" Rhett announces with a sharp clap and quick pivot toward his car. "Reece, you're with me."

I'm too dumbfounded to ask questions or protest. *What in the actual f just happened?*

"No, really, *what* just happened?" I wonder again, apparently out loud this time, Rhett's laughter snagging my attention.

"Quit worrying." He opens the passenger door, motioning me in with a jerk of his chin. "I'll tell ya exactly how this is gonna play out on the ride over."

"The ride over?" I parrot, settling into my seat.

He shakes his head and grins as he closes my door, not responding until he's in and has the car started.

"They'll rebound fuck 'til they both feel better, then Jarrett'll let her have the apartment when he asks me to go back out on the road. So stop stressing. Your friend'll be thoroughly satisfied, over her heartbreak, and have a place to live in no time. Believe me, if I had any doubt this wouldn't work out, I'd step in. He is my little brother."

If I thought I was confused before... *On the road*? Investigation all but over, the Fred Jones theory proving as unlikely as I already suspected. But then why...

"I can smell your brain smoking, Reece. You're worrying needlessly. So they both thought they'd found love, they hadn't. Not exactly a shocking plot twist. Give 'em a couple weeks to sweat out their revenge and disillusionment and they'll be as good as new. Only a free soul can thrive, wild and untamed. We step back while they fuck like crazy for a while, everything'll be fine. Trust me."

"Rubik's Cube." The random, but accurate, analogy pops out of my mouth of its own volition.

"What?" he asks.

He heard me. Might as well explain. "*You*, you're a freakin' Rubik's Cube. Just when I think I have one of your moods, which we'll refer to as 'yellow,' sorted out, you talk again... and it's like flipping over the cube. Sure, I've got all the yellow together, but the red, blue and orange are still a mess. And if I start trying to figure *those* out, I'll screw up the yellow!" I heave in exasperation but can't contain the rest. "Seriously, Rhett, English isn't my *second* language. It's my *only* language. So I'm having trouble following all your African tongue-clicking. And warning, if interpretive dance comes next, save it. I don't understand that either."

"Oh shit," he chokes out through raucous laughter, steering with one hand and clutching his side with the other. "I gotta pull over." And he does, lost in his hysterics for several more minutes.

"Thank you, Teaspoon. That felt so damn good." He smiles at me when he's finally caught his breath and wiped his eyes.

"I do what I can, but I wasn't kidding. Explain to me the part about two strangers living together being a good idea again? And on the road? For what?" I'm edging, holding on to plausible deniability by a guilty thread, so I switch gears to *all* the other stuff tripping me up. "Or better yet, tell me about you, with me, I just... I know why you danced with me. I even *sadly* comprehend why you left me stranded. It was shallow and deplorable, but I have a general understanding of your motivation. Even the fight in the hall, I get, was much my fault as anyone's. But since you knocked on my door this morning, I've sincerely felt like I've got whiplash. You're tender and introspective, then you're a cocky ass, then you're just talking superficial madness. I can't keep up."

The lingering happiness on his face disappears, his staple guise of pessimistic superiority restored. "Do you pick apart and analyze everything, all the time?"

"Hmph." I cross my arms. How he lures out the boisterous, argumentative, yet playful and engaged version of me, I have no idea. "Do you assume to know everything about everyone, all the time?"

74

"I'm usually right." His gaze bounces over every part of me, then locks back on mine. "Except with you." It's more a thought, escaping in breathless reverence, than a statement...and my skin prickles.

"Psshh." I dismiss his intensity with a wave and shaky laugh. The only other option—absorbing it—terrifies me. "I'm only an exception because I didn't fall into bed with you. Men want what they can't have. *That*, I know, is a chromosomal thing. Men see the forbidden as a challenge and the challenge as a *sign*. It's not. You're smarter than that."

His enigmatic stare bores into me as we sit in silence—very uncomfortably if you ask me, but he seems... content.

"Rhett? Maybe it's not my place..." I take a deep breath. "No, it's absolutely not my place, and very soon you'll never have to listen to me again, but..." I should shut up, having taken a humongous step over the line already, yet I can't fight whatever compels me to continue my uninvited analysis. "You're a thinker, a feeler. *Nothing* is impersonal to you." I dare to lay my hand over his. "Face it, *you're good*. Except at acting." I laugh. "Really, you're wasting your time with all the 'tortured soul' nonsense. Locks have keys and walls can be climbed. I'm not buying your whole grumpy, callous routine for one minute. So unless you have a terminal disease or something, why don't you snap out of it and at least *try* to be happy?" I'm literally trembling, adrenaline buzzing through me so fast, there're little white spots in my vision. That will quickly become a much bigger issue when he tosses me out and I have to see to walk. "If you quit sleeping with just anyone, you'll get better at deciphering the *exceptional* from the *exceptions*."

"Ya think so, huh?" is all he has to say, his expression and voice hollow.

"Definitely. You disagree?"

He completely bypasses my question. "At first I was pissed you turned me down. But now I'm *so* glad we didn't fuck, Teaspoon."

What? I shake off the chill of his cruelty and fire back. "Wait just a dang minute, you, you..." *Now I'm tongue-tied?* "I'm way out of line, and I'm sorry if I got too personal. I mean, what do I possibly know? We just met. But my intentions were kind! There's no need for you to be so hateful and nasty!" I sense tears building; the end of my nose tingles. "You'd be lucky, if I let you do that with me..." I look intently at the floorboard, my angry speech fading off pitifully.

"I absolutely would. But what I meant"—his hand finds my chin and lifts my face—"was I *like* you. I can get laid anytime. But I can't get this." He gestures between us. "Your spice, which you only break out when it'll pack the hardest punch. Your kindness and strength. You intrigue me, *every* part of me, especially the ones others don't take the time or interest to discover. So I'm glad I didn't ruin it before it ever got started."

"Your, uh, sex is ruining?" I stammer faintly.

His lips curl at one side, devilment in his eyes. "Remember how you felt in the hall? Angry, unappreciated?"

Okay, so maybe he *does* know everything about everyone. I nod—no sense bothering with denial.

"I didn't even fuck you, yet I still somehow managed to make you feel two feet"—he smirks—"tall. So yeah, my sex is ruining. For everyone involved."

"Then why—"

"Sshh. Counseling *out* of session for a while." He starts the car back up, looks behind him, and pulls onto the street. "I'm sure they're wondering where the hell we are, then I've gotta get ready for my gig tonight. You're coming."

"I—"

"Say yes."

Not that listening to Landry and Jarrett "rebound fuck" isn't tempting. "Yes."

"Yes." He glances at me from the corner of his eye and gives me a grin that's… ruining.

CHAPTER
seven

Rhett

Good thing Thatcher's the man at Goldsbury Casino Resort, or I'd have lost my gig here. I was late tonight for several reasons. First, I had to get Reece thinking about something that didn't rival "acid burning her retinas." Jarrett and Landry were *rebounding* when we arrived at "their" apartment. More specifically, they were two steps inside the doorway, fucking on the floor—quite the tripping hazard.

When everyone was dressed and once again able to look each other in the eye—meaning Reece agreed to come back inside—Reece, Jarrett and I had to unpack the vehicles while Landry capitalized on the confidence my brother had just restored in her, via his dick, to scream her way through a handful of "wedding's cancelled" phone calls. *If* it was even a handful- must've been some event they had planned.

A dash across town to shower and shave later, I'd backtracked to pick up Reece… and arrived at my show fifteen minutes late.

But Reece's dress… fire engine red and molded to her curves as though she had been born in it? Taking the time to absorb and commit to memory every facet of that sight took ten excruciatingly worthwhile minutes all by itself. I'm doubtless that Landry dressed her tonight as well—Reece's pinkened cheeks and constant tugging on her dick-teasing hem both big clues. And with the taunting smell of honeysuckle permeating my car as she rode with me, all I can figure is God's testing me, seeing how long it'll take for me to desecrate this girl's integrity.

I end my first set with a solo acoustic version of See You Next Tuesday's original, "Unapologetically," my eyes scanning the crowd for Reece. She was sitting with Jarrett and Landry, where *they* remain, but she's vanished.

"Hey, where's Reece?" I ask them when I steal her unoccupied seat.

Landry detaches herself from my brother's mouth to answer, "Bathroom."

"How long's she been gone? You couldn't have joined her? I thought you always went in pairs?" I inject my frustration with their carelessness into my tone.

"Man, relax. It's been ten minutes tops. Good set by the way." Jarrett offers me a high-five, which I return half-assed. "Oh shit, before I forget, you need to take next Friday off if you're booked."

"I don't want a party," I snap, standing to go check on Reece. I'm well aware of when my twenty-sixth birthday is—he's about as stealthy as a punch in the face.

"Dude, I can't tell you a lot without ruining the surprise, but listen to me when I say it's *non-negotiable*. Take. The. Night. Off."

"Whatever," I grumble as I leave, heading straight for the ladies' restroom. "Reece?" I yell from the entrance. "You in there?"

She squeals, and I can picture the bright pink heat of her embarrassment. "Rhett? What're you doing? L-a-d-i-e-s spells ladies. Get out of here!"

"I was worried. You were taking a while. Come 'ere and make me laugh before I have to go back on stage."

"Go away! I'll meet you at our seats."

I hear her stall door squeak open and catch a flash of red as she crosses to wash her hands.

"You're still out there, aren't you?" She giggles, melodious and sweet.

"Yep."

She groans. "I liked you better when you hated me." She appears around the corner, trying to glower menacingly—all five feet of her.

"Liar." I tap her button nose as if I do shit like that every day—which I do not. But now that we've established fucking's off the table, I feel as relaxed around her as I ever have any woman. Except Liz of course. I grab Reece's hand, which is swallowed by my much-larger one. "Have a drink with me before I'm up again."

"K." She simpers, lacing our fingers together.

I stop and lean down until our noses touch. "And I never hated you." Her squeezing my hand's nice, natural and affirming, before it's interrupted.

"Hey, Rhett." Melissa? Monique? *Whoever* rudely inserts herself between Reece and me, forcing Reece backward with a bump of her hip. She presses every inch of her brazen self against me, sneaking her hand in the non-existent space between our bodies to rub my dick through my jeans.

"Um, hey, M, *you*," I snarl, robbed of Reece's hand. I'm left gazing at her back as she hurries faster and farther away.

"Who was that?" what's-her-nuisance asks in sickening baby voice.

"None of your damn business. Why would you get up on me if you saw I was with someone?" I all but scream at her. "And where's your *sheik*?" No shit. If I'm matching her up correctly—difficult with the myriad of nameless faces who matter not—her high-rolling sugar daddy is, in fact, an honest-to-God *sheik*.

"Busy," she purrs, rubbing impossibly closer to me. "And to hell with whoever that was. *I* want you for the night."

Another glaring confirmation—I have *got* to stop fucking them.

"Rhett!" Thatcher calls, quick-stepping our way. "Get on stage. That's what I'm paying you for, isn't it?"

No, I don't get paid. But I do get interference ran when I need it.

"And *Ms.* Marjorie"—he raises her hand to his mouth and kisses the back of it—"what can I help you with, beautiful?"

I silently thank him with an 'atta chin and get the hell out of there as if I'm being chased. I sneak up behind Reece and whisper in her ear, "Hey."

"Done so soon?" she jabs snidely, facing away from me, back pin-straight and tense.

"Funny, but no. Talk to me." I unsuccessfully coerce her to turn around with my hand on her waist.

"You're very good, Rhett. Your music, lyrics, talent. And you were right—Jarrett was talking earlier about how he's ready to travel and play again. Said you're actually a drummer at heart, which I'd love to hear sometime. I can't imagine how amazing that'd be if it's even better than your guitar."

"Reece, look at me."

She does, begrudgingly, with a manufactured smile and one last sip from her empty drink. "Does it still work?"

I let out an uneasy laugh. Her eyes convey the rapid subject change I already know she's focused on. "Does what still work?" Why did I ask? Masochism?

"Sex, your escape, your coping mechanism. Does it still give you a rush of power, enough blessed numbness to outweigh the regret in your eyes right now? Or has it officially become just a really bad, unbeatable habit?"

"As much as I'd like to hear how you have me all figured out, *again*, I can't do this right now, Freud. I have to go on." Why does this girl keep prying and openly analyzing the shit out of a guy she barely knows? And why am I not angry about it? *Shit*, because I'm too impressed to be offended. Not only does she have the brass balls to call me out, repeatedly, but she holds *real* conversations, with multi-syllabic words used correctly. "Later though. Hold on to all those big thoughts?"

"I'll be here. Unless of course another one of your *friends* comes along and butt bumps me off the chair."

Ah, that's what's prompted her "examine Rhett" replay. Yeah, I can see how that would get a chick's dander up. And where the hell did Jarrett go? I'd rather not take the chance of that happening again with her sitting alone while I'm on stage.

"Play me something good."

"Stay put and I'll see what I can do. Yes?"

She rolls her eyes. "Yes, I'm fine, go."

Play her something good, she says. That narrows it down. I do love a challenge though... let's see if I can get inside her head the way she's snuck into mine. I take the stage, adjust the mic unnecessarily, and say hello to the crowd as I sit, still contemplating the perfect song choice.

With the strap of my Martin six string over my head and body settled in my lap, I clear my throat. "Thanks for sticking around. This first one goes out to a tiny blonde with emerald eyes that see more than they should."

I play her "The Fear," an eclectic rendition of Ben Howard's styling with a bit of Rhett blended in—aptly appropriate I'd say. More importantly, I'd rather put it out there myself than have her boast anymore in revelation. I'm not a mystery to unravel; surely we can find something else to talk about.

She squirms in pinned unnerve, but those eyes of hers bridge the space between us and tell me that the gravity of my blatant, complicated message isn't lost on her. She orders another drink but remains focused on me—every note, every word—so I keep right on hitting home with my next choice. Funny thing is, I'm no longer convinced that I'm trying to get in her head, but rather my own.

"This is one I wrote, called 'Make Me Believe.' Hope ya like it." I close my eyes, letting the strum of the chords ignite me and each word rasp out with all the provocation I intend.

> *"Do you wonder what I haven't told you?*
>
> *Are you scared I'm not all that you need?*
>
> *If you knew I'm a shell of a liar*
>
> *Would you long for a different sort of me?*
>
> *It can't all be exciting*
>
> *Brand new wears away*

And you're left with the old, the plain, the mundane

Can you keep inventing reasons to stay?

You beg me to open my soul and give you my pain

You swear that you see me, all that I hide

And you say you won't run, won't fall apart

And I want to believe you,

So make me believe.

If it somehow came down, to only the two of us

Our storm to face, our wounds to bleed

Nothing can touch us that we don't let in

And we both find the who that we've always been

Are you strong enough to hold me up

Stronger still to fall

Are we brave enough, when war comes to call

To sacrifice it all

You beg me to open my soul and give you my pain

You swear that you see me, all that I hide

And you say you won't run, won't fall apart

And I want to believe you,

So make me believe.

I need you, to make me believe."

I'm not sure if the crowd liked it, nor do I care—it's white noise if they're even making any. I am sure I'm supposed to play another song, still wondering what the hell I was thinking playing that one. But when she wriggles her finger for me to go to her, I do. Well, at least we know I'm not pussy whipped, and I'm pretty sure there's no such thing as "haven't been anywhere near the pussy" whipped, so it's just a walk then.

Just a walk.

I saunter up and give her a loaded smile. "You need something, Teaspoon?"

"What was *that*?" she whispers, eyes wide and appraising.

"Couple songs." I shrug, shoving my hands deep in my pockets. "Why, you didn't like them?" Fuck me, I'm a fisherman now too? I need to get laid. *This* is why you don't "talk."

"They were both incredible, especially the one you wrote. No surprise there. But you know what I mean." Her head dips.

I do nothing to move her face up, needing reprieve from… whatever. "Honestly? I have no idea what you mean. Or why I played 'em." I expect her to respond, but she doesn't. Much like before, she's fascinated with her straw—I'm on to her hiding spot. "So where the hell are Jarrett and Landry? I can't seem to keep the three of you in one place."

"I doubt I want to know the answer to that." She snickers, finally glancing up. "What now?" she asks as though I, and I alone, hold the answer to life's every riddle.

"Now we have fun. What sounds good first, gambling or heading over to the club?"

"Surprise me," she whispers, her expression alive with delight.

I offer my hand, and she slides her own in it without thought, letting me guide her to the counter. I cash in money for a slot machine card and one hundred dollars in chips.

"Do you have a particular poison?" I turn and once again take her hand.

She beams. "It's my first time gambling, so you lead the way."

I walk her around the place, holding her hand. Lots of people know me here, and I'm positive if I paid attention to anything other than Reece, I'd find looks of shock upon more than a couple faces. I just don't give a fuck—what they think, who sees, or what it means that her hand entwined with mine feels as if it's always been there.

The virgin gambler, everything fascinates her. I don't even have to try to show her a good time. She flits around and creates the good time. In fact, it's not long at all before she's actually dragging me from one game to another, asking how to play each and finally deciding we should get comfortable at… a nickel machine.

"Reece, these are five-cent bets. You can't win any big money on them."

"I don't care if I win a lot or not. I just want to have fun. Look!" She points at the pay scale at the top of the machine that's caught her eye. "If you get five Nemo fish, they swim into little caves for a bonus round! How cute is that? Sit down." She pats the seat beside the one she's already warming.

Please let her get five Nemo fish. She'll be thrilled, which I won't mind watching, then we can move on to something else.

"You want a drink?" I ask as she fumbles through sliding a twenty in the feed tray.

"Sure, something refreshing." She doesn't look at me, mesmerized by the bells dinging and lights flashing as the machine tallies up her credits. "I'll be right here."

Quite a while later, she's hit the bonus game several times, and I've refilled our drinks at least as many. Her starting twenty has become $486 and her ass is threatening to fuse with the seat. But her face is illuminated, her little hands clapping as she bounces up and down and liquor loosens her tongue—which has run non-stop the entire time. No way will I so much as think about grimacing in boredom.

"There you guys are!" Jarrett yells, walking—a generous description considering she's more laying on his side—over with Landry. "Y'all about ready? This one's done for the night." He tips his head her way. "I need to get her home."

I laugh, partly for the predicament quick-to-recover lover finds himself draped in, but more because Reece is completely oblivious to the fact they're even standing here.

Her nose is an inch from the screen as she rubs her hands together, chanting, "Here, fishy, fishy. Come to Mama."

"You two go ahead. I'll drive Reece to your place when she's caught her limit."

"Really?" my brother asks, overstatedly mystified. Subtlety is nonexistent in his repertoire. "You're just *hanging out*?"

"Yes, really. You okay to drive? I can get you a cab."

"I'm straight. One of us had to do the walking." He chuckles. "So I guess I'll see ya later then?" He glances disbelievingly between Reece and me.

"If you're still standing here in ten seconds, I'm scheduling you a Pap smear."

"Aight"—he puts the hand not holding Landry out in surrender—"we're going."

S.E. Hall

While I watch him drag her out, it humorously dawns on me that neither of the girls—Sloshed and Spellbound—know any of that just happened. Thank Christ, because they'd think we were far too in touch with our feminine sides. Jarrett was giving "Best Dramatic Actress" a hella try.

I sit and watch Reece play a little longer. Any time she doesn't win in three consistent spins, she asks me to push the button to "change her luck." It doesn't, and in just over another hour, she's out of credits. Gotta give it to her though—she might've just set the record for the longest-lived twenty-dollar investment in the history of Vegas.

She squeals, standing up, wincing, and rubbing her ass unashamedly. "That was fun! What do you wanna play now? Your turn to pick."

"I'm good. We can head out if you're ready." My phone chooses then to chime with a text and I hold up a finger while I dig it out of my pocket.

Jarrett: Landry's sobering up, take your time.

Two of the most inconsiderate, self-serving people on the planet... I *never* think like that of my brother. But damn, Landry invites Reece here for a visit and abandons her *twice*? From what I've seen, Reece is a damn fine friend. So far she's helped Landry move, with no lingering anger whatsoever from being abandoned, consoled her with empathy and kindness and offered to loan her money. Jarrett should know better than this shit. Tap out your however many minutes of fun, then give the girl a place to sleep. And Reece should seriously consider making some new friends.

90

Me: Take your time, I'll take care of Reece. Not fucking cool of her friend, or you, though.

Jarrett: WTF?

Me: Not gonna explain human decency to you right now, I'm on a date. Gotta go.

"What is it?" she asks in a timid voice.

I look up from my phone, her head ducked as though she has a pretty good idea of what's coming. "Oh, um, Jarrett was just asking our plan. And I have one. You hungry?"

Her head lifts, glee no longer gracing her features. "They don't want me there, do they? I swear, I'm going home tomorrow. This is ridiculous." She heaves a sigh of frustration, dropping back in her chair.

Jarrett: I may need to explain "date" to you— not what you're doing.

Me: Night.

"Can you see if JC can get me a room? Not free though. I'll hit an ATM." She fails to hide a slight wince when she says it. "I'll worry about dealing with the questions later."

"What questions? From who?" I ask, definitely interested in the answer. This is where she pops my bubble of foolishly thinking there's *something* about her and casually mentions the fiancé or husband… she forgot to mention.

"My father, mainly. We're in business together, sorta, and he'll grill me over the withdrawal. That part doesn't bother me as badly as what he'll say about Landry though. He already thinks she's flaky, a horrible influence, whatever. I've been trying not to give him any ammunition, sticking to the cash I brought."

She surprises me again. That wasn't the answer I was expecting, and an honest one I've no doubt. Her father's not exactly wrong on a few points, but I don't say so.

"I asked you a question." I pull her up by the hand. "Are you hungry?"

"Rhett, it's fine. I'll just get a room. You've entertained me long enough."

"Okay, let me try this another way. I'm hungry, and you just don't want to admit that you can't live without my company. So we're going to eat. Say yes."

"Rhett…" she dawdles.

"Say yes." I'm already leading us to the door and she isn't even attempting to pull her hand from mine.

"I guess I could eat. But you drank. Should you drive?"

I laugh. "Mine were Coke."

"Coke and…?"

"Ice. Come on." I speed up our steps.

"You order the same thing every time you come here, don't you?" she asks, coy little grin and confident twinkle in her eyes mocking me.

"And you order something different at every restaurant, every time," I counter, having already decided that this time, we're dissecting all things Reece for a change.

"Basis for your theory?"

I'd forgotten how fucking sexy intelligence can be. "You're really gonna let me have a turn, huh? Okay." I put my elbows on the table and lean closer to her across the booth. "You order something different because it makes you feel free, spontaneous. Your tiny consolation of empowerment that you refuse to forfeit, that last saving grace between what you want and what's wanted for you."

"How'd you know that?" Her mouth remains agape after she asks.

The waitress brings our food and we both thank her.

"How'd you know all that stuff about me?" I ask.

I take a big bite of my sandwich, giving her time to formulate an answer and because I'm starving.

"So I was right?" she challenges.

I keep chewing but nod. She was right, on all nosy counts. I can't deny her affirmation.

"Intuition, I guess," she replies, blasé and popping a shoulder.

I swallow and take a drink. "Well, Teaspoon, I'm equipped with some intuition myself."

Her phone vibrates on the table with an incoming text and I can see Landry's name displayed from here. "What'd she say?" I ask after she's had time to read it.

"She, um, asked if I was on a date?"

Jarrett's big mouth.

She's still typing, looking at her phone. "And said I was welcome to come stay there tonight."

Of course I don't have the definitive "read" on everything yet, but I know Reece deserves better than being someone's afterthought, burden or consolation prize when they're done with whatever's obviously more important to them.

"What'd you tell her?" I use the ketchup on her plate, since mine is gone, for my fry and pop it in my mouth.

She says nothing and turns the phone toward me.

Me: I think I may be? And no thank you.

Landry: Jarrett said Rhett doesn't date. It's a show to get in your pants. Come stay here.

Her green eyes are waiting, filled with a hopeful trust I haven't earned.

"Your friend's kinda shitty. And wrong," I deadpan.

She reaches for the ketchup bottle and squeezes some onto my plate for me. "She's actually not. Landry didn't desert me for selfish reasons. Took me a minute to figure it out, but I got it now."

"Care to fill me in?" I use her ketchup again and laugh at her small scowl.

"She thought if she forced my company onto you, well, that maybe I'd be forced to live a little."

"And?"

"And she was right. I've had a lot of fun. I'm still not sleeping there though. She needs to learn to polish up her good-hearted tactics. I'll get a room and give her a wake-up call."

"Stay with me." I hold up a hand to thwart her upcoming attempt to argue, her mouth already open.

"I'm *not* going to Hawaii with you." Her eyes narrow to fiery slits, and her lil' bowtie-shaped mouth twists.

"I didn't invite you to." I arch a condescending brow. "You *are*, however, more than welcome to stay at my place for the night. And before those eyes roll out your head and you say things you don't mean, know this. Not only do I *never* use my apartment to partake in activities of the Hawaiian variety, but we've established that's off limits for us. You'll be respected, I promise you, and you'll avoid any hassle with your father. I'm well versed in what that's like. Now say yes."

"Rhett?" She nibbles on her bottom lip.

"Say. Yes," I repeat.

She releases that tortured lip, enabling her face to split into a blinding smile. "Yes."

"Yes." I hold out my hand.

CHAPTER *eight*

Reece

I defied my father and Warrick's high-handed, forbidding demands by even making this trip to Vegas, but if they knew that I've progressed to spending the night with an insanely hot man who's all but a stranger? They'd both fly here to forcibly drag me home—five minutes ago.

What they don't know can't control me. That thought alone adds an extra, exhilarating zing of liberation to my decision.

"You okay?" Rhett asks as we walk to his car. "Your brain's steaming again."

"No, yeah, I mean…" I tsk at myself and giggle, a rambling mess. "I was just thinking that I don't have my stuff: clothes, toothbrush, pajamas." To be honest, I was deliberating between this being an act of freedom or just a dumb choice. Do I *really* believe I can trust him to be a gentleman if I crash at his place for the night?'

Absolutely.

But what does my agreement say about me? Ladies who are responsible and professionally poised don't have a few drinks and dinner with new acquaintances and then go home with them. Then again, being whoever I'm expected to be is boring as hell.

He gives my hand a reassuring squeeze. "I have stuff you can sleep in and probably an extra toothbrush. We'll have you back to your clothes tomorrow. Sound livable?"

I nod, my pulse racing with my myriad of scandalous musings… such as sleeping in his clothes, items saturated with his scent against my naked flesh. When he opens the car door for me, I falter, my knees as shaky as my nerves, but he's right there to catch and steady me.

"Relax." He dips his head and speaks comfortingly in my ear. "I told you, I never let people into my home, my one sanctuary. If I'm inviting you there, I swear to be a platonically accommodating host. My childhood best friend was a girl, and I'd have been furious if she went home with a guy she barely knew, so I can guess the range of concerns in your head right now. But I give you my word, you'll be safe."

"Why?" It comes out as blunt and rude rather than the appreciatively shocked I intended and I shrink back in embarrassment. "I meant, if you don't ever, ya know, invite anyone, why me?"

"Several reasons. If you're with me, I don't have to worry about you. And like I said, it saves you from an inquisition from your dad." He turns me to face him and tilts his head. "I've proven I have the ability to enjoy female company while keeping my hands to myself. I'm rusty as of late, I'll admit, but I'm diggin' deep for ya here, Reece."

"Lizzie…" I whisper with heated inquisitiveness laced with biologically natural—I'll tell myself that excuse anyway—jealousy. No girl wants to hear about other ones, from any guy, no matter what. *Platonic smonic.*

"How do you know about Liz?" he asks in a weak attempt at nonchalance, seemingly distracted with helping me get in the car and shutting my door before I can answer.

We're on the road a good five minutes before the color returns to his blanched knuckles that are clutching the steering wheel and I feel comfortable enough to reply.

"I don't know much about Lizzie, just her name mostly. Jarrett was talking about your band earlier and mentioned her."

He stares ahead. "Hmm…"

"So?"

"So what?" he snaps with a quick glimpse my way.

"You're stewing in thought over there. Why don't you tell me about her? Did you, or um"—I look out my window—"*do* you love her?" The blonde girl staring at me in the glass is unashamed of intruding ever deeper into none-of-her-business territory.

He sighs and shifts in his seat. "How do we always end back up on me?"

"I'm not sure, but you keep answering me, so I'm gonna keep asking." I snicker softly. "Talk to me. Doesn't it feel better to get it off your chest?"

"Maybe," he grumbles. "I think you may be drugging me—only explanation for how you're doing it—but yeah, it does feel good to air out loud. So to answer your question, yes, I love Liz very much. I always will. But not like you're thinking. Liz, her brother, her uncle, our band; we were a family, all each other had. I loved it. Then a new guy joined, loved her in the forever-and-only kind of way I never did, and now I have twin nieces. Stella and Sophia, my angels."

I feel as if I've cracked a code. Rhett Foster is openly sharing things that are making him more than obviously uncomfortable. I'm honored he must think enough of me to entrust me with his ghosts.

"Are you happy for her?" I ask quietly, teetering on the tightrope of pushing too hard.

"Of course. She deserves every happiness she gets and then some. Cannon adores her, as do I, but I was never *in love* with her. She's a mom now, a wife, part of a *real* family. I might be a bit jealous at times, but I'm never not happy as hell for her, for them. All Liz's ever done is give, nurture, and protect. Cannon gives all that back *to* her now. If I wasn't confident in that, he'd be dead."

"Then what are you jealous of?"

"I think *you* should've bought *me* dinner." He laughs. "I'm feeling rather violated."

"How 'bout if I make you breakfast? Not just for asking a follow-up question, but for buying me dinner—thank you very much for that by the way—and letting me stay over. Oh, and for swearing not to 'violate me' of course." I snicker.

"Deal, but only because I haven't had a home-cooked breakfast in… shit, I can't remember when. So I'll humor you a bit. I like French toast by the way. You got that on your menu?"

"Perhaps," I needle him in a drawl. "Now talk."

He exhales extendedly, once more fidgeting in his seat, then spits it all out in one rush of vulnerability. "I miss being depended on, needed. I knew Liz inside and out, same as she did me. We didn't have to speak a word to know what the other was thinking, saved a lot of painful conversations. Like this one." He winks my way with a coy grin. "But most of all, I miss our band, the camaraderie, being a part of something that mattered."

The car's stopped, parked in front of what I assume is his apartment building. The only movement and sound is him turning off the car and pulling out the keys. I don't have to ask why the gigs he does now don't fill the void of which he just spoke; I know the answer. I definitely abstain from prompting him for more information on that topic—sharing all that took too much out of him. Instead, I wait for his lead.

Long minutes later, he runs a hand through his hair, the dark locks in front sticking up and out perfectly imperfect, and turns fully to look at me. "That enough to earn me a couple slices of bread dipped in egg?" He smiles, and I swear it lights up the whole interior of the car.

"Definitely," I affirm with a curt nod.

"Thank fuck," he breathes out heavily.

"I'm not taking your bed from you," I counter with my best impression of authority, standing in the middle of his hallway with my arms crossed. "Just give me a pillow and blanket, and the couch will be more than sufficient."

Obstinate stance of his own and scowl firmly in place, he sighs loudly and lets his head fall back to stare at the ceiling. "You're a smart sprite, Reece, a people reader. Any part of me screaming 'make the female take the couch' at you?" He drops his head back down and anchors me with those imposing blue eyes. "You're taking the bed. End of conversation. Sweet dreams." He turns and walks toward the living room, leaving me rooted stubbornly in the same spot, mouth agape in aggravation.

I'm already shamefully interloping on his time and space, not to mention I'm currently wearing his oversized T-shirt and boxer shorts—I'm not taking his bed too! I do have some semblance of decorum left in my helpless, deserted self. Between his shifts from grumpy manwhore to open, considerate conversation guy, coupled with his clothes and his bed saturated in the pheromones the man can't help but exude, I fear I may collapse from sensory overload.

"Go to bed, Reece," he growls, jolting me out of my thoughts.

I lean around the corner to peek into the living room at him situating the cushions and blanket for his makeshift bed. The moon, that blessed ball of light in the sky, sends down the perfect amount of romantic glow, highlighting the vision of Rhett getting in, or rather *getting out*, of his sleep attire.

Nine out of ten men would reach behind their neck and yank that bad boy off over their head with one hand, exactly as he did when we were moving. But not tonight. No, tonight he torments me—either aware I'm watching or utterly the master of sexiest ways to undress. He grips the hem of his white T-shirt, pulling it up agonizingly slow and finally, at long last, off. He jerks open his jeans and slides them off, revealing a pair of black, short-cut boxer briefs that hardly contain his robust thighs but still manage to showcase all the right *areas*.

Man, oh man, when the angels got together on this design—what a product meeting that was. His perfectly proportioned, tall physique could literally be displayed at the front of an anatomy class and used to learn every muscle in the body, ideally delineated. His skin is a light tan, as if kissed daily by the sun, his chest hairless, and I think I'm counting three lines of definition... easy multiplication… that's a six pack! He's delectable, truly the embodiment of masculine beauty.

"Reece?" His throaty rumble, spiked with feral warning, startles me, and a mortified heat of embarrassment rolls up my entire body. *Caught.* "Do I pass inspection?"

I teeter back off my tiptoes, the wall hopefully shrouding me more now than I stupidly thought it already was, and I clear my throat. "Sorry, I was gonna… just… come get a glass of water." He doesn't need to see me to know I'm lying—and badly.

"Give me a minute to get under the blanket, then you can come get your water. Yes?"

"A-alright," I mutter lamely at the beige wall.

"Trust me, Reece. Listen and do it. Because if you spend one more second eye-fucking me from the shadows, with those sweet little nipples poking out high and hard through *my* shirt, we're *both* taking the bed. I'm only human. But you had a few drinks tonight and would regret it in the morning. We decided that when you were completely sober and not adorably swallowed up in my clothes, remember? So play fair. My resolve is wavering."

I glance down and gasp. He wasn't lying—my nipples are visibly peaked.

He chuckles softly. "Yeah, imagine how I feel. They're pointing right at me, just begging to be in my mouth."

I hear the rustle of the blanket, the couch squeaking under his weight, and the juncture between my thighs pulses from the erotically tempting sound.

"It's safe now, you lil' peepin' Tom. So either come get your water and go straight back to bed, or come attack me, all at once, no hesitation, not a hint of uncertainty in your eyes. Those are your only options."

Wordlessly, I shake off any unclear thoughts and do what the Reece I can't help but be would do—I turn around and head for the bedroom.

"Not thirsty?" he calls out in the darkness.

"No, I changed my mind. I'm fine. Goodnight, Rhett, and thank you." I rest my forehead on the doorjamb of his bedroom, calming my breathing and full-body tingles as I await his response.

"Goodnight, Reece." His sigh is distinct, bouncing off every surface and wall between us. "And you're more than welcome."

Am I imagining the innuendos of my options in that sentence?

I grapple for sleep, perhaps harder than I've ever sought anything in my life, but the room's too hot and the sheets are annoyingly infused with his intoxicating aroma, which has been branded in my nostrils since I first met him at the door of the club. My fitful unrest must be making a commotion, keeping him awake as well, because I hear him doing some noisy tossing and turning of his own.

"Rhett?" I call.

"Teaspoon?" he calls back in sarcastic mockery.

"What're you doing?"

"Chanting the Serenity Prayer in my head repeatedly. You?"

I don't stop my giggle. Recalling the words of such prayer, I ask, "What things can't you change?"

"That you're magnetizing, angelic, and absolutely gorgeous. And the fact I'm a moody, selfish bastard and you live across the country."

Candid, honest... and the most titillating words ever spoken to me. I should jump up and go to him, have one tawdry night of all that I'm not, never have been and more than likely never will be again. I should leave with the memories of the one time he'll give me, armed with the creed "What happens in Vegas stays in Vegas." But what I opt to do, predictably, is stay frozen, cowardly tucked in his fragrant bedding, and ask more about the applicability of the Serenity Prayer. "You seem courageous. What things *can* you change?"

"Nothing I just listed."

"You sure about that?" I'm already up, propelled by a baser instinct I didn't know I possessed. I saunter to him, scared and unsure but tempted beyond reason. I'm burning from the inside out at the possibilities of what might happen when I get there.

"What're you doing?" he grouses, damn near wails, scrubbing both hands over his face when he spots me standing over him. "Reece, even God took a day off, and I'm hanging on by a string of dental floss here. I'm an asshole. I fuck random women and never look back. I know it, you know it." He sits up and takes both my hands, looking into my face with solemn anguish covering his own. "I *will* *not* treat you so callously. Everything about you screams unequivocally that you deserve better. Better than me."

"You seriously meant it." My flattered shock is audible. "You don't want to just sleep with me. But how is that possible? We hardly know each other."

"Not true and you know it. Have you told me more about yourself than anyone else in a long time, if ever?"

"Yes, no contest."

"That revelation you just had? Multiply it by ten and you'll be where I am. I barely know their first names, let alone their middle, last, and birthday. I've never even *wanted* to know their minds, souls, little tics. But we know each other, no matter how much you downplay it. So please, I'm begging you, go to bed, lock the door, and do not come out in that outfit in the morning."

Amid my slight embarrassment of being denied, far greater is my astonishment and respect. I turn to go... but not before catching him off guard with a surprise hug and kiss on the cheek that I was still hoping he'd turn his face into, but didn't. "Thank you again."

"Tea," his grunted plea is strained, "go. And you're welcome again."

Shuffling down the hall, disoriented but still tingling, I *almost* turn back to tell him how wrong he is. I'm far from angelic; I'm a farce, a liar by omission, the prototype of what probably built up his walls in the first place. It's good he didn't succumb to my pathetic, wanton invitation. It'll be all the easier to retreat from this enticing town of what ifs as the unrewarded imposter I am.

I just pray Landry keeps her mouth shut long enough for me to quietly disappear.

CHAPTER
nine

Rhett

The next morning, I wake from a vivid dream of her. Dreams—when the mind is left to its own accord to do major damage, freely straying—to things such as the fresh scent of her hair as crisp as if draped in my face, her sweet whimpers of pleasure ringing in my ears, and the beautiful vision of her curled in a miniature ball in my sheets. I was imagining her soft sighs against my pillow, her little toes digging in under the covers, until the smell of… food, an oddity, must've woken me. Oh, that's right—somebody owes me French toast. I can't get dressed and into the kitchen fast enough.

I expect to come around the corner and find her cute little ass twirling around, plating up the breakfast I've been looking forward to since she promised it.

Instead I find a note on the counter:

Rhett,

Thank you again for giving me a place to stay last night. I was able to navigate your kitchen without waking you. There's a plate of French toast in the oven, should still be warm. I hope you like it.

And yes, I turned it off so your place didn't burn down.

I made the bed. The clothes you let me borrow are folded and on top of it.

Thank you for everything. This weekend, while interesting, was also perhaps the best one I've ever had. I'm going to blame my embarrassing lapse in judgment last night on you... for being so enlivening. I hope you stop with the acting and pick up some drumsticks!

Take care,

Reece

Okay, one thought at a time.

I can't believe she was in here, digging around and clanging pans, and I didn't wake up. I was asleep in the next room, didn't even take anything... first good night's rest I've had in forever, of course. I mean, why wouldn't it have been last night?

I bet those clothes smell twice as heavenly as the food, but walking in there to sniff them would tell me so much more about myself than I'm ready to acknowledge.

Also, where the fuck is she and how'd she get there? Breakfast and scenting her aside, I rush to find my phone. I just want to make sure she made it safely to Jarrett's; she doesn't know this town or even his address.

I notice the red 1 next to my email icon, but I ignore it for the time being.

Me: Reece at your place?

Jarrett: Nope. Landry took her to the airport about an hour ago. Why, w'sup?

Airport, gone.

And then there's that.

Me: Just checking.

This morning's shaping up to be real damn shitty real damn quick. I might as well ice the cake. My finger hovers over the email icon, dark anger constricting my chest before I've even read it. Only one person sends correspondence to this account, so I take a few deep breaths, send up a silent prayer that *this* is the time, and open it.

Mr. Foster,

Hope this finds you well. Our team found your song "Timeless" to be exactly what we're looking for, and we're ready to proceed immediately with buying the rights to the work.

I'll have a contract couriered over by close of business Tuesday, the same legal and payment terms as our last transaction, but of course, feel free to read over it carefully. If you have any questions, please don't hesitate to contact me.

As always, Mr. Foster, the entire Crescendo family appreciates your talent and would like to thank you for allowing us the opportunity to be a part of it.

Sincerely,

Preston Waterman, CFO

Crescendo Records

Same monotonous load of bullshit in every email. I don't even know him, let alone everyone at the label, so I seriously doubt they requested their thanks be conveyed. And be a part of what exactly? There's no "part" left for me—the song is theirs now. I'm just meaninglessly richer and on my own.

This makes the third piece I've written and sold to them. I have no idea how they found me and don't care. I'm not allowed to know, or even ask, which artist will record it or when. Don't give a fuck about that either really, except how the denial of even basic knowledge reiterates my insignificance.

I don't need the money. I sold the first one in hopes they'd see my potential and want *me* along with my songs. That's what I was hoping would be different about today's message too. But it wasn't, and deep down, I've known all along it never will be. Some boy band composed of ex-Mouseketeers whose balls haven't dropped yet are going to strike it rich off my work, and sniff it up their noses or sue their parents for it. Songs written for See You Next Tuesday—the three childhood friends who I'd have sworn could never be parted: Liz singing like an angel, Jarrett ripping chords that gave verve to my thoughts, and me banging the drums—will now be the background noise to choreographed routines geared toward the hormones of thirteen-year-old girls worldwide.

They can fucking have 'em. The songs are nothing more than painful reminders now.

Me: Heading to the gym.

I go get ready while I wait for Jarrett to respond; the plate in the oven and clothes on the bed both remain untouched. I can almost taste the cinnamon-sprinkled, syrupy goodness, and damn if I wasn't looking forward to it, but a man gives you his bed and keeps his promise—not laying you wide open and eating you like his last requested meal on death row, especially when you press your sublime little body against him, pert nipples poking his bare chest while your soft lips rest on his cheek—and you can't even say good-bye in person? I'd rather fucking starve.

The gym will help me work off some aggravation. One thing I refuse to let happen, no matter how entrenched I become in my own internal demise, is for my outsides to remotely resemble my lackluster insides. So I splash my face with cold water and brush my teeth then throw on some work-out clothes. I grab my keys and phone to head out the door when a text chimes.

Jarrett: Be there in 30.

"Rhett," Tracie croons when I walk in the gym about fifteen minutes later and approach the counter to swipe my membership card. "How're you today, handsome?"

Tracie's hot and a *superb* lay, but she's not worth breaking the rules. Flashbacks—some with my dick in my hand, some not—will have to tide us both over. Said memories aren't hard to conjure up when she leans over the counter like that, double D cleavage that I've enjoyed up close and thoroughly begging to pop out for a rematch with my tongue.

"Any better and I'd be somebody else," I reply, veering my eyes away from the twins of temptation.

I should probably ask the same polite formality of her, bluffing the most basic of manners found in anyone capable of using a fork instead of their fingers to eat, but instead I keep walking straight for the dead lift. It's always my first choice, working every part of my body at once, thus releasing the most aggression with one exertion. Shockingly, I have more than my usual abundance of it to work off today. The email from the record label pissed me off as usual, but I can't lie to myself—Reece's vanishing act is what really has me tied up in irate knots.

The one time I keep it in my fucking pants and *I'm* snuck out on?

I'm gonna feel this workout tomorrow, careless with my warm-up, or lack thereof, and not fully extending and resting on my reps. I'm really just a frenzied shit-show of needed release.

Oh fuck me. "Dark Horse" blares overhead. Surely they know other songs do, indeed, exist.

"Hey, sunshine," a jeer comes from my left.

I don't need to look to give my brother a grunt in response.

"I'd say you need to get some, but we both know *that's* not the problem. So what gives, man? Why the hell are you so damn miserable? I mean, more than usual?"

"Not," I clip on an exhale, no break in my sporadic rhythm.

"Are," he counters adamantly. "You're a shit liar, always have been. So either you didn't tap it last night, you *did* and regret it, or you're mad she left before you could leave her first. Which is it?"

"You're wrong on all counts, not that I'd tell you if you weren't, and don't fucking talk about her like that. Thought I'd already given you plenty of warnings about that shit?"

"Which brings me to my next question. *Why* have you given me plenty of warnings? You've jumped my ass about the way I talk *to* her, *about* her, way too many times for just meeting her. What is it with this girl?"

I glare at him, silently warning him to drop it *now*, but he doesn't take the hint, testing me with a defiant grin. "She's gone now and you're the only one still talking about it. Don't make a big deal about something that isn't."

"It isn't?"

"Fuck no. Jesus Jarrett, you need to go have your testosterone levels checked."

"Okay." He backs up, hands out in surrender. "So is this about the band then? 'Cause I was thinking I might be ready to give it another go."

"What band?" I set the bar down and grab my towel to wipe my face and neck. "Only two members are left standing, and I really don't see us pulling off a Sonny and Cher thing, so I'll ask you again. *What band?*"

"We could find new members."

"Then why haven't we already done that?" I raise a sardonic brow, calling him out. He and I both know damn good and well he wouldn't even entertain this idea if Vanessa hadn't cheated on him. The fact my dreams are *again* his consolation concern and distraction pisses me off more than just a little.

Jarrett ducks his head and shifts in place, knowing exactly what I'm thinking. "What do you want me to say? Yeah, I'm crawling back. And no, I didn't care about the band when I had her. But at least I took a chance, put my all into what I hoped was the real thing."

He's right, and I truly wish like hell it would've been. I want nothing but happiness for my brother. I'm proud as hell of his optimism, zest for life, and ability to bounce back as open-minded and hearted as ever.

"It's alright, really." I walk over to the bench press, and he follows, ready to spot me and helping load his end with weights. Which he can stop doing anytime. "Jarrett, one-fifty's good, man. You trying to kill me?"

"Sorry." He laughs, pulling one of the discs back off. "But seriously, let's do a few local gigs a week and see what happens. I'm worried about you."

"Couple problems with that plan." I lift, my voice strained with exertion. "I already do a couple gigs a week. Nothing happens other than the songs get bought. By the way, I sold 'Timeless.' I'll wire your cut as soon as they pay me. Anyway, doing gigs more often or at different places, it'd just be more half-ass, pass-the-time bullshit, and you know it. I'd rather give it our all"—I lift back down and up—"or just keep doing what I'm doing now. A one-man set has a chance at pulling off urban eccentricity. Two-man duo? Just looks like the band forgot to show up." I do ten consecutive reps before saying any more. "Done." I guide the bar to its bracket with his help and sit up. "Any *decent* musician we'd want to sign on should feel the same way. Go big, go home, or go broke."

"Let's do it then. Audition people and hit the road, balls out!"

"Maybe." I shrug. "I'll think about it." I gather my gear, waving over my head on my way out. "Later."

I don't move the car, sitting in the parking lot with my forehead resting pathetically against the steering wheel. I thought this Rhett died, the "deep thinker," the "old soul" who felt things and paid them prose to melody. But in one weekend, Reece awoke hibernating parts of me, *didn't want me,* and didn't even say good-bye. Liz got loved and Jarrett got screwed over. Now he's talking about the band again, but some of my best songs are already sold. This version of myself I was sure was so well buried is clawing his way up and out of the grave—I need a shovel to ensconce the pansy-ass motherfucker down a little deeper this time.

I've got "In the Air Tonight" blaring, but even it can't drown out his voice.

"Your son is 'creating' again, Margaret. Too flowery to be any son of mine. This is your doing, coddling him when he should've been taught how to be a man."

Fuck you, Dad... any day, night, or *second* I choose, I can have my choice of pussy. Not rank, honky-tonk bottom-shelf-whiskey or stuffy, saving-herself-for-marriage debutante shit either. No, I have my pick of the perfectly manicured and prime, the mistresses of men who could buy any woman they wanted. The grade-A likes of which you've never even had a sniff, and it doesn't cost me a damn thing—not even sweet talking, let alone a five-star dinner and "getaway weekends."

Yeah, Pops, I've got your "man" hanging.

Hell yes, this is more like it—anger with a vengeance. I start the car I love, zero to sixty in under six seconds, three hundred horses powering the good vibrations humming through my body, and drive to the Goldsbury—my buffet.

Less than five determined, predatory steps inside, and it's game time.

"Wanna play?" A hand snakes around my arm, the fingers and their talons searing their claim into my skin. They belong to none other than what I'm almost positive is "Jenny," a frequent "guest" of Mr. Rotti, the highest roller of them all. CEO of Rotti Industries, a diversified conglomerate buying up every electronics company possible, the man donates some serious coin to Goldsbury at least once a month. He's married with children older than Jenny; same song and dance as all the others.

"Sweetie, I just finished working out. Don't have it in me." Lie. I could bust out my fly with one stiff breeze.

I haven't fucked anyone in… I don't know in how long exactly, but it's been more than a day—too long. But oddly, and quite disturbingly, now that an offer is right in front of me, I'm not feeling it. That usually happens *during*, when they say something that's a total turn-off, or *after*, when they whine or get clingy and send my regret ratcheting. But never before. And isn't this exactly what I came here for? Easy, willing ass?

"Thank you though, gorgeous." I smile, letting her down gently, and pat her hand as I peel it from me. Picking up my pace to the exit, the bitter vengefulness I ambled in with loses steam.

Again, I sit in my car, staring out the windshield but seeing nothing. I have no idea why I just shot that girl down, highly flammable and a fire I've refused to hose down far too many times, but shoot her down I did. It's undeniable—somehow I've wandered into a weird headspace I don't like, a commotion of mystified confusion. Your mind is the trickiest, most deceitful bastard of any nemesis you have. If you don't stay in control of that relationship every single second, it'll drift in a direction of its own choosing and turn on you the first chance it gets.

I know when, and why, it happened. All that's left is figuring out the "how to fix." And there's only one way to accomplish that. Enough pussy-footin' around.

Grabbing the keys, I jump out, slam the door, and jog back inside. She's in the vicinity I left her, on a quarter machine at the end of the row, sitting pretty.

"Twenty minutes, Sherwood Forest, sixth floor," I snarl in her ear, guessing Thatch has the Forest unoccupied in case one of us needs it. If not, I'll take the one he does; theme the least of my concerns.

Her head falls back on my shoulder, eyes closed. "Finally." She moans, sliding her thighs back and forth as I rush to find Thatcher and grab the key card from him.

Fifty-two minutes later, I feel worse than I did before.

"Why not?" she sulks, hair askew, lips swollen, and the scent of her want still pungent in the room.

"Why not what?" I ask as I hurriedly get dressed.

"Why can't we do it again? He won't be looking for me yet." She folds her arms, eyes squinted with venomous courage as she tries to wheedle an encore from me.

Every. Single. Time. Really, I should probably quit fucking them.

"I never go in twice, I told you that. You said you understood completely. Remember that part?" I recite mechanically. "Can you be cool about this?" I glance over my shoulder one last time. "I had a great time, and I'll think about it often. Thank you."

I barely get the door closed before something smashes against it; my guess is the lamp. I thought those things were bolted down?

CHAPTER
ten

Reece

As the plane taxis at LAX, I turn my phone back on. I have a couple of text messages from Landry; she misses me already—probably because we spent next to no time together—and a request to let her know when I land safely.

One voicemail from my father, droning on about how I'm being irresponsible and asking if I'm done with my selfish escapades yet—delete. I *could* call him right now and tell him I'm back in L.A., thus lowering his blood pressure, but I don't.

And lastly, dousing any hope for at least a *decent* return home, I have four texts from Warrick.

Warrick (2:17pm): I miss you so much. You come home today, correct? What time?

Warrick (2:51pm): The least you could do is reply, tell me you're alive. After all we've been through, you owe me that much.

Warrick (3:23pm): I can play immature games too. Her name is Jillian and she answers the minute I call, gives me anything I want.

Then by all means, I'm begging you, call her! Again! Now, now works for me.

Warrick (3:27pm): Found your flight. I'll be waiting and YOU WILL TALK TO ME. I'M MORE THAN HAPPY TO END US BUT YOU WILL NOT SCREW ME OUT OF WHAT'S MINE!!

Welcome home, Reece. I never should've come back. I could've gone anywhere, started over, hid out. But things have changed, and I'll endure whatever they throw my way long enough to right certain wrongs.

And *us*? Who are these "us" people of which he speaks? Warrick's insane, always has been, but this is a new level of all-out hallucinatory.

Even though I'm seated in row three, I'm the very last person to de-board, dreading what awaits me inside the terminal. I trudge down the tunnel on tense legs and uncooperative feet that feel weighted with trepidation, much like battling my way against the current.

Sure enough, when I round the final corner, waiting on the other side of the glass door as threatened, arms crossed and volatility his only expression, stands Warrick Tyler. I summon up a timid smile and adjust my carry-on to offer him a friendly hug, which he shuns. Instead he takes the bag with one hand and my elbow, forcefully, in his other.

"Nice trip, *darling*?" he snarls, dripping of toxic, misguided possessiveness.

"Lovely, thanks for asking. How've you been?" I ask as I would of anyone, refusing to engage his pompous attempt at demeaning control.

"We'll talk about it in the car. Your father's waiting."

"In the car?" I can't taper my surprise. My father can hardly ever be bothered with my existence, so that he's here spikes my suspicion.

"Yes." His sneer's conniving. He loves the gang mentality he's orchestrated for reasons yet unknown.

They're up to something even worse than usual—I can feel it in every intuitive nerve ending—and "usual" is disturbing enough.

As Warrick opens the car door for me, he hands my bag to Ozzie, our driver. He's much more than a driver to me though, and I don't miss the worry in his eyes. He feels the trouble brewing as well.

"Reece," my father greets me.

I slide in, my apprehension almost paralyzing, and accept my father's dry, insincere kiss on both cheeks.

"We're so glad to have you back home where you belong," he says. "I trust your trip went well?"

Warrick joins us and gently rubs my leg. I shift away from him, unaware of when exactly we progressed to him touching me at his will.

"Where's Mother?" I ask, a rhetorical and awkward gap-filler at best.

"Off raising money for something." My father waves dismissively. "How was your friend's wedding?"

Your friend. He's known Landry as long as I have. Why he thinks it's classy or "so very upper echelon" to slide in exasperating little digs like that, I'll never understand. You can say it in a British accent while sipping tea with the queen, but if you pretend not to know something you do, especially someone's name, as if they're of no consequence—it's ignorant and pretentious; plain and simple. And it makes my skin crawl.

"Wonderful, it was a beautiful ceremony. Landry made a gorgeous bride," I lie with a straight face. I refuse to give either of them the satisfaction of the truth. Landry, with her countless interpretations of "friendship" aside, *is* my best friend. And I'll be damned if I give them an opening to lambaste her. *I* can say or think whatever I want about her—they can't.

"Speaking of gorgeous brides..." My father and Warrick share a conspiratorial grin, and my stomach rolls. "Warrick has asked permission to marry you."

A shrill laugh pops out of me. I didn't know my father had the ability to joke... or drank this early in the day? But he's not holding a drink, and his scowl is anything but reciprocal of my laughter. The vile disgust of realization spreads from the pit of my stomach throughout my body, contracting every last muscle.

"Wh-what?" I choke out.

"Yes, I was more than pleasantly surprised too, dear, but thrilled of course. I readily gave him my blessing. This sensible union is long overdue. Why, your mother can hardly wait to start making plans. Congratulations." He leans in to once more to chafe my cheeks with his sandpaper pecks.

I was only gone for three days! Surely that wasn't long enough for Warrick to completely lose his grip on reality and my father to travel back in time to *betroth me. To Warrick?*

"A fall or winter wedding, either is fine with me, my love." Warrick folds my hand in his and smiles. "Your choice."

Fall is... now. Winter, right after that. Wait, who cares? The season's not the problem—their hallucinations are!

The car, and my lungs, fill quickly with suffocating panic, but I school my expression and breathing. I need to play this just right. They think they're so clever, trying to marry me to Warrick to ensure their control of *my control.* Obviously they're not crafty enough to count though—they're too late. My twenty-first birthday has come and gone. Maybe they're in denial or don't know my birthday—which wouldn't surprise me in the slightest, my father didn't comment *on* the day after all—but either way, they've fallen short on the timing of their insane plan.

It doesn't matter to them that Warrick and I struggle for amicable proximity at best. In their cold, calculating minds, this is a logical business decision. Marry her and put her on a shelf in the corner with all the other possessions while you reign over that which isn't yours.

In three days' time, my father became a high-dollar pimp. I don't even know what to say.

And in the midst of these thoughts, a rich, tranquilizing voice echoes in my head. *"Your spice, which you only break out when it'll pack the hardest punch. Your kindness and strength."*

Suddenly, I'm no longer concerned with playing this mindful of their reactions. A fight I wasn't sure I had in me surges up and out of my mouth, empowered by the memory of a certain anomalous acquaintance. "How do you get married without being proposed to? Which I wasn't! And had I been, I would've declined, right after I stopped laughing. I'm no more interested in a life with Warrick than I am with being domineered, tricked, or coerced into things I don't want for myself." I keep my chin raised, jaw set in firm adamancy. "Warrick and I aren't anything! How exactly did we get from not even dating to marriage?"

"You're exhausted from your trip, not thinking clearly. Let's get you home for some rest," Warrick placates me with a condescending grin.

My father hums his agreement as they decide on the only possible explanation and solution as though I'd never spoken.

"Don't patronize me! Did you two honestly think I'd fall for this... this... bullshit?"

"Reece, calm down, dear." My father clicks his tongue and shakes his head disapprovingly. "This behavior, and that language, is beneath you. I apologize, Warrick, and she'll be sure to do the same when she's recovered from her trip."

"Of course," Warrick says.

I save my breath and stare out the window for the remainder of the ride, truly exasperated. I bolt from the car when we reach my penthouse, leaving my luggage and purposely eliminating any opportunity for Warrick to invite himself up. Cause who knows, maybe he does that now too; it seems anything's possible.

Emotionally and mentally exhausted and, quite honestly, a bit afraid that I'm actually the one who's lost her mind, I run a hot bath and grab my phone while I wait. I have a call to make that can't be postponed another second. Of course Oz answers on the first ring, not because he's paid to do so, but rather—we've always had this kindred, unspoken bond—an invisible, comforting barrier from those around us.

"Can you talk?" I ask quickly. The privacy partition was up when I got out of the car, and I'm praying that's still the case.

"Yes," he says quietly. "I'm sorry I didn't get a chance to warn you, sweetpea. I only caught the tail-end of their conversation right before we arrived to pick you up."

"Ozzie, they're full-on delusional! They actually suggested that Warrick and I are gonna get married! What exactly did I miss?"

"I understand, I'll call you back with that information as soon as I have it. Thank you, sir," He responds in his professional monotone then hangs up.

The partition came down.

I soak in the tub 'til I'm pruny and relaxed. I'm too weary to wait any longer for Ozzie to call me back, so I dry off and crawl under my covers. I'm just about to drift off when my phone finally rings.

"Alone at last?" I answer.

"Just dropped that sniveling idiot off at the apartment of one Ms. Zais, *a business associate*. Boy thinks I'm stupid," he growls.

"Ozzie, I don't care at all. You know I'm not even slightly interested in Warrick."

"But he's interested in you. And your father's going along with it! You're his little girl. I've got a good mind to—"

"Not important. There's no way I'm cooperating, so it doesn't matter. Now tell me something that does. Did you check on that thing I asked you about?"

"You know I did." He chuckles. "And you already know what I'm gonna say. Had your answer before you called me."

Of course I did. I knew the truth the minute the words "on the road" left his mouth. And with each

129

subsequent affirmation, I felt a bit guiltier. "I needed to be absolutely positive. Kind of a big deal."

I sigh, feeling more unresolved than ever and terrified of how to proceed. But as always, the longer Ozzie and I talk, the stronger and more capable I feel. Our plans are intricate, based mostly on faith, and it'll be amazing if we actually accomplish them.

I go to sleep feeling... spicy.

I spend the week rushing around in an endless, covert flurry. I field a few especially scrutinous phone calls from my father and Warrick, but I think I pull everything off undetected—as usual. Thankfully, those two don't give me near enough credit, never have... makes it a lot easier for me to keep my finger on the pulse.

On Thursday night, I'm drained, riding the paper-thin edge between deviously proud and paranoid, when in classic Landry fashion, her "Fancy" ringtone blares through my otherwise quiet bedroom. I hate that song, but she loves it.

"'Lo?" I garble.

"Reece, I need you to come back to Vegas. Pleaseeeee," she whines.

"I'm great, thank you for asking."

She huffs in my ear. "Sorry, how are you? Can you come back?"

"What could've possibly happened in the last four days that would warrant me flying back?" I say a little too snippily.

Landry wears me out. I truly believe, if she *really* tried, she could drive the pope to killing puppies. She didn't spend any time with me when I *was* there, and now, disaster strikes again. It could literally be *anything* that's wrong, and I do mean anything.

Once, I walked out of a board meeting, crying hysterically from the terrifying briefing I got from her because she thought letting the tiny piece of paper with "a cute lil' snowman on it" dissolve on her tongue was a good idea. Babysitting your best friend while she comes down from an LSD trip? Horrific and definitely worth a flight… except she'd have been far safer in the ER than waiting the three and a half hours it took me to fly to her.

Or the eerily similar phone call I once got because she thought some guy had "given her something?"

It was an ingrown hair.

"Landry, what is it?" I ask with as much genuine concern as I'm still able to contrive after years of friendship with   her.
"I don't want to talk about it over the phone."

"Are you hurt?"

"No, nothing like that."

I'm never one to be unsympathetic, I'd like to think, and I breathe a sigh of relief at her calming response. But I swear to God, if she just scared ten years off my life because she queefed really loudly or something as asinine, I'll strangle her with my bare hands. Yes, that happened. You can't make that kind of thing up. "Call me in the morning. If this is still a catastrophe then, I'll be there."

"It will be, Reece. You're going to have to come, *please.* I love you, best friend ever."

Now she's got me worried again, and I'm suddenly *hoping* it's the queef thing—add that to my recent, and rapidly growing, list of things I never thought would happen. Maybe I can talk her down in the morning when we're both thinking more clearly.

But I won't. If she calls in the morning, I'm Vegas-bound again… because only Landry can convince Landry something's not really a big deal. So I hang up and roll back over, planning what to pack, as sleep creeps upon me once more. Landry's annoying sometimes, but far worse are my father and Warrick.

And Vegas… isn't annoying at all.

As predicted, I wake to over ten missed calls and texts from Landry, still needing me to come back ASAP. I call her to confirm it wasn't a bad acid trip, an embarrassing bodily noise incident, or anything just as insignificant, and agree to be there as soon as I can. She promises to give me an explanation the minute I step off the plane.

Next I call my main man Oz, and together, we do what we do best—devise plans, and the excuse for him to offer my father and Warrick when they realize I'm once again not at their disposal—*I'm off preparing myself mentally to be a wife.* Makes me queasy just thinking it. As far as my location? Well, we've made an arbitrary list of places that start with "B" for him to rattle off. He's assured me ten times that he will in fact be able to say all that with a straight face and/or a mocked bout of oncoming Alzheimer's, whichever the situation calls for. There's no telling what deception those two vultures might be keen to.

So while I throw non-matching, perhaps clean, perhaps not, items in an easily carried-on bag, I book a commercial flight under the alias no one other than myself knows and head out the door.

Ozzie's waiting with a supportive, paternal grin, holding open the door for me. "Landry sounded all right today?"

"Yep, I'm sure it's nothing."

"Then why are you going?" He grins, razzing me since I *may* have let a few personal, motivational details slip while we carried out our "plans" this past week. Who else am I gonna run it by—Landry? No.

"I can't believe you're teasing me, mean old man." I faux pout in jest. "I thought you were on my side?"

"Always. You have nothing to worry about, so stop."

"But you don't even know h—"

"I know *you.* I've watched you grow into a fine young woman whose taste and judgment I trust impeccably. If you like him, I like him."

My eyes moisten. I wish my actual father could be half as faithful and understanding as Ozzie, and I thank him around a sniffle.

"Oh, don't go hugging me just yet, little one. I'm still gonna put the boy through the wringer. If he messes up in any way, he'll need the forgiveness of more than just your sweet self."

I laugh, a bit tense. "Either way, it's Landry I really am going back for."

"Uh huh." He nods and helps me in the car.

Yeah, I didn't quite buy it either.

This talk's most likely all for naught, but it sure feels good to know my Ozzie loves me unconditionally. I spend the ride to the airport wondering what Landry's gonna tell me. If it's another wedding—a do-over with her ex-douchebag, some fly-by-night sham with a new douchebag, or Jarrett *(oh God, surely not already)*—I'll kill her.

Pregnant? Not the end of the world. I'll help her.

New job? Nah, she'd have spilled that over the phone… unless it's as a stripper or a porn star. *Anddddd, I'm again rooting for queef.*

I simply can't guess, so I give up and go back to pondering the one thing, above all, that's got my stomach in a perpetual nervous cramp and my chest constricting tighter with each anxious breath. *Does Rhett know I'm coming back?* And if so, how does he feel about that? If anything at all... I haven't asked Landry about him once, and she hasn't freely shared. Then again, I haven't had a chance to tell her any specifics about our whirlwind of non-specifics, and I highly doubt she picked up on anything herself, what with her failed engagement/hot new roommate extravaganza happening simultaneously.

When the car stops, I throw on my ball cap, pulling my ponytail through the opening in back, pop on my sunglasses, and get out before I have time to talk some sense into myself.

Ozzie takes in the additions to my attire, one brow rising. "Something concerning you about this trip?"

Even though I think he's the softest teddy bear in the world, with a smile and laugh that could bring about world peace—when he uses them—my Oz is one very large and in charge man. If he thinks for one second that harm's even looking in my direction, I truly pity the person who tries to stand in his way.

"Just my gut." I shrug one shoulder. "Things are changing, on my terms and timeline. I'm not taking any chances of that being ruined."

"You need anything, you contact me," he grumbles. My cryptic explanation isn't to his liking.

CHAPTER eleven

Rhett

And here I was thinking all I had to do today was lay in bed and catch up on my *Breaking Bad* DVDs. I'm hoping I can get through the whole box set and caught up before *someone* realizes what a bad idea ending the show was and miraculously brings back a whole new season. Seriously folks—only fix shit that's actually broken—leave brilliant alone.

No such luck though. Jarrett's text is a grueling reminder of his top not-at-all secret plans for me tonight.

Jarrett: Picking you up at eight. Be ready. And act happy fucker.

Granted, he's by far a more pleasant person than I am, but he's never such a party planner. Why is this so important to him? It's not as though I have that many friends busting down the door to come to my birthday party. My bubbly personality isn't exactly a magnet, so how elaborate could this scheme of his possibly be?

Me: I'll give you $200 to forget the whole thing.

Jarrett: I'll buy you $200 of liquid enthusiasm to get through it. Don't ruin this.

Party it is then.

I guess it couldn't hurt to hang with my brother for one night. Honestly, I could use a reprieve, anything other than my two option—alone or just finished fucking and ready to be alone again—monotony. I spent some time this last week going back to the regimen that silences the voices in my head, but it didn't work for even a second. If possible, it made me feel worse. A new, unexplainable cloud of guilt attached to each girl.

I drag myself out of bed and head to the shower, determined to find the right frame of mind for tonight. If it's this important to my brother, it's important to me. When I'm dressed, I call him.

"Birthday boy!" Jarrett answers with over-exuberance, as though we didn't just converse twenty minutes ago.

"I'm ready."

"Well stop the fucking presses." He laughs. "I said eight though. That's when the little hand's on the eight and the big hand's on the twelve, bro."

"Who uses clocks with actual hands anymore, nut funk? I'm ready now." I could just as easily crawl back in bed, and I might do that if we don't get this shit started. "I'll meet you there. Where we going?"

Jarrett's never quite mastered the concept of whispering, but everyone in the background apparently sucks at it too. One of those faint voices, I could pick out in the midst of the apocalypse.

"Put her on the phone," I bark. No, not *that* her. With the complete radio silence on that front, and not a word from Jarrett and Landry's camps, I'm starting to think I imagined her.

"Who?" He plays dumb, humor lacing his pathetic attempt.

"Jarrett," I warn, "let me talk to her."

Liz. Came for my birthday. No doubt with Cannon in tow—which is fine, he's a great guy. With authority, Cannon Blackwell had busted in and swept away all the cobwebs and demons holding Liz hostage, and now... she's happy. And I'm happy for her.

The part I didn't tell Reece, the perplexing little pixie I may or may not have imagined, is that Liz'll always be mine in a way. She'll always be the first girl who taught me that females worthy of admiration do exist, and when found, they're to be protected and coveted with every ounce of strength you possess... but I wasn't made to *love* her. I wasn't created to be her change. Just her best friend.

"Rhett?" Her sweet voice rings in my ear.

That's what "found" sounds like.

"Liz, how's my girl?"

"Very good. How're you?"

"It's my birthday, so I'm even more chipper than usual, if that's possible," I joke. "Seriously though, I can't believe you came."

"Of course I did, it's been too long. Besides, when Dad, Laura, and Alma teamed up and offered to watch the girls and keep Conner away from open flames for a whole weekend, I was out the door before they had time to ask me twice." She laughs, and every dark cloud in this hemisphere dissipates with the sound. "So are we coming to get you or what? I'm ready to get my Mommy's Off Pamper Duty party on!"

"Hell yes, come get me. Tell them to hurry up!" Now I'm excited. Honest to God excited.

"On our way!"

This is the good stuff. The times a man commits to memory and pulls out to revisit when everything else goes to shit.

Liz shines with a new vibrancy, a light in her eyes that's unmistakable, even in the dimly lit club. And her boobs? She's definitely still breastfeeding or pumping or whatever keeps your tits triple their normal size. Honestly, I didn't even have time to avoid looking and they were right there- front and center. Cannon looks dog tired, which brings me much needed amusement. An added surprise, Cannon's sister Sommerlyn has accompanied them on the trip. And while she's hot as fuck, body banging harder than Bonham, certain streets don't need a "No Parking" sign for you to know—Keep. Fucking. Driving. *The other way.* If only she agreed with my sensible, and safe, reasoning. Which clearly, she doesn't, draped all over me like very drunk, tacky curtains.

Jarrett thinks it's funny as hell, sloughing off my many "help me" glares. Landry and Liz are, um... I look around... dropping it like it's lukewarm on the dance floor, Cannon standing vigil over them.

That leaves me fending off Sommerlyn's advances by myself, until the birthday Gods take pity upon me and JC finally arrives.

"That's one helluva present," he says, raking grateful eyes all over Sommerlyn. "Who got ya that? Was there a bow on it?"

"I've told you about my friend Liz, right? Married Cannon. My nieces." I roll my hand, urging him to speed up the connecting of the dots.

"Oh yeah." His bewildered memory scan fully loads.

"Uh huh, well, this is Sommerlyn, *Cannon's little sister.*" I send him an S.O.S. in my tone. "Sommerlyn?" I turn her, up and *off me,* toward him. "This is my single, not almost your family, friend JC. You guys get to know each other. I've gotta hit the head. Don't leave her alone, man."

I dart toward the men's room. First things first, and then I'm drinking. Heavily.

A few shots—*not* taken off any part of Sommerlyn's body, despite her encouragement—later and the karaoke hath commenced.

"Dude, you need to up your game. Her hand *accidentally* brushes my cock one more time, and I'm out," I tell JC as the girls take the stage.

"Do you not see me trying? Girl's only got eyes for you."

"Shot!" I bang my hand on the bar, needing one severely as Sommerlyn takes the lead vocals on whatever this shit song they chose is.

My brain weeps with her first caterwaul. Why not let Liz sing it, *please*? I tip back my deafening elixir while JC rattles off excuses for his digressing prowess and Jarrett flips through the binder, deciding what "us men" should sing.

"You guys go ahead," I decline. "I'm good right here."

"Drink more, whatever you need to do," Jarrett says, "but enjoy your goddamned party, and I mean it."

He and JC head up to the stage, Jarrett snagging Cannon's arm to join them. The girls bound back, all hyped up from their "performance." *If that's what we're calling it.* I quickly pull Landry onto my lap.

"Wh—" she gasps.

"Just go with it, I'm begging you. Sit still and remain strategically placed between my dick and Sommerlyn until the guys get back," I request.

She giggles. "Okay. Very wise decision, I'm impressed."

"As am I." Liz stands beside us now. "What's her name, and when do I get to meet her?"

Landry turns her head to give me a twisted smile and widened, curious eyes, waiting to see if I'll say...what I don't. "Not Sommerlyn, your husband's sister, for damn sure. He could keep a better eye on her, by the way."

"Didn't ask who it *wasn't*," Liz counters. "Very nice try though."

Landry says, "Her name is—"

"They're starting," I interrupt and jostle her with a move of my leg.

Sommer's shooting me the stink eye. I feel it boring into the side of my face like a heat-seeking missile, but I stare at the stage and will the guys to hurry up and cover Liz's inquisition with some noise.

"Black" by Pearl Jam starts, and I jerk my brother a "good choice" chin-up. Jarrett can nail the vocals on this song and Cannon's a great blend... if JC wasn't backing them up. Poor guy can't catch a break tonight. I have to laugh at the looks they both throw JC every few words, destroying their musical mojo, and Landry knocks me upside the head.

Just when I was beginning to less than detest her. "I shouldn't have to tell you this, but you can't be hittin' men that aren't yours."

"I just did. Now be quiet, Jarrett's singing." She sighs wistfully as she watches him, enraptured.

Huh.

When they finish, Landry springs from my lap to wrap her entire being around my brother, falling into his mouth before he's cleared the stairs. Guess who wastes no time sliding herself over my way?

"Are you gonna sing one?" Sommerlyn attempts a flirty purr. Gotta appreciate her tenacity.

"Nah, I—"

"The hell you say," Jarrett interjects. "Someone else is up, then it's all you, birthday boy!"

"Shot!" I shout, waving to get the bartender's attention.

An inexplicable surge of heat works its way from the base of my feet to the tips of every hair on my head. *What the...* I do a quick scan in all directions as the eerie sense of being watched builds in intensity. Seeing nothing or no one overtly out of the ordinary, I turn back to the stage.

Well happy motherfucking birthday to me... I steel my jaw from dropping as I watch. Hard-wired to the very center of my desolate, cantankerous core is Reece Kelly, climbing the steps to the stage on shaky but mesmerizing legs. She takes the microphone off the stand with a trembling hand.

"Happy birthday, bro." Jarrett chuckles and slaps my shoulder. "Didn't even have to blow out a candle. You're welcome."

Nosy, sneaky motherfucker...love the hell out of him. I'd tell him that, but I can't look away. Even more fascinating than, well, *her* is her song choice. From the first word that leaves her miniature mouth, I'm entranced. Again with the deceitful packaging—the girl's got a huge, beautiful set of lungs on her. Where she fits them I haven't the first guess.

And she *sees* me.

Her green eyes never once stray from mine as she sings "I've Got This Friend" by The Civil Wars, one of my favorites. She lends her own beauty to the song in this solo rendition, but I'd damn sure love the chance at a duo with her. Before she's even finished, I'm up and making my way to her, blocking her path at the side of the stage.

She fidgets, head dipped, as she speaks softly to the floor. "Happy Birthday, Rhett. Nice to see you again."

I take liberties with my finger under her chin and lift her face, smiling when her gaze belongs to me. "Thank you, Teaspoon. What're you doing back in town?"

"Long story." She rolls those emerald eyes as her shoulders slump. "Landry sort of tricked me. Not that I'm upset. I, uh—" Her eyes flicker to everywhere but me, then she snickers softly. "Never mind. Happy birthday."

"Never thought I'd say this, but I'm pretty pleased with Landry. She's on a roll tonight." I dip my head to once again snare that attention she keeps refusing me. "Pretty intrigued by your song choice too, which you sang beautifully."

Her teeth slowly torture first her bottom lip then the top, ending her innocent seduction with a gentle swipe of her tongue that has me feeling anything but innocent.

"So which do you feel like explaining first, why that song or why I didn't get a good-bye?"

"You did get a good-bye. I left a note. And the breakfast I promised," she mumbles, shifting from one foot to the other.

"Hmmm." I lean in, my mouth stopping short of the taste of her earlobe it craves. "Not sure a note qualifies. You slept in my sheets, so I'm thinkin' I deserved at least a wave on your way out. And I was too pissed to eat the breakfast." I blow a hot breath along her skin and savor her shiver. "So I'm still waiting for a taste."

She gasps and falters back, but I'm already moving in to eat up the space, pressing against her. I don't know why I'm so drawn to her, which is almost as annoying as it is exhilarating. She isn't anything like the only other female to ever garner my attention for more than…an hour tops. She's not a bottle blond—the flaxen hue of her locks is God-given—her eyes aren't brown, and she's as far from brassy and brazen as one gets without literally being a mute. Well, except for that one sexually frustrated, uncharacteristic outburst in the hallway… which apparently, I still find adorable enough for just the memory to get me hard. Her allure hit me sharp, fast, and seemingly out of nowhere, like being struck by lightning with not a storm cloud in sight. What the hell is it? I've truly listened to every word she's said, anticipating the next; only having wondered what color her little panties are once this entire time.

"Rhett, you're up!"

I somehow comprehend the DJ's intrusion.

"It's your turn for karaoke," she whispers.

"Not happening," I whisper back.

"That works too."

"Why are you here, Reece?" I involuntarily growl, dragging her tighter against me.

Tense and eyes on the run from me again, her words slip quietly past her lips. "We need to talk. But it can wait. I don't want to spoil your party."

"You couldn't spoil anything if you tried." I shake my head and laugh, at her yes, but more at the realization that I'm hedging closer to unrecognizable with each Reece encounter. "You're not big enough." I tap her nose then take her hand as she giggles. "Come on, meet a few of my friends, then we'll find somewhere to talk. Yes?"

"Yes." She grins... but not fully.

I'm not real sure what a "we need to talk" talk could possible entail when we haven't fucked, but I'm sure it can't be good. I tighten my grip on her hand and lead us at half the speed of my impatience, knowing her little legs wouldn't be able to keep up. After helping her into a seat at the bar, I ask for a water, needing a clear head as soon as possible. I finish the whole glass in large gulps and spin Reece's chair around to face our audience.

"Everyone, this is Reece Kelly. She's Landry's best friend." I look at Liz while I speak.

"Hi, I'm Liz Blackwell." She steps forward with a smile, pulling Cannon with her. "And this is my husband, Cannon. I grew up with Rhett and Jarrett."

"Very nice to meet you both. I've heard wonderful things."

Liz's smile brightens at Reece's reply. "Wish I could say the same." Liz nudges me with her shoulder. "Really though, it's nice to meet you, Reece. So you know Rhett through your friend Landry? I don't think I got the story how she knows him either."

"That's because nobody told you yet." Cannon laughs and wraps an arm around her shoulders, squashing her interrogation. "Dance with me."

"To karaoke?"

Yeah, even I laugh at that. *Thanks for trying, Cannon.*

"Fine, siren, we're really just going to find anything else to do before you scare Reece. Catching on now?" He winks at Reece. "She's harmless. Nice to meet you."

Liz's chewing him out as they walk away, her flapping arms and scowl unmistakable as I chuckle at them.

"So, *the* Lizzie, huh?" Reece murmurs.

"That'd be her," I grumble. I'm not sure why, but I'm uneasy about those two worlds colliding.

JC props one elbow on the bar, giving her a smile. "Hey, Reece, glad to see you back. Staying a while this time?"

"Hello to you." She beams, too big, and replies, too friendly. "Not sure yet, but probably not very long." She glances at me from the corner of her eye.

"I give up!" Sommerlyn, apparently still lurking nearby, huffs. "Can we go home already?"

"Excellent idea." JC inches up to her side. "I'll take you."

No way Cannon's letting that happen—*if* he finally cues in on the fact his sister's even here tonight. All of them getting caught up in that debate *on the other side of the damn building* is more than fine by me. I love my family, but Reece is two inches away and driving me insane with her "need to talk" and sweet scent of honeysuckle.

This party needs to wrap the hell up.

However fucking long later, Liz and Cannon offer their departure excuse, calling it an early night because "they're exhausted"—code for "we never get to fuck without one part of our brains focused on the baby monitor right beside us." I stand to give Cannon a handshake good-bye and Liz a long overdue hug.

That's her chance to critique in my ear. "I like her a lot. Adorable and subtle, great singer. And I *love* the look she puts on your face. Wasn't sure your eyes still knew how to sparkle."

"That so?"

"Excellent choice, Rhett. She has class."

"Which means one thing—she's out of mine."

Liz leans back and frowns, her eyes glistening with unshed tears. "I pray you don't really believe that. You're as classy and fine a man as ever's been made, despite your bullshit quest to prove otherwise."

"Sounds a lot like the last speech I got from Reece." I laugh.

"See?" She slaps my arm. "I knew I liked her!"

"Come on, love," Cannon hurries her, desperate to get laid.

"I gotta go." Liz starts to walk away then pivots and speaks softly in my ear again. "Show her the *real* Rhett, just once, for me?"

I nod then dodge her eyes, done with the introspection. I catch a glimpse of them walking out, hand in hand, Cannon bent to her ear. *They don't make it look so bad.* In fact, Sommerlyn's the only picture of misery here, trudging along behind them—*alone.*

JC's quick to say his good-bye as well, and I have no idea where Jarrett and Landry disappeared to long ago… and that's all of them.

She's pretending to be enraptured by the person on stage when I walk back over and sit beside her.

"Just us," I point out.

She's obviously well aware, the rapid pulse in her neck her Judas. "Be right back." She jumps up. "Ladies' room!"

Reece

I hide in the bathroom much longer than necessary, scrubbing my hands twice to the entirety of, ironically enough, "Happy Birthday"—learned that tip on Oprah. Then I touch up my makeup and give myself a quick freshener spritz. It dawns on me that I've been in here awhile, working on settling my nerves, and he probably thinks I'm… *Oh God*! What if he thinks I was pooping? *So attractive.* Even more humiliating is that according to my current reasoning, he must have thought the same thing the last time I left him waiting outside a restroom!

Men do basic things in the bathroom: pee, *the other*, and if you're extremely lucky, a quick swipe of their hands under water, wiping them dry on their pants—done.

That's all the knowledge he's equipped with, so he'll have no choice but to conclude, once it's clear I didn't actually "fall in," that I must've been pooping. How do you explain to an insanely gorgeous man that you don't have nervous bowels, he simply makes you nervous? I scan my options, of which there are none. No back entry to the restroom and absolutely no chance of being able to reach the window, let alone hoist myself through it.

Maybe he got distracted by one of his frequent "fly-bys" and left.

I like that option least of all.

I peek around the door, and of course he's propped against the wall, arms crossed and staring right at me, a glorious, smug smirk alight his handsome face.

"Come here," he mouths, coaxing me out of hiding with a sexy crook of his finger and raise of his chin.

Denying *that*—not an option. I'm blushing feverishly, scorching heat on my neck and cheeks, as I amble toward him, eyes focused on my feet. When I'm near enough to smell him, his own scent that never quite left my nostrils and brain, I stop, still gawking at the floor.

"I wasn't pooping, I swear." I cringe at my astounding grace, dying a little inside as the words fall, unapproved, from my mouth.

His laugh is loud, joyful, and sincere, the first time I've heard it exactly like that, and I bask in it before realizing he's laughing *at* me and shrink further back into my shell.

"I know." His voice is deep and unarming as he leans in and tips up my chin. "But that was classic,

Teaspoon. Been needing a dose of your special brand of humor so bad. Thank you."

So glad I could be of assistance.

"No, you were adding mascara and lip gloss, neither of which you need. And"—he leans nearer and inhales—"putting on some smelly good. You don't need that either, especially since you weren't pooping." He takes my hands and rubs his thumbs along my knuckles. "Washed these *at least* twice too. Am I right?"

I nod, diverting my eyes from his all-seeing ones.

"You done stalling? Ready to go have that talk now?"

"Sure." I gulp, nerves fully reinstated. "Should I tell Landry? Do we know where they went?"

"If I'm not mistaken, I believe my brother escorted her into the men's bathroom."

"*The bathroom*? Why not go to their apartment?"

"Sometimes you just can't wait." He grins and shrugs one shoulder.

"Or you *can*." I grimace. "I don't care if you're Long Dong Silver and repeatedly growl the sexiest words I've ever heard—being bent over to stare into a public toilet has *got* to kill the mood!"

"Oh shit," Rhett wheezes, laughing so hard it's soundless, his breath caught in his chest.

"Are you okay?" Should I... pat his back, do the Heimlich, what?

"Fuck." He comes around, still gasping for deep breaths. "You're hilarious, Teaspoon. And you can stop worrying. I'm sure he's got her up against the wall."

Still not even remotely sexy. Mid-heave, I change the subject. "So how was it, seeing Liz?" I toss the question out there and walk around him, back to the bar, our knees touching when he joins me.

"If we're starting the twenty-one questions portion of the evening, I have a really important one," he says.

"Okay." I fiddle with my hands. "What is it?"

"Could you love me in a Bentley?"

I roll my eyes and laugh, delighted and temporarily relieved. "Only if you could love me in a bus," I tease him back, glad he's forgotten about "the talk" for the time being.

"You got it."

"I wouldn't have pegged you for a 50 Cent guy. Rubik's Cube, I swear."

"Most of that album has killer rhythm. Manufactured and no real instruments harmed in the making of course, but good beats nonetheless. *And* now that you're relaxed, tell me what you wanted to talk about. You didn't think I forgot, did ya?" He leans back, arm stretched across the back of my chair.

"I was sure hoping." I sigh. This is the perfect time to just say it, but I'm having trouble digging up the courage. Talking to him, his dark blues eyes constantly engaged, a smirk always hinting at the corner of his mouth, an undeniable virility his perpetual cloud... I don't want to risk him never treating me to all that ever again, even if just on the occasional visit.

I would miss it.

I would miss the thrill of the possibility.

"Reece?" He shatters my disheartening thoughts with his murmur, his forehead now resting against mine. "You came back to me. Tell me why."

Did I? No, I came back to *Las Vegas. To do what's right.*

Who am I trying to kid? You can say you eat Cracker Jacks because they're fabulous, heaven in your mouth all on their own, all you want. Everyone knows you're looking for the extra surprise in every box before the first bite.

Much like Ozzie, and obviously Rhett, I can't fool myself either—I'm here for the extra surprise.

I have him in prime conversation position—no fortified macho bullshit, just straight up discussion, which I think we've both been craving—and I'm wordless.

"What's something you like to do for fun, to escape everything else, your... remedy?" he asks.

"Sing," my instinct answers.

"And you're excellent at it." He chuckles. "But that might not work for what I have in mind. What else?"

"What *do* you have in mind exactly?" I ask, a bit worried but oh so free, and I realize I'm completely okay with any answer he gives.

"Just name something else, impromptu, that you could do right now."

How can I refuse that boyish smile, the clever pride dancing in his eyes? "There's one thing, but... I don't know why I'm telling you this." My eyes roll themselves.

"Spit it out." He tickles my sides. "You know you wanna tell me, so say it."

I'm squirming, laughing and forgetting to feel self-conscious. "I people story. Like—"

"Bet I got it. Let's see if I'm right. Come on." He rises, pulling me up by the hand and tossing a few bills on the bar. Placing his hand on the dip of my back, slightly brushing my butt as I move, he leads us to the exit.

"Where are you taking me and why?" I ask with an excitement I can't conceal. I'm already having fun, whatever we're actually gonna be doing, 'cause there's no way he guessed what I meant correctly from the few words he let me get out.

He looks at me over his shoulder but continues walking us forward, outside now. "If you're conscious of the effort, it's work. You and I has yet to ever feel like work, and I'll be damned if we're ruining that now. Have a seat." He guides me down on a bench and joins me, sliding his arm around my shoulders. "So you people watch and make up their story, one that's probably, hopefully, better than their reality. That about right?"

"No." I peer up at him, sure my blatant wonder's on full display. "That's *exactly* right."

"Very cool. Show me. Tell me what you have to say but don't want to say while you show me. Get lost in your thing and just think out loud."

He makes it sound so easy. Maybe it can be.

"How about him?" He points at a short bald man wearing purple yoga pants.

"Um, no. Her." I motion to a young girl with blond hair, about twelve years old, obviously with her parents.

"Okay, her." He takes my hand and rubs his thumb along the inside of my wrist. "I'm ready."

I inhale, mentally tracking the lungful of bravery's path through my body, and blow it out slowly. "That little girl wants to be a star when she grows up. Her whole life, she's been watching her dad make ordinary people into extraordinary people, and she wants to show him that she's extraordinary too. She's been begging him, for as long as she can remember, to listen to her sing. Tomorrow, he's gonna find himself in a jam and finally give her a chance."

I wait, but he doesn't say anything, so I steal a sidelong peek at him. No, he's not asleep, just silently watching me with palpable consideration.

"Go on," he encourages.

Looking back at the crowd bustling up and down the Vegas sidewalk in both directions, I spot her. "That young lady—blond hair, tan leather jacket? She's in one of her father's girl groups, called My Mama Said. Their first single, 'When He Looks at Me,' has been very well received, but no one notices there's anyone in the group besides the lead singer. That girl gets a solo career almost immediately, and all the promo and hype for the group album is quickly forgotten. So is the girl in the jacket. Almost overnight, her father forgets she exists."

He tucks me deep into his side and rests his chin on my head. "Hey, this was supposed to be fun, make things easier. Not make you cry."

I sniffle and peer up to offer him a weak smile. "It was a great idea. Please, let me keep going."

His brow wrinkles, and he hesitates but nods.

I scan the passersby and focus on a woman standing still and looking into a store window. She's taller than me and I can't tell her eye color from here, but I can sense her longing for something she wants but can't quite grasp. "Her, at the window." I point. "For most of the last decade, she's been dancer A, B, and C in some videos, a back-up singer in two quickly failing bands, and the invisible keyboardist/songwriter for one very nasty male star."

"We should go buy her whatever she's eyeing in that store." He laughs shallowly; he's very much attuned to this particular round of people story.

"No, she doesn't want you to pity her. Everything gets better. You see, Nicki—oh, that's short for her middle name, Nicolette, by the way—Nicki has two very big plusses in her favor."

"And what might those be?" Yup, he's keen, his tone low with recognition and cynicism.

"Nicki was always her grandpa's favorite lil' munchkin, the *only star* in his eyes, and he made sure what was his would one day be hers. She just had her twenty-first birthday not too long ago, and that means Nicki can now do what she wants, like recording and going back to using her real name, which is—"

"Reece," he finishes for me.

I bob my head and keep my stare directed on the woman at the window, bracing for what I know will be the loss of his touch. "Since she's of age, she's now in control…" I swallow hard and squeeze my eyes shut. "Of Crescendo Records."

I wait several excruciating minutes. The only sounds I hear are that of our heavy breaths comingling. I don't dare look at him to gauge his reaction. I'm afraid of the hurt and disappointment I'll find on his face. But he hasn't let go of me, and I'm soaking up all he'll give me while I can.

"So…" He clears his throat. "Your name's Reece Nicolette Kelly, I'm guessing from Connecticut originally, still not even close to 5'3", and you own Crescendo Records, the label I've sold three songs to. That about sum it up?"

"Three?" My head flies up and back so I can look in his eyes. "Ozzie checked and said it was only two."

"I signed the contract on 'Timeless,' but haven't received the payment yet."

"Nor will you. That contract will be shredded or returned to you, your choice. The payment terms you've been being offered are not near what you're worth, and some contractual points don't work for me either."

"Why?" His voice is monotone, no cloaked accusation or anger.

I shift back into the crook of his draped arm, pleasantly surprised that he allows it. "You play this round with me." I whisper my plea, praying it's a good idea. "There, that couple sitting on the edge of the fountain. See them?"

"I see them," he murmurs.

"They randomly met one night, and everything from that point on's been really confusing. She can't believe the impact he's had on her in such a short amount of time and why it's so important to her that he never think badly of her. She's scared he thinks that she somehow planted her best friend in his city so she could one night happen to catch him at the door of a club where he doesn't even work."

"He doesn't think that for a second."

I relax marginally when he plays along, hugging me impossibly closer.

"He knows what Fate looks like."

"But he told her his name, and she recognized it *almost* instantly. She wanted to be sure though, before she outed her private affairs, so she did some digging when she got home."

"Before she left though, he told her about his band, his dreams, even sang her one of his songs. She wouldn't try to deny being sure then, would she?"

I have to try to answer him twice, the first attempt lost between my rapidly heaving chest and threatening tears. "No, no, she wouldn't. She should've said something before she left. She knows that, and she's very sorry."

His lips brush my ear, rubbing back and forth in warm comfort, and a tremor racks through me.

"Is that why she left, she was afraid to tell him? Did she think he'd misplace coincidence as blame on her?" The tip of his tongue traces the shell of my ear. "He doesn't look like the kind of guy who would've done that."

I nod at the couple. "Look, she's begging him to believe her, forgive her. She omitted, and she knows that's *technically* lying, but she's not a *liar*; she just needed to get things lined up. And see? Now he's telling her to stop feeling guilty." A nervous giggle escapes me. "How could she be sure of his reaction, that he wouldn't hate her?"

"She couldn't, until she tried. It's called faith." He sighs, his hot breath hitting my skin.

Before I collapse under the weight of his words, I try for levity again. "Let's not discount his crazy mood swings though. Which included leaving her alone to pursue *relations* with a hussy after sexy dancing with her. Actually, now that I really think about it, *wow*. Poor girl. Yeah, I totally think he should forgive her. What about you?"

"Look at me," he growls.

161

I let my head fall his way, quivering down to my DNA.

"I sold those songs willingly, for the price offered," he says. "I wasn't stolen from or duped. You could've mentioned the whole double persona, owning a record label part, yes, but it's not worth leaving without saying good-bye and not a word for four days."

"She thought—"

"No." He glides a hand up my cheek and demands my undivided attention. "We did your distraction thing, and it was cool, glad it helped. See why your singing choice wouldn't have worked? Might've gotten awkward for us to sing all that back and forth."

He laughs, and I sigh minimal relief at the sound; he's not absolutely furious. Rhett could yodel the Gettysburg Address and anyone within earshot of his throaty, graveled message would listen—but yeah, I see his point.

"We're doing things my way now," he decrees in a low rumble. "You left some shit unsaid. You're sorry, and I forgive you, but truth is, Teaspoon, I wasn't exactly honest with you either."

"About what?" I stammer, tension creeping back into my joints. We just full-circled to square one, and the thought of anything destroying our "start over" is daunting. I'm just not ready to give up on what might be.

"I've spent the last four days wondering what happened, or didn't happen, between us… and why I even cared. I wasn't lying when I said you intrigue me in a way no one has in, possibly *ever*, and conversations with you are indeed my favorite. But when I said I was glad we didn't fuck, that was a flat-ass lie. *No guy* is ever glad about that. Would it be cool to be able to sleep with you *and* stay your friend? Sure. But, Reece"—he scoots closer, surrounding me, his leg pressed against the mine, his arm around me, his hand on my face—"truth is, I want inside your hot little body so goddamn bad I can hardly think of anything else."

CHAPTER thirteen

Rhett

You can't say things like that." She chews her lip, staring at me with those big green eyes filled with a smoky innocence she can't hide any better than she can decide on.

"Just did," I growl, shoving my hands through her hair and pulling back her head.

I crash my mouth over hers, any semblance of control extinct. At first she resists me, lips clamped in a firm line, but for this particular girl—I'm willing to work a little for it.

"Stop thinking. Open for me," I hum upon her lips then trace their seam with the tip of my tongue, urging her to surrender.

After a few more seconds of stubbornness, with a breathy moan, she does. Her mouth is small, warm, and tastes of sweet liquor, and the longer I slide my tongue along hers, the deeper into the kiss she falls. She's only listening to her body now, letting it take over. Her arms wrap around my neck, and her fingers creep into my hair and tug.

Never leaving her mouth, I hoist her into my lap and yank one short leg up and over so she's straddling me. *Much better.* This way I can feel the heat between her legs as she wriggles against the hard-on in my jeans and she can feel what she does to me, what she's been doing to me since I met her. She wants this as badly as I do—there's nothing indecisive about the way she kisses me now. She gently bites my lip, and her throaty moans drive me crazy as she writhes harder against me, as though fighting her way through the non-existence space between us. And her little noises, fuck me but her little noises have me struggling not to take her right now, right here on this bench.

"Reece," I groan into her mouth, about to forget that we probably need to continue this elsewhere.

I grab her ass with both hands, squeezing, moving her faster. It's not as though we'll get arrested for public indecency. This *is* Vegas. I nip across her jawline, sucking down her neck... which means I left her mouth free.

"I thought we agreed we weren't gonna do this?" She tries to sound resolute, but I hear louder her latent want, that she's silently asking me to vindicate, as she scoots back and off my lap. "Now you're messing up the yellow too."

"*I'm* messing up the yellow?" I scoff, adjusting some painfully neglected parts. "Teaspoon, I've been stopping on green since the night we met."

"You have?"

"You felt the answer to that, just rubbed yourself all over it." I grab her thighs and pull her back to me. "Don't play coy with me. And don't act like I'm the only one on this bench thinking about my dick sliding inside you right now."

She sucks in a sharp breath, but it's followed up immediately by a low hum. *She likes dirty talk.* But I know, without question, she'd deny it if I asked. My closet naughty girl—I can deal with that.

"*Would* it slide right inside you, Reece? Are you nice and ready for it?" I husk in her ear, moving my hand higher up her thigh.

"Yes." She doesn't realize she's moaning, her forehead dropping against my shoulder, making her ear even more accessible.

"Yes what?" Hand now there, I press two fingers exactly where she wants me, and she shudders for me with a soft whimper, parting her legs slightly. "Yes what, Reece?"

"Yes, I want you. How could I not?" She rocks her hips into my hand. Her breathing quickens, face still hidden in my shirt. "You have... you have to stop," she pants.

"But you don't want me to. You want me to make you—"

The loud, intrusive backfire of a car startles her... and stabs me in the dick. No, I mean it; it actually feels as if someone reached over and cut my dick off, just for ironic shits and giggles.

The moment's gone, de-fucking-stroyed, and the only thing in her expression as she jolts backward and out of my grasp is recognition. Of where we are. What she almost let herself get lost in. I can see I'm losing her. The rate of her rising and falling chest is approaching dangerous, the sweet flush of her cheeks now a fully enflamed, scorching red, and that little tongue is working her lips so hard and fast they're gonna chafe.

She's five seconds from crying, running... or coding.

Only one thing I can do at this point.

"Rhett! Have you lost your mind? Put me down!"

She's squealing, her arms and legs flailing wildly from the second I throw her over my shoulder. Not that she's bothering me; all of her rubbing against me, tits bouncing and ass wiggling, is more than enjoyable.

"Settle down, or people are gonna think I'm abducting you and call the cops." I swat her squirmy ass, and she shrieks.

"You are abducting me!"

"And I'm okay with that. Not sure the cops would be though." I quicken my pace toward my car and set her on her feet when we're there.

Goddamn, she's adorable, and I take a second to appreciate it before I fuck it up, literally. Her hair's tousled, and she's fuming like a little one-woman storm as she pats it down. Her whole body trembling, eyes narrowed, and mouth all twisted up—she's the vision I didn't know I was looking for… until I saw it.

But this little fit she's feigning… she can't fool me any more than I seem to be able to fool her.

"Why are you looking at me like that?" she asks with just a touch of snark.

"I think I've covered that."

"Rhett, we can't. Especially now." She stops my advance by pressing a shaky hand against my chest.

"Now that what? It's my birthday, you came back to me, sang to me? Or maybe now that I know you kiss with all that spice of yours? No, I know—we can't now that I'm standing here timing my pulse in my dick. Is that it?" I cover her hand with mine and start to guide it southward, but she tears it from my hold.

The consideration in her eyes morphs to indecision, and I feel a shift in the air between us the instant she reaches a verdict. "I have an idea. A different remedy for you this time."

I'm almost sure she doesn't mean a blowjob, and yet I still find myself anxious over any possibility. That's the thing about Reece that's most perplexing—and reconfirmed every time I'm around her. Whatever she has in mind, I'll enjoy it. Look forward to it. Feel alive with it.

"You're fun, Teaspoon." I didn't mean to say that aloud.

"As are you," she responds instantly, voice warm and sincere. "Thank you for being so understanding about everything. I really am sorry, and I'm gonna do my best to make it up to you."

Just keeps testing my resolve—little minx.

"Stop!" She swats at my chest when I wiggle my eyebrows. "I don't mean fellatio!"

So the thought *did* cross her mind.

"Did you really just say fellatio?" I laugh and open her door. "We're gonna have to work on your dirty talk. You love when I talk dirty to you; don't you think I might enjoy hearing some back?"

As I round the car, I don't have to look this time. I hear her pop up the lock on my side.

"Where are we going?" she asks when I'm in the driver's seat—figuratively and literally.

"My house."

"But I was gonna get a room here, at Goldsbury. I didn't feel safe depending on Landry for a place to stay— we've seen how well that works out."

"You feel safe depending on me, staying at mine?" I start the car with hopeful confidence.

"Yes," she confirms softly, triggering a wave of possessive pride in my chest. "What about my bag? I left it in the back of Landry's car."

"Which is parked right over there." I point. "What do you want to bet it's not locked?"

We're both hungry, so I swung through a drive-through, where I could've sworn I ordered nuggets and she ordered some salad wrap thing. But now she's sitting cross-legged on my living room floor, wearing her own T-shirt and shorts—not quite as sexy as seeing her in mine, but damn close—popping *my* chicken nuggets in her mouth with an antagonistic smirk.

My first mistake was politely waiting to eat, instead pouring us both drinks, while she changed into something more comfortable. The second was dumbly answering "yes" when she asked if nuggets were what I always ordered. Next thing I knew, we had switched orders. Or rather, she had grabbed my nuggets, shoved the wrap thing in my hand, and run from me around the apartment. She'd already popped three in her mouth by the time I caught her, so I swatted her ass—I was looking for an excuse to do that again anyway—and let her win.

"Mhmm." She wipes her mouth and rubs her belly. "So good. How was yours?"

"Delicious." I refuse to admit it was tasteless and unfulfilling.

"Hand me your trash, I'll throw it away." She calls over her shoulder, "Hey, do you have instruments here?"

"I have a few guitars and maybe just a knock-around keyboard. Drums are in storage. Why?"

She returns from the kitchen, staring at her miniature pink toenails. "Can I use one of your guitars?"

"Sure." I stand and hold out my hand to her. "Come pick one."

I lead her down the hall and open the door to the spare bedroom where I keep my instruments, some sound equipment, and all my lyric books. I wish I could have my kit here with me, but there's simply not enough space.

"Can I play the Taylor?" she whispers, running her fingertips softly across the sleek body and up the fret.

"Of course, might need tuned. So what all do you play?" I let her walk out first and shut the door behind us.

She goes for the couch, and I sit beside her. "Guitar, piano, violin. Pretty much everything except the drums." She laughs. "What about you?"

"Very little piano and no violin. What do you like playing best?"

Happy with the tuning now, she settles my favorite guitar in her lap. Her eyes drift away in serious pondering before she responds. "Lyrics are my favorite part of any piece, and I love to sing. But if I'm gonna play, I'd have to say piano. It was the instrument I learned first, and I guess it stuck." She smiles. "I already know your answer. Drums, right?"

"Definitely. Even if I'm on guitar, I'm tapping my foot. The beat, it's the pulse pumping all the other parts. "

"Yeah," she says softly, nodding. "I get that."

She's looking too closely, so I clear my throat. "You gonna play for me or what?"

"Are you neighbors gonna care? It's kinda late."

"Fuck 'em," I grunt and force myself to scoot over some to give her room to wow me. "What're you planning to serenade me with, Teaspoon?"

Her answer is the first chord, then the second, of "If Only That Were True," one of the songs I sold to Crescendo. "Sing it with me," she whispers, eliminating any possibility of refusing her. "I'll take the top."

Well, I would hope so. I can't hit those high notes. More importantly, does she really not realize how often she pops innuendos into a sentence?

She begins to sing in a rare voice, so well suited for my words it's uncanny, and erases all my other thoughts.

"I've done some of this, a lot more of that

Too much of most, and I'm starting to see

Everything I've tried lately, hasn't brought you back

It's only made a bigger mess of me."

I make my way through the accompaniment of the next stanza, even half the chorus, but then I stop singing. I'd rather *listen*. My words, her voice… it'd bring a lesser man to his knees.

When she comes to the end of the song, she reaches up and touches my mouth, tracing it. "See, it worked— you're smiling. Your remedy."

"So it would seem, Teaspoon, so it would seem. Is that the one you're gonna record first?"

She rises without replying and walks over to her purse on the kitchen counter. Watching me carefully, she returns to sit beside me, an envelope in her outstretched hand. "Nope. That's the one, I'm hoping, *we're* gonna record together first. This is your new contract, selling Crescendo, well me, fifty percent rights to both songs you were already cut a check for. The other fifty percent is yours. Here, take it." She taps the envelope on my hand.

"What's your father gonna say about this?" I have no idea why I'm asking. I don't give a damn about her father, but my heart's racing with an enthusiasm I thought I'd never feel again, and I don't trust myself to say anything else just yet.

"Oh, he'll have lots to say, loudly." She laughs. "But other than just annoying noise, it really has no bearing. I haven't cut him out yet, and I won't if he can get on board. We'll see." She shrugs happily, as carefree as I've ever seen her, and presses the envelope into my hand. I guess I'm silent too long for her comfort because she stands quickly and talks even faster. "Read it, think about it, let me know. So am I staying here all night?"

I nod, doing nothing to hide the slow sweep of my eyes over her, and growl purposefully.

"You gonna fight with me if I try to refuse the bed again?" she sasses, hand on her hip.

"Absolutely. And, Reece?" Her brows arch at my huskier tone. "I'm only gonna say this once, and we both know I'm praying you don't listen, but if you wander out of that room this time, I *will* take you."

"O-okay." Her voice trembles, as do her legs, as she slowly turns and walks away.

I fight the urge to watch. Her sweet little ass heading toward my bedroom is more than any man should have to resist.

"I haven't forgotten I owe you an in-person breakfast, don't worry," she calls.

"We've got a good-bye breakfast with Liz and them in the morning," I counter.

"We?"

"We. Say yes." I chuckle. Our dynamic is so new, but oddly natural.

"Yes."

Yes she says. With less hesitation and more instinct every time.

CHAPTER *fourteen*

Reece

This morning has been unusually silent and awkward and the car ride less than informative. Rhett has yet to mention a word about the contract or my proposition, and for some reason, I don't think he wants me to bring them up either. It's a big decision—I can understand he needs some time to deliberate. But the drive turns delightful when he cranks up "I've Got This Friend" and starts singing. I join in, grinning so wide through our entire duet that my cheeks ache.

Huh, I guess the ride's informative after all. My song choice seems to have struck a chord with him.

After parking, he helps me out of the car and holds my hand as we enter the restaurant. Five familiar heads turn our way when the bell above the door chimes our arrival in classic diner fashion. Rhett immediately firms his hold on my hand, twining his fingers through mine. The blond

175

sister from last night, Sommerlyn if I remember correctly, lasers in on me with her scathing glare immediately.

I lean into him and whisper, "Did you 'visit Hawaii' with her?"

"I've never visited anywhere with her, so I'm not real sure where that shit's coming from. But Liz will fix it fast, you watch. Come on." He tugs me toward the table.

"Well, if it turns out looks actually can kill, don't you dare let my mother pick out what I wear in my casket," I mutter as we reach the group.

He bends down to kiss the top of Liz's head then grins at the guys. "Morning, gentlemen, what's good?" He's downright... *jovial*. He pulls out a chair for me then his own.

Liz leans forward, looking down the table at him. "Rhett, sorry we left early last night. I forgot to even give you your present." She passes down an envelope, and I watch from the corner of my eye as he opens the card with a two-hundred-dollar Music Center gift card inside.

"Thank you, and Cannon," he says.

"You're welcome." She smiles while Cannon grumbles the same into his coffee.

Not that I know him well enough to recognize his "happy" look, but I'm going to venture to say...it's not the one he's wearing. He's in a better mood than his sister though—I can feel her stare still pinned on me. I'm giving myself a headache from purposely avoiding looking in her direction.

"It meant a lot to me that you guys came down, but I get the whole 'kid free' thing, no worries," Rhett tells Lizzie, reaching under the table to caress my leg.

"Oh," Cannon pipes up, "I don't think you do get it!"

"Stop," Liz chastises him. "Mouth shut."

"What?" Rhett eggs Cannon on with a devilishly innocent grin.

"Rhett, decide what you want to order," Liz snaps at him, then does the same at her husband. "You too! You know better than to invite curiosity with those two." She nods at each Foster brother.

I can see Jarrett's wheels turning from here, his head toggling furiously between us as they bicker. Smoke practically blows out of his ears as he waits for his opening to jump in on whatever action is brewing.

"Oh, oh!" Jarrett snickers, eyes positively glowing the second he thinks he's got it.

I'm really hoping he doesn't.

"I know what we're talking about. Check it out." He elbows Landry. "Pilot Cannon was denied his red wings. Ha, I'm right, aren't I, Blackwell?" he yells across the table.

What did he just say?

Rhett bends his head to my ear. "No telling what's coming next. Brace yourself."

"You"—Liz points at Jarrett with a shaky finger—"zip it. And you"—she focuses back on Cannon—"answer him and see what happens. Everyone ready to order?" she scream-chirps way too happily.

A waitress runs over, wide-eyed and ashen from Liz's volume and tone if I had to guess. I'm sure I look about the same.

I don't think Jarrett knows how to whisper—that or he's not even trying in the interest of antagonism—but we *all* hear what he says next in Landry's ear. "Liz started her period on their *one* night of solitude and denied him access. No red wings for Cannon. He's so bound up over there, he might climb the building and start shooting. Earning your red wings means—"

"Got it." Landry slaps a hand over his mouth, to cease all our pain, then she knocks him upside the back of the head with the other hand just as Liz slams her menu on the table.

"Jarrett Paul Foster, what the hell's wrong with you? Are you versed in anything *besides* menstrual cycles? And for the love of God, learn how to whisper! Did you ever go have your hearing checked? We're in mixed company, you crude, freaking—ugh!" Liz screams 'til she's out of breath, stands, and marches out of the restaurant.

Rhett pins his eyes on his Jarrett. "Really? Bit much, even for you. And, oh, I don't know, when we're about to eat? I just can't imagine why they don't come visit more often. Now get your ass out there and apologize."

Jarrett, still rubbing the back of his head, gets up and goes in pursuit of Liz.

"Sorry, man," Rhett offers Cannon.

"Yes, very," Landry adds.

Would you look at that—she's already apologizing on Jarrett's behalf. That triggers an inkling of guilt. I want, more than anything, for Landry to find happiness; maybe I jumped the gun on my plans.

"Shit, I'm used to Jarrett. Don't be sorry he said it. Be sorry he's right," Cannon grouches into his coffee.

"Breathe." Rhett does just that in my ear. "Liz is more than used to Jarrett too. They'll be back in five minutes."

"Are your gatherings always this colorfully uncomfortable?" I ask inconspicuously, head dipped.

"No, they're usually worse." He laughs. "Nothing but love though, Tea. We'd do just about anything for each other."

"Um…" Oh shit, the waitress is still standing there, her mouth open in shock, eyes glazed over with stunned abhorrence. "Should I, uh, come back?"

Cannon sighs. "Sommerlyn, you ready to order?"

Between watching the Jarrett "situation" unfold and glowering at me, she probably hasn't even looked at the menu. She continues stewing, letting out a "hmpff," and poor Cannon rubs his forehead and sighs louder.

"Um, we're gonna need a minute." Landry gives the waitress, who can't disappear fast enough, a pity-filled smile then turns a smug grin on me. "So, Reece, good visit?"

"Um, yes," I mumble, shifting in my seat.

"Glad to hear it," Liz adds from behind me. She and Jarrett have returned, both seemingly back to normal. "Where is it you live, Reece?"

Landry's eyes go wide. She knows I don't usually like people delving too deep into my specifics, but she doesn't know I've already told Rhett.

"I live in Los Angeles," I lift my head, refusing to speak to the table, and meet Liz's eyes.

"L.A.," she repeats with a whistle. "What do you do there?"

Landry gasps, raising in her seat ready to jump in and save me, when Jarrett saves us all.

"Fleaver, babe?" he asks Landry.

Again, what did he just say?

Rhett groans. "I'm already sorry, and I apologize to the whole table in advance, but I just have to know. What the hell does fleaver mean?"

"You know, when a woman's sitting down and farts?" Jarrett looks at Rhett incredulously, positive everyone knows random stuff like this. "If they're on their ass, especially if their pants are tight, sometimes a fart is forced in a new direction and fluffs its way up their beaver. A fleaver." He puts up either "ta-da" or "duh" hands—I'm not sure which. "It gives 'em a shocking lil' tickle, like oh, *ahhhh.*"

Rhett lets his head drop forward and shakes it slowly. "Did you read Urban Dictionary on the way here this morning? Seriously, man, information overload for one breakfast."

"Dude, I already knew that. No reading required," Jarrett boasts.

"Landry, I'm actually starting to worry about you. He's my brother and all, so I have to hear it, but you're making a conscious decision to put up with"—Rhett waves animatedly in Jarrett's direction—"*all that.*"

"Well, let's see," Landry drawls, tapping her chin with one finger. "Most of what he says is crude, yes, but also funny as hell. He's kind, plays guitar, sings like an angel, body by Ford"—she leans across the table on her elbows to meet Rhett's eyes dead-on—"and being brothers, you've seen his dick, right?"

Dear God. I can't imagine what lunch conversation, when everyone's had some caffeine and are really feeling lively, would entail.

"Okay!" Liz claps. "Now that we are way too thoroughly educated on vaginas and their many fascinating tricks, thank you for that Jarrett, I *believe* I was asking Reece about L.A."

I don't know why I tense under Rhett's hand, which has never left my leg. I'm comfortable talking about L.A., but I don't get the chance.

"Can someone please explain to me why we're all so fascinated with Rhett's fuck buddy? Apparently I missed it," Sommerlyn snipes.

"Cannon," Rhett rumbles, grip clenching my thigh.

"No, no Cannon needed!" Liz slaps the table so hard everyone's silverware clanks. "Sommerlyn Blackwell, I'm not sure what the hell's gotten into you lately, but if you don't snap the fuck out of it, Imma do the snapping for ya! If you're miserable, fix it, but don't take it out on everyone else. And by that, I mean you'd better aim that *unresting* bitch face away from Rhett and Reece and apologize right now for your rude assumption!"

"Assumption? Yeah right," she sneers.

"That's what I said." Liz is standing and leaning over the table, braced on both hands, and I'm shaking, deathly uncomfortable in my role in a family war. "First of all, you hardly know Rhett, so why you think you're an expert or even give a damn about what he is or isn't doing, I'm not sure. But you're wrong and making an even bigger fool of yourself, so how's about some shut the fuck up to go with your breakfast?"

"Wrong? Who's assuming now?" Sommerlyn also stands, going head to head with Lizzie, which even I already know is a very bad idea.

"That'd still be you." Liz turns from Sommerlyn to regard Rhett; every secret, story, memory, hug, moment of comfort they've shared alive in her gaze, then turns back to her sister-in-law. "He's fighting really hard right now not to tear you a new ass for disrespecting Reece. Which means he *does* respect her and therefore hasn't done anything to the contrary. You will respect her too, even if I have to teach you how."

"I didn't marry you, *siren.* I don't jump when you say so," Sommerlyn says with such contempt, it hurts me for her. That is one severely unhappy woman—she's not angry at me, Rhett, or Lizzie specifically—just miserable in general.

Lizzie shuts her eyes and takes a deep breath then reopens them. "Cannon?" She turns to him. "Please take your sister away from my family meal and figure out what the hell is going on with her. I'm offering you up your red wings in return. I love you, but I'm done. I don't get to see them very often, and I'll be damned if it's ruined. And Sommerlyn, I love you too, but I suggest you find your Zen real fucking quick, or it's gonna be a *long* trip home for you, sister."

Cannon rises and kisses his wife's temple. "I love you too." He takes an extra second nuzzled against her then casts angry eyes on Sommerlyn. "You heard her; let's go. 'Bout time we had a talk anyway."

"Some sister-in-law you are," Sommerlyn gets in one last jab.

Liz opens her mouth, ready to verbally slaughter her, but Cannon places his hand on his wife's arm. "I got it. Everyone, enjoy your meal." He nods at each of us and holds out an arm for Sommerlyn to lead the way. He sends the traumatized waitress back over on their way out.

Liz breaks the ice with the waitress with an exasperated, but good natured, sledgehammer. "So since we both know that you know I'm having *my time*"—she quickly scowls at Jarrett then smiles back at the waitress—"it shouldn't surprise you that I'll have a number one with scrambled eggs and bacon, and a number ten with hashbrowns and blueberry pancakes. Next!" She yells.

The rest of us take our turns ordering timidly, eyes straight down at our menus… except for Jarrett, who hasn't quit laughing.

"You okay?" Rhett asks me quietly, worry prominent in his expression.

"I think I may be after some intense therapy. You?"

"I'm great." The corner of his mouth quirks in amusement. "Actually, I'm enjoying this. I've missed it. Not one thing about this whole morning has surprised me. Except Sommerlyn—definitely something off there."

I look around his shoulder and see Liz sitting alone. "Hey, Liz, why don't you move down here by us?"

She looks at me for a moment, then smiles and scoots down a few chairs.

"Thank you, for that, um, defense? I didn't want to start any fights," I tell her.

"You're welcome, and you didn't. I'm sorry I had to discuss your and Rhett's business, but dammit, I won't have her taking out her whatever on everyone. I'm especially not willing to let her downplay things that I've been waiting to see happen since—"

"Alright!" Rhett throws an arm around her neck and tugs her in for a kiss on the head. "Enough. Tell us about the girls. How are my Sophia and Stella? And Con Man?"

"Yeah, how the hell is Bubs?" Jarrett rejoins the discussion with love in his eyes.

And just like that, Liz's face lights up. We talk about the kids for the rest of the meal, passing around the plethora of pictures she has on hand and oohing and ahhing over two of the most beautiful little girls I've ever seen. We share laughter over some heartwarming stories of what sounds to be a wonderful brother. When we've all finished eating and it's time to say good-bye, I step back with Landry while the three old friends share some alone time.

Landry uses the opportunity to trample her way into my private business. "Jarrett's packin'. His brother hung too?"

"God, you're awful." I shove her playfully. "And I have no idea. Not that I'd tell you if I did." I don't mention that the bulge I shamefully rubbed against felt sizable.

"Reece, I know you, and you like him. That's why I didn't hesitate for one minute when Jarrett asked me to get you back here. Admit it. You. Like. Him."

"I most certainly do, a lot, for a list of reasons that do not include the words packin', hung, fleaver, or red wings. Seriously, I've never met a group of people more vocal about their bodies and its functions. And by people, I mean you and Jarrett! Now ssshh, here they come." I straighten, painting on an innocent smile.

"It was so nice to meet you both." Liz's eyes hold mine though she speaks to Landry as well. "I hope to see you again."

"Likewise." I smile, and Landry agrees.

Liz doesn't hug me or anything, but she takes a long moment just… considering me, then turns on her heel. "Be good, boys!" she calls as she gets into the car where Cannon waves from behind the wheel.

The four of us watch them drive away, then we turn to one another.

"What now?" Jarrett asks.

"I have to get to work," Landry says.

"You got a job?" I ask, thrilled. "Where?"

"The casino. Jarrett's friend Thatcher hooked me up. I'm gonna be a drinks waitress at the card tables!"

"That's great." I pull her in for a hug. "I'm so proud of you. So then, Jarrett, are you free?"

Looking confused, he nods. "Yeah, I guess I am. Why?"

"Why don't you come hang out with Rhett and me? I'd like to talk to you."

CHAPTER fifteen

Rhett

I scan the lot and spot Jarrett's truck. Landry's leaving in her own car, so I quickly intervene. "You know what? Go ahead and grab your truck and meet us at my place. Sound good?"

My brother's as caught off guard as I am, but he's doing a worse job of hiding it. "Whatever you say, I guess. Hurry up though, I haven't got all day."

Yes, he does.

"Okay, let's go!" Reece chirps. She's nervous, and bounces off toward my car.

I slide up right behind her, a move she knows, and press into her while grabbing her hips. "Not much on the blind side, Teaspoon. Care to fill me in?" I gnarl in her ear. Her hair smells of *my* shampoo today. Maybe most men wouldn't notice something like that, but I sure as hell do, and I like it… *primitively.*

"I thought we should discuss things with your brother. The contract, and ya know, all the other stuff, details."

I whirl her around to face me, and she leans back, staring into my eyes with worry in her own. "Why would *you* need to discuss things with *my* brother? Especially since I didn't even give you my answer yet?"

Her face shifts, and she straightens. "You didn't read it?" She shoves my arm. "Glad to see it's so important to you."

"I don't know if you noticed—I'm guessing not— but since you gave it to me, I haven't had a lot of free time. I took a cold shower, miraculously went to sleep, woke up, took another cold shower, and just finished breakfast. Obviously I'm gonna need the Cliff's Notes since Jarrett's waiting. Get in." I gently pull her away from the door and open it. "Explain it to me on the way."

"I wasn't trying to be presumptuous, figured you read it," she says softly when I'm in the car.

I can't look at her while I pull out, but I don't need to in order to hear the insecurity in her voice. "And what would I have read that pertains to Jarrett? Just me leaving? I'd need to tell him that? Which, again, I've yet to agree to."

And that's the real reason I haven't made the time to read or agree to anything. I'm gonna need to think long and hard about doing this without my brother. Something—

no, *everything*—about that doesn't sit well with me. Granted, when he had Ness, it wouldn't have mattered to him what I did. In fact, he would've refused to go without her, as he's already proven. But that doesn't mean that's how I work.

"Rhett, the contract covers Jarrett too. If you want him in your band and trust his abilities, I would never exclude him. And… I may have looked you guys up on YouTube." She laughs nervously. "He's amazing, we'd be lucky to have him."

"We?" I barely get out, some weird emotion I'm unfamiliar with clogging my throat.

"We. You and me." She lays her hand on my leg. "I believe in you, you believe in Jarrett, ergo, I believe in Jarrett."

It's like someone gave her a map to Rhett. Every secret tunnel and hang-up inside me, she knows how to navigate flawlessly.

"I guess all that's left—" her words so quiet, I lean over and still *feel* more than actually hear them, "is if you believe in me?"

We're in front of my building now, and thank fuck for that, because this girl's got my brain spinning so badly that I shouldn't be driving. I shut off the ignition and turn into her. "Look at me." I refuse to physically make her do it. I want her to *give* me her gaze. "Reece, look at me."

She does, tears brimming on her bottom lids. I can't take it another second. I capture her mouth with mine all at once, delving my tongue inside without permission. She accepts it, moaning for me and pulling my hair to tug me closer. When there's a loud rap on my window, she squeaks and jolts back. What the fuck is it with noisy interruptions every time I finally get her mouth?

"Am I here for a threesome? If so, you're either gonna need to get out or let me in," my brother jokes through the window.

I hold up my middle finger behind my head and yell at him to wait inside. Shithead's got a key. Reece moves to scramble out the door, but I stop her. "So let me make sure I have this straight. You included my brother in the contract, in the future of our musical deals, because you knew it was important to me?"

"Yes." It's a breath, her eyes searching mine for a reaction.

"Shit." I scrub my hands down my face then back through my hair. "Is this the part where I'm a bird too? I'm not sure I'm quite there, Teaspoon."

It takes her a second, but then she beams and laughs melodically, beautifully. "*You* watched *The Notebook*? Was that before or after *Black Swan*?"

"Before." I grin. "*Many* times before. You find yourself sequestered on a bus with Liz, you'll be more than willing to sit through that damn movie however many times it takes for her to go from crazy to putty in your hands."

"I can see that." She snickers again. "And no, we're not at the 'you're a bird' part. Calm down."

I think she may be wrong…

Jarrett… is not reacting at all how I expected. He's pacing back and forth in my living room, his voice rising each time he interrupts me from reading the contract aloud. Reece left, intimidated as all hell, and is currently hiding out in my bedroom. When I've read the whole thing—which is *more* than fair in my opinion—Jarrett's still trying to breathe fire through his nose, hands on his hips and saying nothing.

I finally break the tension, puzzled as to why there is any. "What do you think?"

"*What do I think*? I think this girl, who's somehow put a goddamn hex on you, set you up! And her power card is tacking on a spot for your poor, pitiful little brother to ensure you agree!" he yells in one breathe.

I'm stunned stupid, not a single word to be rounded up. I'm the skeptical, cynical, self-loathing one; I don't know how to respond from the opposite side of the fence. I won't deny Reece does seem to have some weird "way" with me, but his timeline is off. It didn't become a full-blown hex per se *until* she respected me enough to include my brother…the guy dogging her right now. And set me up for what? She already had the songs free and clear!

I find my voice and try to tell him all these things, but he just laughs me off condescendingly. "Dude, are you blind? Her pussy can't be that good!"

"The fuck you just say?" I'm up, over the coffee table, and nose to nose with him in seconds. "Getting real sick of that mouth of yours, bro. You need to start thinking before you speak again, Jarrett. You're my brother, I love you, but you talk about her like that again, I'm gonna fuck you up." And I will. He's being a little shit. I just haven't quite figured out *why*.

"You're gonna get in my face for some chick you just met?" he seethes.

"Yeah, I am! You're talkin' out your ass about someone you don't even know!"

"Neither do you!"

I lose steam, as frustrated as he is and sick of talking in circles. I take a deep breath and scrub both hands over my face before I respond. "I know her enough to know you're wrong. You are, Jarrett, you're just *wrong*. Think about it, she had nothing to gain here. The songs were already hers. And those negotiations were on the up and up; I accepted what was offered! You're just not making any sense."

"Probably. Lord knows I'm wrong about everything else. But what if... I don't know," he huffs, dropping into the armchair.

"What if...? Oh, now I'm hearing ya. Jesus, Jarrett." I take a seat on the end of the coffee table. "You're afraid to leave because you think Ness may still come back and you'll be gone. That's it, isn't it?"

He shrugs, refusing to look at me.

"That's pathetic." I regret the words before I'm even finished and try to pull them back, but it's too late.

Jarrett's fist smashes against my jaw with a loud crack and I hear Reece's muffled shriek as I shake off the blow. Jarrett's already stomping toward the door.

How did this possibly go...here?

"Jarrett, wait." I grab the back of his shirt and stop him. "I shouldn't have said that. I didn't mean it like it sounded. I'm sorry. And I'm not doing this without you."

"Fuck off, Rhett," he snaps, back still to me, and walks away.

Now I finally understand what Liz meant when she always bitched about how Yoko ruined The Beatles. *Women.*

I wait a few minutes after he's slammed the door to see if he'll come back. He doesn't. I wait a few more to go find Reece, to see if some brilliant, consoling words will pop in my head. They don't.

Unprepared, I trudge down the hall, a lead lump in my stomach, and slowly open the bedroom door. The noises outside hit me and I don't even have to look around—she's gone, out the window. *What the fuck?* Is this day really happening: Sommerlyn's hormonally unhinged behavior, Jarrett having a nervous breakdown, and Teaspoon going all cat burglar?

I climb through the window and down the two flights of the fire escape, scanning the area... in time to catch sight of her jumping in the back of a cab. Shit! I don't have my keys. I run back up to my apartment, growling a string of expletives that I make up as I go, and grab my phone.

Me: What's Landry's number? No fucking around. Reece is gone.

I wait at least twenty seconds with no response and grab my keys to go to Jarrett's apartment. No, wait, Landry said she had to go to work. I flip an illegal U-turn and smash down the gas pedal. The Goldsbury is just a few minutes away.

When I walk in the casino, I spot her instantly, back to me. She's slumped over the bar, but Landry's eyes go big and wide when she spots me. I see her mouth move subtly to warn her friend, and Reece's head pops up. She turns to look at me, eyes red-rimmed and puffy, lip quivering.

"I'm sorry," she mouths as I stalk closer and takes a deep, shuddering breath.

"Unlock your phone and let me have it." I stick out my hand when I'm right in front of her.

She doesn't even flinch, let alone ask questions and quickly unlocks and places the device in my palm.

I program in my number then call myself. It rings once in my pocket, and I hang up before handing it back to her. "One problem solved. Now let's talk about your daredevil escape routes. Windows, fire escapes... you've been a very busy girl."

"I never intended for you to fight with your brother. Or Liz with Sommerlyn. I'm gonna get the hell out of here as soon as there's a flight available, and I'll quit causing such a mess. I swear, I never meant for any of this to happen."

"He knows that! Jarrett's just being an asshole!" Landry spits.

I didn't even realize she was still standing there. "She right, on both counts. If you heard the fight, then you heard me tell him I don't doubt your intentions at all. Landry, I'm taking Reece with me. You tell my brother I'm not done talking to him. Come on." I offer Reece my hand, unsure what I'll do if she refuses it. Luckily, she doesn't, sliding her own into my palm. I let my clenched-up shoulders drop for the first time in an hour and roll my neck.

"Yes," she breathes, walking beside me.

I laugh, a relief that dulls everything else. "Yes what, Teaspoon?"

"Yes, I could go for some R&R."

I halt in my tracks and look down at her. Where did this girl come from? "And what does R&R mean to you this time?" I ask in graveled astonishment.

"Takeout, whatever you usually order, and movies, what I want to order." She smiles up at me

and I have to remind myself—*still not a fucking bird.*

Her first movie selection is Dane Cook's newest stand-up routine, bless her good taste.

Except she hits pause to get my perspective on *everything* he says. It'll take us all night to finish the show at this rate, and yet, I'm okay with that. When Dane teaches the audience how to learn their significant other's phone passcode (information that would've been helpful an hour ago) by breathing on the screen and looking for the smudge marks, we have to pause, switch phones, and try to crack each other's codes. She gets mine on her first attempt— 6969. Made that way too easy. But hers? The finger smudges are clearly on two, five, six, and eight. How many combinations can there possibly be? I could swear the answer is twenty-four options. I could also swear I've tried them all.

Apparently not.

"Are you sure these aren't just smudges in general, your grubby lil' fingers smearing everything?" I ask, snarling at her phone. She's howling in laughter, rolled on her side, as I cuss, fluently, and finally toss her "locked for 60 minutes" piece-of-shit phone to the end of the bed.

My bed, where we lay together.

"I'll tell you the code when the sixty minutes are up so you can have your closure." She snickers, all too pleased with herself, and pushes play on the movie again.

Three minutes later, I see her finger twitching. She's just about to hit pause to ask if I agree that women are far superior texters and ask whether I use emojis.

I still her hand. "Yes, women reign supreme on texting. Congratulations, next stop, global domination. And no, I am unversed in emojinese."

"That's not what I was gonna ask," she frumps.

I laugh. "It absolutely was. Now watch the movie."

The next bit starts, and I'm fully prepared for a grand inquisition of the etiquette on how to end a relationship, which I've never had the need to learn, but it doesn't come. Dane's still talking and I'm still laughing when a tiny snore makes me look down.

Reece is asleep, blond hair fanned across my chest and one tiny hand on my stomach. She's absolutely breathtaking, and I smile when I realize I don't want to banish that thought. Instead, I stay perfectly still and watch the quiver of her lips as puffs of breath float across them, the slight twitch in her eyelids, and the occasional shift of her legs. I turn off the movie, the lamp, and somehow manage to maneuver us down—me lying flatter on my back, her half draped over me—and pull the covers over us without waking her.

The last thoughts I remember having are: I never imagined I'd bring a girl to my bed. And if I ever did, I definitely didn't think it'd be to laugh, talk, and fall asleep.

"Rise and shine, your sleepiness!"

I roll over and grapple for comprehension of the chipper sound waking me. I sit up and scrub my eyes with the heels of my hands, then look to find Reece standing at the side of the bed.

"What's that?" I ask in a gruff, sleep-laden voice.

"Breakfast. French toast to be exact. Now sit all the way up so you don't spill it." She sets the plate in my lap. "What do you want to drink? You had coffee yesterday, but I wasn't sure if that was an everyday thing?"

"It is. Black. But I can get it." I start to set the plate aside to get up.

"Hush and stay put. I owed you. I'll be right back."

Man, she's perky in the morning. Once again, everything I know about myself says I should find it annoying, and I probably would if this French toast wasn't warm, sweet, and melting in my mouth… yeah, I definitely would.

She returns with a steaming mug in her hand. "Here you go, one coffee, black. My flight's in a few hours, so I have to get going, but I wanted to be here to give you breakfast this time."

I hurry down my mouthful. "I can take you to the airport, but what about everything? I need a chance to talk to Jarrett again."

"I know, but I've got to get back before the vultures come circling. It'll be better for you to talk to him without me here anyway. Just let me know. You have my number. Is it good?"

I moan around another mouthful, and she smiles proudly. I'm about to ask where hers is, surely we have time to eat together, but there's a knock at my front door. I almost can't admit it, but my stomach plummets with the sound.

"That's Landry. She's giving me a ride."

"I said I'd take you."

"No, you finish eating and get some more sleep. She's already here. And Rhett?" She climbs onto the bed, one knee bent, one hand braced. "I had a lot of fun. Thank you." She leans in and kisses my cheek. "See you soon, hopefully."

Reece

I can't believe I had the audacity to call him out on *his* acting skills! Could I have been any more "Sorority Girl on crack" this morning? I just hope my nauseating over-exuberance wasn't as transparently fake as it felt.

I don't want to leave, so I rushed my departure. I toss my stuff in Landry's backseat then climb in the front beside her, letting out the substantial sigh I've been holding in. This trip went *so* much differently than I planned and hoped. In my wake, I'm leaving people hurting and fighting. That's not my martyr, that's truth—I was here, spoke, and fighting ensued.

Landry pats my leg and laughs. "You still not get any?"

"Does your vagina ever stop talking?"

"Only when there's something in her mouth!" She makes an O with her actual mouth then some lewd movement with her fist to emphasize.

"*Way* too early in the morning for that. Just start the car and get me out of here before I cause any more damage," I grumble, slouching in my seat. I can feel him watching from his window, the weight of those tumultuous blue eyes aimed right at me, but I don't look. I'm not scared of what they'd tell me; I'm terrified that I'd want to do something about it.

"What damage? You talking about Jarrett?" she asks.

"Mostly yes. I mean, let's not forget the ordeal between Liz and Sommerlyn at breakfast, also about me. But Jarrett and Rhett fighting is my main concern. Jarrett *punched* him, Landry!"

"Yeah, he told me. Trust me, babe, they're brothers; it's not the first time punches have been thrown. Jarrett's just in a funk. He'll get over it, and when he does, what then? Have you told your dad about all your big plans?"

The mere thought of that conversation—and by conversation, I mean all-out threats-and-insults warfare— makes me cringe. But my father's never chosen me. My journey might entail a little more work, but it ensures raw talent and passion prevail.

"No, what's the point of getting him all worked up if Rhett and Jarrett haven't even agreed yet? Landry!" I scream, instinctively covering her with my left arm and

S.E. Hall

grabbing the edge of my seat with my right. "That was a red light you just ran!"

I don't hear her excuse, only... *"I've been stopping on green since the night we met."* His words pop into my frazzled mind and calm the havoc.

And speak of the wordsmith... my phone dings with a text.

Rubik's Cube: And she cooks too.

He programmed himself into my phone as "Rubik's Cube." Yes, I'm composed of all girl parts, so of course I'm already wondering what my name is in his phone. Any female who denies they'd do the same thing is lying. No-you don't have to be thirteen years old to appreciate the "little touches." It's those kind of cynical thoughts that are killing romance!

"What was that giggle/sigh thing you just did?" Landry asks, popping my bubble. "Is that Rhett texting you?"

"Yeah," I whisper, staring at my phone.

"Then never mind, I know what that sound was."

Me: She does? Sounds like a great girl, this she. Anyone I know?

"Reece?" Landry drawls my name condescendingly, once again barging into the moment I'm *trying* to have. "Babe, you know I love you. You're my best friend, and I'm totally on board for your hookin' up with that hottie and letting go some. But promise me you won't get too attached."

202

Rubik's Cube: She's an exception...al girl, the prettiest of remedies. And now she's gone again. At least she used the door this time.

"Too late." I sigh. "Turn around!"

"What? No, that would most definitely fall under *getting attached*. Make him come to you."

"Psshh." I flit a dismissive wave at her. "All girls do the wait for him to come to them thing. I'm *an exception*." I smile. "The strong woman who isn't secretly waiting to be rescued is hot. It's going to be the new trend, I can feel it. Now turn this car around!" I'm flying on instinct here, no practice at this sort of thing whatsoever.

Rubik's Cube: Too much?

I got so caught up in my crusade, I forgot to text him back, and now he's thinking he spooked me; which he did anything but. My fingers are a little shaky with adrenaline, and Landry's weaving in and out of traffic like a maniac, looking for a place to turn around, but I manage to type out a reply.

Me: Not at all.

Rubik's Cube: Good. Starting out the day with breakfast in bed...Idk Reece, but I want to.

Me: I think I know exactly what you're saying.

Should I tell him I'm coming back or surprise him? My phone vibrates again. Decision made for me—neither.

Rubik's Cube: Wish me luck, I'm heading to gym with Jarrett. Gotta talk 2 him, worried.

Leave him alone, Reece. You've given him plenty to deal with that's more important than your romanticism. He needs to sort things out, not be distracted.

"Wait," I yell to stop Landry from turning at what appears to not be a turning lane. "Never mind, just go on to the airport."

"Your white steed decide to go in the shop there, Juliet?" She laughs, but only slightly, and flips an illegal U-ey in the middle of the road. "Listen, that plan *may* have been a bit impetuous, but it doesn't mean things won't still work out. Rumor has it Rhett doesn't do relationships or encores, but if anyone can change him, it's you."

Me: Good luck. Ttyl.

By the grace of God, in direct opposition to Landry's driving, I make it to the airport alive.

The trip to LAX isn't a terribly long flight, but it's long enough for me to reorganize my thoughts. What do I do if Jarrett doesn't change his mind? What am I willing to sacrifice in search of "what if?"

Ozzie greets me at LAX alone, which makes me as relieved as it does leery. Not one call or text from my father or Warrick the whole time I was gone, and no "welcome home" barrage this time?

"Sweetpea, missed you." Oz sets my bag aside and hauls me into a burly hug. "So how was your trip?"

My shoulders slump. "Ugh. Confusing, rocky, wonderful, back to confusing."

"Your calendar's empty today. We'll take the long-cut home, and you can tell me all about it." He opens my door and ushers me into the backseat.

First thing I do is kick off my shoes then flop back on the long, plush leather seat. "Where are the jackals?" I ask when he's in the car.

"Closed door meetings. Have been since you left. They smell trouble. Thought you'd marry Warrick, play wifey, and let him run the show, and now I think they've figured out that plan might not run as smooth as they'd hoped. What about you and the boy? How'd that go?"

I throw my arm over my eyes and groan. "He's not a boy, Ozzie. He's a twenty-six-year-old, gorgeous, intelligent, creative man. And I'm not sure yet. I think he wants to be on board, but his brother, not so much. They need time to sort it out."

"What's your gut tell you, sweetpea?"

That I'm a ninny who dreams too big. "To have faith. There's something way down under the surface with him. Something deep there, Oz. I just… I just know it."

"Okay, then what are you gonna do?"

"I'll tell ya what I'm gonna do." I sit up and lean over the back of the seat, closer to him. "I'm gonna let that faith steer."

"That's my girl. World wouldn't run without *some* of it somewhere." He chuckles, deep, and robust. My Oz knows me, so he knows that's all I have to say for now, and he heads for my apartment.

Once I'm inside, I leave the unpacking for later and head to the kitchen for a glass of wine. But first, I stop by my idock and turn on some Civil Wars. It's always warm enough to sit outside in L.A., so I take my glass of moscato out on the patio. With my feet propped up on the railing and music wafting through the open french doors, I realize it's not a bad life. I'm only twenty-one, so there's no hurry to figure it all out, right?

Then why do I feel so close to having it all figured out...my forever kind of happy brushing the ends of my fingertips yet just out of reach?

By Tuesday afternoon, still not a peep from Rhett. Landry's clueless as to what's going on there because she's working nights and sleeping days, so I'm beyond impatient and in the foulest mood I can ever remember being in. I've typed out a text to him who knows how many times, but deleted it just as many. That damn Dane Cook is wrong by the way—texting is just as daunting for women. When I've got myself all geared up to ask—in all caps—how you go from "She's an exception" to days of incommunicado, I chicken out and play Devil's advocate. I don't want to push too hard or make him feel as though he has to choose between me and Jarrett.

Considering all that, the ugly turn this board meeting's taking probably doesn't need saying.

"Darling, really, Warrick and I are happy to handle this if you have things you need to do. I'm sure your mother would love to take you shopping. For wedding items, perhaps?"

I blatantly roll my eyes at my father and scoff. "No wedding, no items, and quit trying to get me to leave. You and I both know I have more rights than ever to be here. Now what's next on the agenda?"

Oh, pick your jaw up, Warrick. Yes, I have a brain, a backbone, and you by the balls. Spicy—that's me.

"All right." My father pins me with his glare and clears his throat. "I'm proposing we sign Little Bone T to a one album deal with our option to renew. His demos were something fresh for us, appealing to a younger market and also the hip-hop genre, in which we're not very strong. Thoughts?"

"I have one," I pipe up.

My father has the nerve to drop his forehead into his hand. "Yes, Reece?"

My name rolls off his tongue like acid, and... it hurts. I haven't stirred up any real trouble yet, and I wouldn't if he'd respect me. I've grown up in this business, do my research whether he realizes it or not and have some valid points and ideas. Not to mention I *am* the younger market he's looking to target!

"Father, with avenues such as YouTube, Vine and Snapchat, undiscovered, talented, young people are much easier to find. I literally watch independent clips with more views than some of our signed acts have in album sales.

These outlets help two-fold. With global accessibility, these new artists know all their competition are being seen too, so they work harder to come up with original, eye-catching, memorable samples. *And,* companies such as ours can be choosier. For example, the young man you're proposing? His name is 'Little Bone!'" I look into the sea of blank faces and have to stifle my laughter. They're far from ready to help me mold innovation. "That name is generic hoopla that he got *backward*! He's literally insinuating that his male appendage is lacking. Um, not savvy—*stupid*. Not to mention, am I the only one who recently read the article about him punching his last manager, in a bar, that he wasn't old enough to be in any way? Is that someone we want in the Crescendo family?"

"Sir," Asskiss Alan, aptly named by me, holds up his large-screen phone. "Those charges were dropped. And I'm sure T would work with us on a new, or improved, name."

"But there *were* charges, so something happened. And there's no improving that name. My point is, *his mentality is set.* I promise you, millions of people Mr. Bone's age are out there and dying for a chance to prove their ability and passion for their craft. Let me ask you, Alan"—I do nothing to hide my curtness—"can Mr. Bone play an instrument?"

His face goes pasty before it drops to his phone. His fingers fly over the keys.

"And while you're at it, ask about lyrics. Has he ever written any? That can actually be played on the radio as is?"

Ozzie stands guard at the door and flashes me a quick wink. Mr. Waterman, also team "Heads Not in Our Asses" smiles subtly.

"Here's my counteroffer, young lady," my father says. "You have one week, seven days, to bring us demos of soloists, bands, *whoever*, you'd like to present for consideration. We will all listen and discuss them then. Will that appease you?"

Not even close, but it's a start. "Yes, thank you, Father."

"Moving on to financial reports. Reece, do you need to stay for this?"

"No." I stand, meeting Mr. Waterman dead in the eyes before glancing away. "I'm sure it's covered. Pleasure all. See you next time."

Ozzie holds the heavy mahogany-and-glass door open for me, and I saunter through with the dignity I'm gonna keep demanding. I just have to be faithfully patient that's it's all worth it.

CHAPTER
seventeen

Rhett

By Tuesday evening, I've waited two days too long for Jarrett to pry his head out of his ass. Here I am, trying to have my brother's back, and he's unconcerned about forfeiting, *again*, what I thought were *our* dreams. The longer I'm left waiting, forced to make her do the same, the angrier I become.

Looks like she's fed up too.

Teaspoon: I need your help. Can we talk?

I push call without hesitation, grateful she reached out… 'cause I wasn't sure I should without an answer for her.

"Please don't say 'I was just about to call you,'" she answers with a soft laugh.

"Okay. How are you, Teaspoon?"

She groans, in what's meant as the classic sound of frustration, yet doubles as the catalyst for my current battle with a groan of my own... for very different reasons.

"I don't know if you've decided yet?" she asks.

I want to say yes, unequivocally, and jump on a plane right now. I want to say to hell with Jarrett's indecisiveness, putting me and the music on the back burner again, but I can't. Growing up, I was always the target of everything that sucked about our house. I kept Jarrett protected and that older brother instinct, to watch out for him, never goes away. "I haven't. I'm sorry. If you need to move on, I completely understand."

"I don't want to move on. No plans to. But my hands are kinda tied on giving you more time. Unless you're willing to help me out a little?"

I sit up straighter in bed, my interest piqued. "I'll help you any way I can, Tea. Whatcha got?"

"Well... "

I can just picture her, pinching her lip in between her fingers, blinking rapidly as she glances in every direction.

"I have a week to present a demo that I believe in. I know once they hear you, us, whatever, they'll be sold. So I'm not saying you have to decide right now, but I need to seal the deal on my end now. Kinda like, buy you time. You understand?"

"Nope," I answer honestly. "You gave me a contract, so I guess I thought this was a done deal?"

She sighs, and I realize there're dynamics in L.A. that plague her, dynamics I don't know enough about to fix for her. "As far as I'm concerned, it is. And if I have to get loud and ugly about it, I will. But I'd so much rather keep things amicable with my father and prove to him I'm capable of making sound business decisions, that I have an ear for talent and can be trusted with *my* company. I know it's crazy, but his respect is, for some unfathomable reason, still very important to me."

We have more than amazing, late grandfathers and music in common...she speaks now to my similar skeletons; but I'll never voluntarily disclose. And my protective instinct? Of course her five feet of precious goodness sets it aflame. "Tell me what I can do, Reece. Name it."

"There's a studio in Apple Valley, almost mid-way between us. Well, about three hours for you, two for me." She laughs. "But it's fully equipped. We could meet and knock out a demo. I don't feel like I have time to learn one of your originals and do it justice, and he's already bought your lyrics, so maybe we could do a cover we both know?"

Her optimism is contagious. She's talking a mile a minute in an octave three pitches higher than usual, and by the time she pauses, she's out of breath. Her determination and tenacity is admirable, but it sounds as though if I end up in L.A., I won't be welcomed by anyone but her—and I'm convinced, more than ever, that's enough. Reece Kelly is a pint-sized ball of fire when her mind's made up.

"I'll play, or learn to play, anything you pick," I say. "You tell me the song, time, and place—I'll be there."

"Really?"

"Really, Teaspoon."

"Okay!" she squeals, and I can't help but laugh. "Let me call you right back."

And call me back she does, about an hour later.

"Can you do tomorrow night at eight o'clock?" she asks. "The studio suddenly had a three-hour slot open up."

Obstinate lil' thing. "Hello to you too, Mighty Mouse. You're just makin' all kinds of things happen, aren't ya? Remind me to choose my battles with you very carefully." I chuckle. "And yes, I can do that. Just text me the name of the studio, and I'll find it."

"Thank you, Rhett. You have no idea what this means to me." Her small voice carries a sincere respect that makes me anxious to see her again.

"Actually, I think I do." I clear my throat. "Guess we'd better pick a song." I'd suggest "I've Got this Friend," but it doesn't highlight two instruments.

"What about 'I've Got this Friend'?" she asks.

And she just keeps coming with it.

"I was thinking the same thing, but there's really only one instrument in that one. What exactly do you want to showcase: voices, guitar, drums? Up to you."

"He knows what I can play, *I think*, and he wouldn't know the difference between a good drummer and not, so let's do you on guitar and our two voices. It'll be great."

Yes, it will be. "Whatever you say, boss."

213

"So I'll see you tomorrow night?" her voice feathers across the line.

"You will. Good night, Teaspoon."

"Night."

I hang up, a slight zing of adrenaline coursing through me. I tell myself it's a response toward this step in my musical career, and that's true, in part. But the thought of seeing Reece again certainly doesn't lessen my heart rate.

I find the studio easily and park before grabbing my Martin OM out of the backseat, its dovetail neck construction ideal for sliding in some extra stylings. When I get out and head to the glass door, Reece's waving wildly from behind it. I'd take my time perusing the form-hugging jeans she's wearing or the small strip of her belly peeking out from the bottom of her shirt, but something about the formidable, none-too-happy-looking man at her hip tells me that isn't a good idea.

"Rhett!" She pushes open the door and jumps up to fling her arms around my neck. No way can her feet reach the ground right now, so I wrap an arm around her waist to hold her up. "I'm so excited. It's great to see you."

I'd tease her about the fact that it's been less than a handful of days since we last saw each other if it hadn't felt much longer to me too. *Jesus.*

Big Boy clears his throat loudly, so I gently set her on her feet, resenting the fuck out of him already. "Hey to you too, Teaspoon," I say and give her a quick kiss on the cheek, then step to the side and stretch out my hand. "I'm Rhett Foster."

He returns my handshake, ensuring I'm crystal clear that I'm shaking hands with a real man, and shoots me a look I'm guessing he gets paid to give to anyone who gets too close. *Fell down on the job there while she was in Vegas, bud.*

"Ozzie, stop." Reece nudges him with an elbow and giggles. "Rhett, this is Ozzie Riley. He's my friend, driver, bodyguard, surrogate father, business associate and worrywart. He's just trying to scare you."

"Yeah, picked up that." I wrench my hand out of his. "Nice to meet you," I lie.

"Sweetpea, maybe you should go inside and get things ready?" he suggests to her, still eyeballing me.

Sweetpea? If he didn't have thirty years on her and the word "father" somewhere in all those titles, I might be trying that whole handshake thing again—my way.

"Maybe I shouldn't. Stand down, killer. Come on, Rhett." She takes my hand authoritatively, and I follow her inside the studio.

For the entire three hours, Ozzie never takes his eyes off us, so I'm denied a touch of her, a kiss, a sniff… nothing. We nail our Civil Wars cover in four takes, so then we try "Broken" by Seether with her on guitar—which she shreds—and me on the house drums. Next, and maybe my favorite of the night, we both strap up for an acoustic run at "Falling Slowly."

Her singing voice is far different, not necessarily better, than when she speaks—it takes on this mesmerizing, raw quality, with a grittiness that's sexy as fucking hell. And her eyes glaze over with every emotion the song draws out of her. If you didn't know they weren't her own words, you'd never figure it out by watching her perform. She injects so much into her singing that it *feels* personal. I can only pray her father, and Jarrett, come around—I'd give anything to work with this girl.

Ozzie raps on the glass and points at his watch.

"I think our time's up." She rolls her eyes at him and snickers but steps closer to me. "We got it. No way they won't want you, which just makes it peaceful. I wanted you anyway, and I would've made it happen. You know that, right?"

"I do, absolutely. Like you said, they can't deny they approve of my lyrics since they bought them almost three times."

"That's true, yes, but I mean *me*. I need to know that you believe me when I say no matter how, I *will* make it happen. That *I* want *you*."

"Teaspoon, you can't say you want me with your Man-Bear standing right over there. I won't be of much use if all my good parts are broken."

The next bang on the glass is twice as hard, and Reece startles.

"Go," I say, bowing my head to her ear. "I'll see you soon. Find him a hobby before then." She snickers faintly, and I press a kiss right below her ear. "Soon."

"Soon," she whispers.

I give them a head start, then walk out and climb into my car.

That felt...found.

Time to talk, once and for all, to my brother. Enough of his wallowing, almost two days of sending me straight to voicemail, not answering my texts or his door, and conveniently, not being anywhere I look for him. This is exactly the kind of "Jarrett Bleeding Heart" bullshit that proves why God made *me* the big brother.

I get in my car and drive to On Tap. There's only one way to squash this tension in my body and torture in my mind. I scan the noisy, dark club and immediately think of the last time I actually took the time to look around this place...*her*. Any girl who'd ever gotten a number written on her hand knew to stay right there and wait for me, but not Teaspoon. She was immediately up and wandering around, unknowingly drawing the eyes of every fucker in the place that night. And when we danced, her body molded to mine in instant knowledge, ceding all control to me instinctively. I'm not sure there *is* a better first impression to make on a man like me. She didn't throw it at me but made me come find it. Showed me her sexy surrender, impressed me intellectually, then threw on the brakes...denying me access.

But Tea's not here now, so I dismiss my musing and make my way through the crowd, having spotted what I came for.

I come up behind her at the bar and speak brusquely over the music. "Hey."

She swings around, her eyes doubling in size. "Rh-Rhett."

"We need to talk, now." JC's watching, and I shoot him a look that erases any thoughts he might've had about interrupting.

"But I have to work." Her excuse sounds pathetic even to her, which is why she won't meet my eyes. We're *all* amply aware of her work ethic.

"I can fix that problem with one word and you know it. Let's go." I gently take her elbow. "JC, she'll be gone about thirty. Cover her."

Neither of them attempt to argue, and I lead her to Thatcher's office, to which I have a key. We'll be able to hear one another clearly here.

"Have a seat," I tell her as I shut the door and move around behind the desk.

"Rhett, what are you doing?"

"No need to be nervous, Vanessa. You know damn well I'd never hurt you. Yes, I'm mad at you and disappointed. I think you're probably a little of both those at yourself too. Jarrett was good to you, and he didn't deserve being lied to and cheated on, but that's not why I'm here." I lean back in the chair and cross my arms. "I have a few questions, and I need you to answer them honestly, no matter what you think I want to hear. Can you give me that?"

"Y-yes." She nods shakily.

"Are you still in love with my brother?"

She fumbles with her apron, never looking up.

"Vanessa, just answer honestly."

"No. I'm so sorry, I just—"

I hold up my hand to stop her bullshit rambling. "Are you *ever* planning on going back to him?"

"No," she answers low and shamefully.

"What if this new kid dumps you? Or, say, cheats on you? You gonna come running back then?"

Now she's looking at me, disdain in her slitted eyes. "Not that Stephen would ever do either of those things, but no, not even then. Jarrett's a great guy, and *how* I did things was wrong—I know that—but Jarrett and I don't have the stuff that makes for a forever."

"So if Jarrett became famous, won the lottery, started dating someone else, his dick grew seven inches overnight, or he bought you the biggest house and ring possible, still no way? Never, no chance, whatsoever?" I hate redundancy as much as I hate talking to her in the first place, but I have to be positive.

"No!" she yells, gripping both sides of her chair. "Enough! I'm sorry, so sorry, but no, no, no!"

I smile, and that really throws her off-kilter, wary confusion smearing across her face. "Good to hear. I'm glad. You don't deserve him anymore than you deserve any hold on him you may still have. Which is why you're going to tell him exactly what you just told me."

"The hell I am. I don't dance for you, Rhett Foster!"

No, I have a dancer, thank you. "Yes, you are. Jarrett needs to know that you're never coming back so he can move on with his life, his dreams, and toward opportunities that could very possibly make those dreams a reality. You *are* gonna tell him, in a convincing, kind way, and you are *not* going to mention I had anything to do with it." I speak calmly, but she hears the warning weaved into my instructions. "You've moved on. You're happy and still employed; Jarrett is stagnant. The unbalance of power ends now, because you're conceding your power over him."

"Why would I even think about listening to you? And speaking of that, what's in it for you?" she snarls and throws one leg over the other haughtily.

"You'll listen, because if you don't, you'll be fired immediately. I'll see to it personally that you're ostracized from every club, bar, and casino in this town. I know people, and those I don't know, Thatcher does. As for what's in it for me? That's none of your fucking business." I stand, walk around the desk, and cage her in the chair, leaning over her. "I won't let you take anything more from him, *Nessy*. Do the right thing, and do it soon. Good night."

I leave the door open and stroll out of the club, starting the countdown. She has twenty-four hours.

Maybe shoulda told her that.

Jarrett bursts into my apartment the next morning, no knock or formalities, and plops down on a barstool. "That French toast I smell? Make me some."

"Hey, you look a lot like my brother, but he's been avoiding me for days, so I can't be sure," I deadpan, ignoring his demand.

"Yeah, listen, about that... I'm sorry. I was being a dick. But if you still wanna do it, I'm in!"

I sit beside him and start eating.

"Dude, did you really not make me any?"

"I really didn't, *dude*." I shove another bite into my mouth.

He gets up to go cook his own damn food "So you think Reece's offer still stands?"

"I do, but there're some things we need to go over first."

"Like what?" He looks over his shoulder.

"Well, let's see. We could start with the most important part, the things you said about Reece. Not only were they completely unfounded, as wrong as they could be, and rude as fuck, but she heard you. That will need to be fixed before I let you anywhere near her."

He turns slowly, mouth gaping and eyes bugging out. "I'll be damned. *Never*, and I mean never, did I think the day would come."

"And what day might that be?"

"You're fuckin' sprung! Must've finally tapped that? Or no, wait, still *haven't* tapped that and that's what's got you feening. Whichever, holy shit!" He sits beside me, clapping me on the shoulder. "Cannot believe you're still worrying about her so hard."

"Jarrett, brother or no, this is absolutely the very last time I say it. Do. Not. Talk about Reece in terms of *tapping it*. You will never know the answer either way, so stop. Yes, I like her, for a number of reasons, and she deserves respect. You'll give it, starting with an apology that makes all other apologies look amateurish. Not because she took a huge chance that cost her more than you could imagine and offered us the opportunity of a lifetime, but because she's the kind of person who couldn't sleep *until* she offered us the opportunity she believed we deserved. You hear what I'm saying to you?"

"Yeah." His shoulders slump with all the guilt I just heaped on. "I hear what you're saying and *not* saying."

"Good." I take my plate to the sink. "We'll skip over you punching me, since you throw like a girl. That leaves one last thing. I need your word, Jarrett, that the first skirt won't have you running again. Reece is risking a lot on us, and I'm risking a lot by going to her. I have to be sure I can count on you. L.A. is full of musicians. Maybe find yourself someone who thinks what's important to you *is* important, supports it even."

"Why would you assume I'm not bringing Landry?"

"Are you?"

"No."

"Because of that." I laugh. "So can I count on you?"

"Yes, you can count on me."

"Good." I toss him my phone. "She's under 'Teaspoon.' Better make it good. But don't tell her we're coming—just apologize and confirm the offer's still an option. I'm going to take a shower."

CHAPTER eighteen

Reece

I receive the tracks on Friday, and my favorite of them by far is the one I secretly recorded of Rhett going ham on the drums. It was the sexiest thing I'd ever seen—sweat on his brow, a cocky, assured glint in his eyes, and his muscular arms flexing up and down with melodic authority. He thought he was just playin' around, but I thought he was magnificent.

I keep my secret sampling just that, but call Rhett on Skype to scrutinize the others to death. Not that we have time to meet up and re-record now—we're just both dedicated to perfection, so we discuss little tweaks that could've be made here and there. I love that his ear and attention to detail are as freakishly OCD as my own; I think we'll work great together. If that ever comes to fruition. Which he makes no mention of and I don't ask. I'm scared of the answer either way—each for an entirely different set of reasons. I also don't find a comfortable opening to bring up the call I got from Jarrett; surely he has to know his brother called me, *from his phone*, and he evidently doesn't feel the need to discuss it either.

And pardon me if I'm a little gun-shy about making presumptions or speaking them aloud where the Foster boys are concerned. Last time I did that, punches were thrown and the puncher went on a prolonged sabbatical.

I wouldn't know what to say about the phone call anyway, very vague indeed. Jarrett apologized profusely for the accusations he made against me and said he hoped he hadn't ruined his chances of us all working together. I readily accepted his apology and assured him he had not jeopardized anything. And…that was it. No acceptance or declination of the offer just sitting out there, rotting on the table. The call ended with me no closer to having an idea of what was going on than when I answered.

Men. African tongue-clicking.

Saturday drags by because—and I only just took notice of this fact—I have absolutely no friends in the town in which I live to do anything with. Warrick called, blathering about some benefit dinner that my parents "expected" us to attend together. Funny how *my* parents didn't think to call me. No matter. I unashamedly, and quite convincingly, told him I had chronic diarrhea and couldn't make it. Honestly, who calls to invite you to an event the day *of* it? If he's actually still hell-bent on that plan of his, at least he could add some try to his crazy.

My bowing out ungracefully apparently pissed off my father, because at eight o'clock, thirty minutes after the banquet started, the entire board at Crescendo receives a group email changing the demo meeting to bright and early Monday morning. All because I won't play along with the maniacal farce that Warrick should be paid in two donkeys, six goats, and the future of my company for my hand in marriage.

My father *wants* me to fail, wants me to learn "my place," and scamper off do-gooding with my mother while "my man," whom I detest, runs the family business. He's making it extremely difficult for me to try to remain a respectful daughter. He and I both know who's holding the winning hand. Does he actually believe I forgot about the recent shift in power? Or is this just his pigheaded confidence that he can break me?

Either way, it hurts. He's. My. Father.

I pour myself a glass of wine and hunker down under my covers, flipping through the movie channels. Quick recap—I'm twenty-one years old, in bed at nine, surfing movies. A herd—is it a herd? A pack maybe? Whatever, *a whole lot of* cats—should bust in to take over my apartment any second now. We'll crochet Kleenex box covers together.

But—bringing me a small smile and flutter to my tummy—guess what's on? If you search long and hard enough, it's always on somewhere. *The Notebook.* Before, I wouldn't have taken note and flipped right by. Now I'll at least watch "the bird" part...every single time it's on for the rest of my life.

I start to call him then drop the phone with a gut-wrenching thought—maybe he's "out." In Hawaii. Or

Eden. Do I have a right to be upset? I mean, there's been *some* action between us, and I'm not imagining the way he looks at me in that sly, appraising way of his every so often. And what about his *exceptional* text message that morning?

Hell yes, I have the right!

I press the call button and hold my breath while simultaneously trying not to swallow my tongue.

"Good evening, Teaspoon. How nice of you to call. Thinking about me?" he answers with audible cockiness.

"You're so arrogant." I tsk.

"It's not arrogance if I'm right. Am I?" He's now speaking in that flirtatious baritone that he's got mastered. Husky and rich, it's devastatingly effective.

"I did call you, you caught me, so obviously I was at least thinking about you long enough to pull up your name and press the button."

"All I heard was yes."

"So, can you, uh, talk?" I fumble as if navigating my way through the daunting task of placing a phone call for the first time in my life.

"I can." I hear his warm smile. "What's on your mind?"

I launch into my father's latest manipulation and my resulting aggravation.

"It'll be okay," he assures me without a shred of reservation.

"How can you be so sure?"

"Because that demo is great, and I believe in you. If you want it badly enough, I have no doubt whatsoever in what you can accomplish."

I can't suppress my skepticism. "Do you *really*? You sound so positive, but you barely—"

"Not that again," he cuts in. "Are you checking a clock, crossing off days on a calendar 'til we've hit the socially acceptable 'makes sense' mark, or are you going by what you feel inside? 'Cause I gotta say, Tea, I feel sure I know you, and I've been pretty damn open with you in return. Still no idea why, but I have been."

"Well when you put it like that," I mutter.

"I'm putting it like that."

"Okay, I hear ya."

"Do you?"

"Yes, I do, sheesh. So what are *you* doing tonight?" Here's where I get reminded that this is too good to be true and that I *do* know him... and his M.O.

"Why don't you come right out and ask me what you really want to know? No, strike that. Hang up and let's Skype."

His bossy butt's already hung up before I even got my mouth open to agree, and my Skype is ringing. Of course I answer.

"There." His face fills the screen, dark hair mussed, chest bare, thin stubble on his jaw.

God, I have no idea what I look like right now, but I'm beyond certain it's nowhere close to as good as him.

"You look beautiful, as always." He chuckles, a playful twinkle in his eyes. "Quit worrying. Now what were you trying to ask me without asking me?" One sardonic brow lifts to taunt me.

"I was just wondering what you were up to tonight?"

"No, you weren't. You were wondering if I was *at home* tonight. Which, you can now see, I am. And you know I was home last night too, 'cause I spent it talking to you." He winks. He hardly ever does that, making it all the more potent on the few blessed occasions he does. "Ask me, Tea. Open your sweet lil' mouth and ask me."

"Are you, um…"

"*Yes?*" he needles with a coy smirk.

"I probably don't have the right—"

"You do. Ask," he says firmly. "Look at me and ask. I'll tell you the truth."

That's what I'm afraid of. I look directly at the screen, pull in an endless breath, and exhale my rushed question. "Are you still practicing your usual escapism habits?" I duck my head, face scorching with embarrassment, while he laughs and taps on the screen.

"Teaspoon?" He's ceased laughing and speaks warmly. "Eyes up here. I already know you're blushing beautifully, so lemme see."

My eyes glance up much faster than my head follows and he's waiting, leaned back in his chair so all of his bare torso is visible. That faint line of dark hair begs my eyes to follow it down, but I refuse. Rather, I stay connected with his blue gems of devilment.

"No," he smiles at me, a wide, breathtaking beam. "I haven't *escaped* since before you came to see me for my birthday."

"Oh." It comes out as a waft of air, hiding the circus going on inside me.

"'Oh'?" He laughs. "Tell me more than 'oh.' Tell me how you feel about that." He leans forward, elbows on the table, face close to the screen. "And follow that up immediately with any extracurricular activities of your own that you think I may want to know about." His eyebrows furrow and meet in the middle, forming one impatient line.

"Me?" I laugh obnoxiously, stopping myself just shy of a snort. "Rhett, I'm not sleeping with anyone if that's what you mean. And that's not a new thing for me. That pesky little habit spans back *well* before your birthday... like your twenty-fourth one."

"I'm not unhappy to hear that, Teaspoon. Not a bit fucking unhappy. And you?"

"No, it doesn't make me *unhappy* per se. I mean it'd be nice—" I stop when his laughter's louder than I am.

"Oh, woman, you never fail to make me laugh," He wheezes. "I meant how you feel about *my* abstinence."

"I'm not unhappy about that either."

I flush and try to look away again, but he stops me with his domineering voice. And keeps my eyes as we talk late into the night about music, his old band, Crescendo, other hobbies (of which neither one of us have very many), movies and even how we used to do in school. The one subject we both willingly stay away from is family. Apparently that's not a very strong suit for either of us.

We play a few songs together, and as he's finishing up his haunting rendition of "Blower's Daughter," a yawn I didn't feel coming escapes.

"It's late." He smiles and sets down his guitar before stretching his arms way above his head.

If anything will wake me up, that's it. His body isn't bulky, more of a lean, intricately grooved specimen with light brown nipples, a perfect dusting of hair between them and broad shoulders. I'm making an oath to myself right now. When I get the chance to explore that body of his, I will. A lot. *Everywhere...* with my hands, lips and tongue. I groan, clench my thighs together, and my eyes fall closed but pop right back open at his guttural words.

"Me too, Reece. *Goddamn*, me too. Soon. Get your mind around that right now—*soon* I'm not fucking stopping."

I nod and squeeze my legs together tighter in an attempt to quell the tingles between them.

"You're tired. Go to sleep, and I'll call you tomorrow."

"Okay. Night, Rhett," I manage to say without all-out panting and completely embarrassing myself.

S.E. Hall

"Good night, Teaspoon."

CHAPTER nineteen

Rhett

I spot her right away, sitting in the shade of a large tree—an instinctive, effortless task regardless of the throng of bodies in the large park—and sneak up behind her. "That man, gray pants, white shirt, by the newsstand? He's thinking, 'Man, since Ozzie didn't kill me, today's clearly on my side. I'm gonna go find my Teaspoon and do whatever it takes to make her smile for me.'"

"What are you doing here?" She startles and jerks her head around to look up at me. I know she was "people storying" in her head, and as much as I second-guessed intruding, I'm glad that I did. Her tear-streaked face, the evident relief in her question; I'll do whatever it takes to fix it.

"Scoot up." I maneuver in to sit behind her, my back against the tree trunk, and pull her in between my legs. "Better?"

"Much." Her body goes lax with a ragged exhale, and she lets head fall back on my shoulder. "You didn't answer me though—what're you doing here? And how'd you find me?"

"I went to the studio to surprise you, and your Ozzie-guard intercepted me in the parking lot, said I might have better luck looking for you here. Not sure which shocks me more—the fact he let you come here alone, he didn't pummel me on sight, or that he actually pointed me in the right direction. Thought for sure he was sending me to the opposite side of the city from you." I laugh, wrapping my arms around her waist. I cover her hands with my own and interlace our fingers.

She sighs. "You're in L.A. Does that mean...?"

"I am, and it does. We'll talk about that in a minute. Right now, I need you to tell me why you're sitting in the park alone and crying." I sink my face into the crook of her neck, reacquainting myself with her sweet scent. "What happened?"

"We had the meeting at work this morning. Of course everyone loved your voice and the lead guitarist, *also you*, so you're in by unanimous vote."

"Okay?" A rush of pride swells within me, but it's short-lived, because that's no reason for her to cry—she has more yet to say.

"My father wants to hear another sample"—her voice cracks with the sob she tries to swallow—"because he's not sold on the female. Me, *the female*. My own father didn't recognize my voice. So I offered them a live audition. I have to see his face when he sees it's me. I'm going to make him look me in the eyes when he tells me I'm not good enough."

I lift and angle her into me, and she lays her wet cheek on my chest. I stroke her hair and kiss the top of her head. "We really should get our fathers together someday. Something tells me they'd have an instant kinship. It's not just misery that loves company—works for dickheads too. They feed off people who share their fucked up brand of thinking. Or *not* thinking."

I seem to remember vowing to never to tell her of my familial woes, yet I've gone and done exactly that. Without even trying, this girl completely obliterates every boundary I futilely set out to enforce.

"Listen to me." I tip up her chin. "I know it hurt your feelings, and justifiably so, but Reece, sometimes you just have to fortify yourself against certain outcomes. Your father's never going to change. But the good news is he doesn't have to, because he's only where you *came from*, not what you choose *to become*. We're gonna give him that live audition, and one of two things will happen. Either he'll be impressed speechless and prove he's not a complete imbecile, or he won't and you'll put your foot down. Either way, I'll be standing right beside you, trying like hell not to put *my* foot up his ass and rob you of the glory if he makes the wrong decision."

"I'm just gonna fire him now." She delves her face back into my shirt with her defeated murmur.

"No, you're not." I chuckle, swatting the sweet ass cheek pivoted up my way for the taking. "You're gonna give yourself the chance to prove him wrong and make him eat his words. If that doesn't work, then, and only then, you're gonna go all tiny but mighty on him!"

"I am?" she whispers.

I hear her but don't answer. Instead, I wait... for what I know lies within her to make its appearance.

"You're absolutely right, I am!" Her head pops up, feisty courage coloring her cheeks.

Didn't take long. "That's my girl." I tap the end of her nose.

"So you're here for good? That was awful fast." She shoves at my arm with a grin. "And a surprise wonderful enough that I've decided to forgive you for the day of worried silence you put me through."

"Yeah, sorry about that, but I'm new to the whole surprise thing. I couldn't quite figure out how to pull it off, avoid outright lying to you, *and* talk to you at the same time." I chuckle. "It's something to work on."

"Is Jarrett with you?"

If only my brother could witness the sincere hopefulness on her face right now—he'd know, as sure as I always have, there's no "pitiful lil' brother" or sinister motivation whatsoever inside Reece Kelly. If he could see that, maybe then he'd understand why I'm so uncharacteristically, but unstoppably, drawn to her. The fact that she's smokin' fucking hot doesn't hurt, nor has it evaded him—since he feels free to mention it to me all the time.

"He is. He's at the hotel right now. Probably hasn't stopped bitching to himself about it since I left either." I laugh, taking added enjoyment from that.

"Hotel?" she shrieks, scrambling out of my hold to sit up straight. "No, we need to fix that now. What about all your stuff?"

"I got most of what I'll need packed before I left. Wasn't much, I'm pretty low maintenance. JC's gonna ship anything else I need to me when I tell him where. He's subletting my place, and I'm letting him keep the furniture; helps him out and it's easier to just buy new stuff here, so shouldn't be much."

"And Landry? She keeping Jarrett's place?"

"Yep, same deal. Furniture stays, she'll ship the rest when we give her an address."

She crosses her arms, the gesture launching the luscious swells of her tits at me, and crinkles her face in a frown. "I can't believe she didn't tell me you guys were coming! She's *my* best friend! It's a rule!"

"Not when Jarrett made her swear not to in trade for the apartment it's not. A lot happened in one day; you weren't left out that long, and it was important to me to surprise you."

She smiles now. "It *was* a good surprise."

"You mentioned that." I brush her lips with mine. "So you done people watching, talking to trees, whatever? I could use some help finding an apartment or condo from someone who knows the area. I'd prefer it be a gorgeous girl who keeps me on my toes. Know anybody?"

"Maybe." She giggles, and like many times before, I take a moment to reflect on how much I enjoy the sound—*only* when it comes from her. *Very* few girls can pull off a non-nauseating giggle. "I just, I can't believe you're here, that we're really gonna do this." Her whimsical tone complements her eyes, which shine with a belief in things that can't be seen or touched. "I'm really happy, Rhett."

"Come 'ere," I say deeper than intended, weighted down with want that's been neglected far too long.

She shimmies up to straddle my lap, with no instruction or assistance, and curls her arms around my neck. "Here?"

My hands glide up her cheeks, and I lean in to kiss her again. She lets out a small, raspy whimper, and I press harder against her mouth, my tongue seeking the entry she readily grants. My fingers get tangled in her hair and angle her head to give me the access I must have. I swallow her breathy moans as she grinds against the hard-on she provoked, and I groan back. My hands dig into her hips and move her faster, increasing the friction that needs to happen without clothes on *very fucking soon.*

Seriously, it's becoming a problem—as of late, I'm more familiar with my right hand that I was the entirety of junior high through high school graduation. I *have* to know if the images of her I conjure up as I jack off even come close to the real thing.

And fuck if she's not testing me beyond reason, pulling my hair and whimpering her frustration because she just can't wiggle any closer.

I pop the button on her pants and slide my hand inside, desperate for a touch, a taste, affirmation that she's warm and wet for me, but she tenses and pulls back. Wearing a feverish blush, she slowly regains control, too aware of our surroundings. Her boobs bounce with each sharp, deep breath, and I'm tempted to rip open her shirt and shove my face between them. Goddamn, she's sexy.

"We're outside," she says, breathy and nervous.

"Gimme a couple minutes and you won't care." I ease my hand lower and bend to kiss her neck, but she's pushing off my chest, yanking at my seeking hand.

"I think we should go get you a place to live. We have plenty of time for *this* now that you're here to stay, and I don't like you having to live out of a hotel."

"Reece," I growl. "My dick is really starting to hate you."

"Then I'll just have to try real hard to make sure he forgives me, in private. Now come on." She hops up, refastens her button, and holds out her hand. "Let's get you settled in."

"So what song are we thinking of doing for this audition, *at the company you own?*" Jarrett asks, pressing every button to open every compartment in the back of the car. Ozzie's chauffeuring us, since I have limited space in my Mustang, which I'm sure is doing wonders for his already high opinion of me.

"I know it seems crazy—I'm not even sure why I'm doing things this way—but I appreciate you humoring me, Jarrett, truly. Rhett's already sold them on his lyrics, playing, and voice, so that leaves me and you. I vote we put him on drums, you on lead or bass, whichever you feel is your strongest, and I'll take what you don't choose or piano, depending on the song. What's one we all know or can learn quickly that covers all that?"

She speaks to only Jarrett, and I don't interject. They need to connect on not only an artistic level, but on one of camaraderie that confirms for Jarrett he's as involved and valued as either of us. Not to mention, and I don't cause they both know this too; any song can be rearranged around the instruments available. They're still brainstorming when Ozzie stops at our third housing option. Reece, unsurprisingly, managed to wrangle up an over-zealous real estate agent on the spur of the moment, and Cheri's already waiting on the sidewalk when we get out.

"All right," she starts her spiel the second we join her. "These lofts range from seven hundred to a thousand square feet, they're closer to downtown than the last ones we looked at, and there's a twenty-four hour gym. The rent starts at twenty-three hundred dollars a month for a two bedroom."

I look at Reece. "How far are these from you?"

Her face spreads into a wide smile. "Very. Probably half an hour, *minimum*, in optimal traffic. Even farther from the studio."

"Then why are you smiling?"

"'Cause you asked." Her smile grows impossibly, joined by a blush.

"No, don't let me standing here stop you from doing your whole love-poem-out-loud thing. Honestly, I never get sick of hearing it," Jarrett grumbles, and I laugh before I fully realize I'm happy. "Anyway, I'm not paying twelve hundred a month to share a thousand square feet with my brother. We need something closer to work, and her"—he points at Reece—"or Lord knows the new vagina Rhett's grown might start weeping, and we either need a lot more space or two units. Can you make that happen?" He sidles closer to the middle-aged brunette realtor, turning up the charm.

"Let me see," she says a bit huffily, tapping wildly on her phone.

"Try Tuscany, that's my building," Reece suggests.

"I got it!" Jarrett's random thought bursts out as he snaps his fingers and looks at Reece and me. "Rhett, that one you wrote, 'Lone Worth.' We can change the guitar intro to piano, I'll play electric lead, and it's already got a killer drum solo, *imagine that*. Reece sings, and I'll blend back-up."

Reece looks at me with a lively spark in her eyes, and I run through it in my head. "I think you nailed it. I also think you have ADHD, but it worked out this time. It's a great idea, man, if we tweak it out."

"Yay!" Reece bounces a little in place and winks at me. *Winks at me.*

And. Then. There's. That.

Wouldn't play anything else now.

"Okay," Cheri says too snidely and disrupts my reverie. "Tuscany actually has a few units available. Shall I meet you there?"

"Absolutely, thank you, gorgeous." Jarrett's at it again. "How about if I ride with you in case you get lost?"

Yup, surely she's forgotten—in the last ten minutes—that he's apartment shopping because he just moved here and knows his way around for shit.

She's already walking away. "I think I can manage. I'll meet you *all* there."

Three hours later, Jarrett and I have both signed *separate* leases on our new pads. His is a one bedroom in the building beside Reece's for eighteen-ninety-five a month. Mine's a two bedroom with full kitchen, balcony, and twelve-hundred-fifty square feet of space I don't need or plan to stay in... on the *same floor as Reece*. Twenty-eight hundred dollars a month and worth every fucking penny. I go ahead and pay for first, last, and four more months' rent.

When I meet Reece's gaze that I can feel on me, her brows are arched in challenge. "You confident you're staying that long?"

"I am. That okay with you?"

"It is."

She throws her arms around my waist and squeezes me tightly as I bend to kiss the top of her head. Then she turns and does the same to Jarrett, hugging him as if she's known him forever, and he can't help but grin. *He's starting to understand.*

Time to do this all out. No holding back in fear of the worst.

I pull out my phone and shoot a text to JC with the details—and faith in the best.

Reece

These two amazing men, faithful and daring, moved to L.A. on my word, willing to *knowingly* walk into a lion's den with me. I absolutely refuse to stand by and do nothing while they sleep in a hotel room too. Neither of them can move into their new apartment before Friday morning, which is as quick as cleaning, final credit checks, and furniture delivery can possibly happen, but I'm not too concerned. Actually, I'm looking forward to some company.

"You guys are staying with me until your apartments are ready. I insist," I announce while we wait for our dinner.

I've taken them to Chavarin's, my favorite restaurant in the city, and regardless of what either of them may think, I'm buying. I always sit in April's section, but she's especially happy to have my patronage this particular evening—as is every female in the building. Both Foster brothers spiffed up and at the same table is indeed a sight to behold. They could easily pass for twins with their dark hair, steel-blue eyes, and the kind of smile that leaves you guessing as to their secret thoughts. They definitely garner plenty of appreciative attention.

And the sexiest of the pair, with a more considering edge to his eyes and the permanent hint of a curl at the corner of his fuller lips, is caressing *my* thigh underneath the table with his talented hand.

"You won't get an argument from me. I hate hotels. Thanks." Jarrett smiles at me from across the table.

"Reece," Rhett growls, but I'm prepared.

I look him dead in the eyes. "Say yes."

Oh, that felt good! I've been waiting for the chance to reciprocate his bossy catchphrase, and even he grins and chuckles lightly.

He leans into me and rests his forehead on mine. "Yes. But Friday is further away than it sounds, so if you get sick of us, you say something. I mean it."

"Promise," I whisper.

"Yeah, okay, the third wheel would like to make a toast," Jarrett says, holding up his glass. "To..., well shit, what's our band's name?"

Rhett and I bust out in laughter, look at one another, and back to Jarrett.

"I haven't thought about it," I say. "You guys have any ideas?"

"How 'bout See You Next *Thursday?*" Jarrett suggests.

"How 'bout... we keep thinking?" Rhett quips.

So grumpy, so dry... I rub his back and grin.

"What about something with Foster or fostered?" I propose too loudly, excited by what I'm positive is a flash of brilliance.

"Hell yeah!" Jarrett toasts the air and takes a big swallow of his drink. "I like it."

April arrives with our entrees, so there's a natural lag in our discussion, but Rhett is silent long after she leaves and Jarrett's already chewing.

"You okay?" I ask Rhett. "This is your first time here, hence, I know you didn't order the same thing as always. I'm not gonna make you switch with me if that's what you're waiting for." I laugh. "Eat up."

"That's not it." Food literally almost falls out of Jarrett's full mouth as he chimes in. "I'll tell ya what he's doing."

"Could that maybe wait until you've swallowed?" I smile at him.

"Or forever," Rhett grits out.

I glance at Rhett, who's already focused on nothing but me, and the gravity in his half-lidded eyes sends a shiver through me.

"Fusion; coming, melting, *together*. Blending two or more styles of music. Fostered Fusion could work," he says in grave monotone, gaze never straying from mine.

Although you could never tell by his expression or voice—unless you know what he's making you search for—he's touched that I suggested incorporating their last name. I know it as sure as my *own* name. But I won't mention it, because I'm also sure he doesn't want me too.

"Fostered Fusion," I test it on my tongue and grin. "I like it a lot."

"Here, here." Jarrett's glass is back up... and his food is swallowed. "To Fostered Fusion, Los Angeles, and new adventures!"

Beneath the table, Rhett squeezes my thigh and skims his thumb along my prickled flesh, raising his glass in the other hand.

The boys flipped a coin. Jarrett won my guest bedroom, and Rhett got stuck with the couch. As I get ready for bed, I hear Jarrett through the wall, talking to Landry on speakerphone.

Sounds like she loves her new job, the fact that the girl who messed up both their lives quit hers and most importantly, she needs to know how to relight the pilot on the furnace because she has no hot water. I make a mental note to call her soon, then another invigorating one—I finally have my own excitement going on and haven't depended on hers vicariously.

Finished changing and brushing my teeth, I go check on poor Rhett in the living room. He's been doing more than his fair share of sofa surfing since he met me.

I sneak up from the side and sit beside him on the couch. "I'd offer you my bed, but I know you'll refuse."

"You're right." He glances over then snaps his neck for a double-take. "What the hell are you wearing?"

"Pajamas?" I look down at my tank and shorts, not seeing the catastrophe.

"Reece, the only reason I'm refusing your bed, with you, is because my brother's here. The exact same reason you can't walk around in that outfit." He runs a hand through his hair. "I don't want to have to kill my little brother, Teaspoon."

I shove at him playfully. "Oh, please. He's not even out here, and these pajamas aren't indecent. They cover a lot more than a bikini!"

"Irrelevant." He scoops me up in one quick move and plops me in his lap. "He's not going to see you in a bikini either." He pulls down the blanket from over the top of the couch, fluffs it out, then wraps it around me. "There, much better, and now you're warm."

"I wasn't cold."

"You sure? 'Cause your nipples thought you were." He almost smirks but more snarls. "By the way," he dips his head to tickle my ear with his breath, "I wasn't kidding about not stopping next time, so keep it covered 'til I can have it."

My whole body quivers, and he's *all* smirk now. "I'm glad you're here, Rhett. I missed you." I snuggle my face in his neck.

"Did you?"

"Yes, you know I did. Can't you just admit you missed me too?"

"Figured you already knew."

"Maybe, but it's still nice to hear."

"Hey, Teaspoon?" His voice is gravely in my ear. "I'm gonna need you to make up some of the pretty words in your head while I get the hang of the stuff I don't know, and take care of all the stuff I do."

"Like what?" I breathe with a slight hitch.

"Like when I've got your legs spread open as far as they'll go and my tongue and fingers have you begging me to let you come all over my face. Maybe I'll stop to tell you just how sweet your little pussy tastes before I drive my dick inside you, but maybe I won't. So the 'nice to hear,' you might need to improvise. Can you do that for me?" he growls, nipping my earlobe.

"I-I can do that," I say breathlessly, shifting in his lap to feel, and torment, his erection the way he's tormenting me.

I've heard his lyrics, he's excellent at "pretty words," but I'm willing to pick up his slack during certain times. No problem. He's every bit as good at the dirty words that make me come alive—fast, hot, and pulsing—as he is the pretty. As my heart threatens to beat out of my chest, I can't decide which I like better.

"Good girl." He slides his tongue down my neck, kissing and sucking my skin expertly, then works his way up to ravage my mouth.

"Who wants to practice?" Jarrett comes bounding, and screaming, down the hall.

Having his hearing checked really wouldn't hurt.

Rhett cusses his brother under his breath as I scoot off his lap, hopefully pulling off nonchalant versus volcanic. And hopefully pulling off "I'm wrapped up in this blanket tighter than a burrito because I'm cold" versus "Your brother thinks you wanna see my boobies."

"Crazy, I know, but I don't have any drums handy and couldn't bang 'em at midnight anyway," Rhett tells him, not nicely.

"Just keep the beat on the table or something. Reece and I need to work on our parts." He hands me the keyboard he obviously found in the spare bedroom closet where I store it, then runs back down the hall, presumably to grab one of the guitars.

"When is the audition?" Rhett asks while he's gone.

"Haven't told them yet. Later in the week, I guess? I thought tomorrow I'd just give you guys a tour of Crescendo, introduce you to a few people, stuff like that. We can really practice in the evenings; everyone clears out fairly early. Now that Ozzie is warming up to you, he can help with reconnaissance."

"Speaking of *Green Mile* guy, what's the sudden shift there about?" he asks.

I laugh softly. Michael Clarke Duncan, God rest his soul, and Ozzie do have an uncanny likeness. "You took a big chance on me, coming out here. He just needed to see for himself that I wasn't making up all the great things I told him about you. Not that he doesn't trust me—he was simply waiting for me to be right instead of disappointed. Unfortunately, he's more familiar with the latter."

"Let's do this!" Jarrett's back, toting my Breedlove... *nice choice.*

I warn him it'll need some serious tuning, and he gets that done how he likes it while Rhett pulls up the lyrics for me on his phone. We do over a dozen run-throughs of - "Lone Worth," the compilation of melody and message as poignant as I'd expect, beautiful and hauntingly provoking, as are all Rhett's songs. Losing myself in the piece is effortless, so I struggle to focus, to convey the emotions with which it was written.

Rhett sings along a few times, as though he can't help himself, and it only enhances what I already consider perfection. But by a quarter after two, I'm exhausted and my throat could use a rest, so I call it a night.

No idea how much later, I barely wake up enough to register the warm body flush against my back, the solid arms coiled tightly around me, and the heavy, hot breathing on my neck. Okay, so I'm more than awake, aware of every splendid detail.

"I heard a noise, figured you'd be scared," he murmurs, sleepy and sexy.

"Very gallant of you. However can I thank you?"

"If I can hear you talking, I'll be able to hear you fucking!" Jarrett yells from the next room. "Not that you'll bother me, just a courtesy warning!'"

Rhett buries his face in my hair and grunts. "*Now* his hearing's stellar? Is it Friday yet?"

I snicker. "Three more days, but you're more than welcome to stay right where you are and hold me. You could use this time to practice the pretty words."

"Or we could sleep."

"Or that."

CHAPTER twenty-one

Rhett

This is why I don't stay, talk, invest… 'cause when I wake up in the morning having needed no sleeping pill and find her tiny little body draped across me, it's very emasculating to discover… I really fucking like it.

I have hope though, that my dick is still, in fact, a dick, because my next thought is of morning sex. And not the "oh, she looks all sweet, sleepy and rumpled" version. No—the "that pussy was on simmer all night" variation, hot, wet, with all the natural lubrication built up. Rolling her onto her side and throwing her leg up and over me to slide into my Teaspoon from behind would be the best damn thing I've ever felt in my life, I've no doubt.

She *feels* me thinking about it and giggles. Maybe she'll say something sappy and send me running from the room, completely cured.

She wriggles against my morning wood, obviously jabbing her in the stomach. "I'd get off you, but I'm a little afraid. One false move and I'll impale myself."

Shit. Not sappy. Witty and signature Reece. I'm screwed.

Test two—morning breath. No way she won't be frilly and high-pitched about this.

"Kiss me," I grumble.

She lifts her head, eyes half-lidded, groggy, and… opens her mouth to blow a huge breath in my face. "Want some of that, do ya? Well, come 'ere' then."

Fuck me… there's that.

I'm laughing so hard I get a stitch in my side, and she uses my incapacitated state as her chance to escape.

"Get up, we've got a big day. You can bring your sword with you if you promise to play nice and not jab any of the other kids with it," she teases over her shoulder as she flounces into the bathroom.

I quit laughing long enough to respond. "I think you may be funniest first thing in the morning, Tea."

"Yeah?" She peeks around the doorframe, toothbrush in her mouth. "Are you convinced yet I'm not gonna tie you to the bed and bring in a preacher to marry us while you're trapped?" She disappears, spits, and pops her head back out. "'Cause the instant you woke up and realized you were in bed with me, I'm pretty sure you were seconds away from official tachycardia."

I look at her, *really* look at her, and blow out a deep breath. "Yeah, I think I am."

"So heart rate back to normal?" Her grin slowly grows.

"Yep, all good."

"Then it's okay for me to inform you—don't think for one minute I didn't notice you had your shirt off." She blows me a kiss and shuts the bathroom door.

The driver Reece called for this morning delivers us to the Crescendo Records building by nine, (I had five hours of sleep tops, yet I feel rested) and we find Ozzie waiting out front for us. Ozzie's less adverse to Jarrett, who walks right up to the man and shakes his hand as if they're best buddies—after saying maybe ten words to each other while Jarrett climbed in and out of the car yesterday. After Ozzie's done receiving Jarrett's greeting, being as jovial as I bet he ever gets, he offers a lesser greeting to me.

"You ready for a tour?" he asks.

"I can do it," Reece offers.

"No, you can't, which is why I offered. Meeting's been called." He checks his watch. "Starts in thirty minutes, Board Room B. I'll take good care of these two, sweetpea, promise."

She huffs, a little scowl marring her face as she looks at me. "Sorry."

"Don't be. Do your thing. We'll be around," I assure her with an easy smile.

"I'm okay with it too. Stop worrying," Jarrett kids her.

She pokes Ozzie in the chest—well, as close to his chest as she can reach. "Be. Nice."

He grins down at her, the love there indisputable. From what she's told me about her father, I'm glad she has Ozzie, even if he isn't my biggest fan.

"You have my word, now go cause some noise." He scoots her along and she turns back once with a shaky smile and waves.

"Well then," Ozzie rubs his hands together. "Let's get you boys caught up. And you?" He glares at me. "Don't watch her walk away like that anymore. I'm standing right here, trying real hard to like ya while you're breathing."

I give him a curt nod while my brother stands by and thoroughly enjoys the interaction.

"Okay, let's go. And don't stare at my ass either." The big guy actually laughs with that one.

The building encompasses six floors, the first four all furnished in a grossly pompous fashion—to impress who, I don't know—they're all empty. Nothing but endless vacant offices, board rooms, and overpriced furniture that looks as if it's never been used.

But when we reach the fifth floor, I'm engaged. This is the home of the actual recording, and everything is state of the art. From the computers, miscellaneous racks, sound booths, down to the mics, it's damn close to how I'd outfit my own studio. Ozzie introduces us to a man named Zephran, the chief sound engineer, and after his knowledgeable and in-depth presentation, I know we're in good hands. He walks us through each setup, a selection of fine instruments to choose from, but I'm quick to explain that any recording I do will be on my own kit, which is on its way and he seems to respect that.

I expect us to ascend to the sixth floor after we leave Zephran, but Ozzie hits one when we get back in the elevator. Jarrett asks before I can, and Ozzie doesn't even attempt to conceal his disdain as he explains that the first floor houses the meeting room where Reece is right now and he's tired of the tour, ready to check on her.

When we're back in the main lobby, the rumble in Ozzie's chest grows which each step he takes toward a sawed-off pretty boy talking on his cell phone.

The guy notices us, ends his call, and offers up the most self-righteous farce of a smile I've ever had the displeasure of seeing. "Ozzie, good morning. Care to introduce me to our guests?"

"Gentlemen, this is Warrick Tyler, CE something of something," Ozzie drones.

"That's COO, chief operating officer, of Crescendo Records," Needledick says, shooting Ozzie a tight grin, and offering his hand first to Jarrett. "And you are?"

"Jarrett Foster."

I stifle a laugh at the expectant look on COO's face as he waits for Jarrett to continue, which I know he's got no plans of doing.

"And you might be?" Warrick asks when he turns toward me.

I accept his outstretched hand and make damn sure he knows I shook it. "I might be Rhett Foster, his brother." I jerk a thumb at Jarrett.

"And to what do we owe the pleasure of your visit today, gentlemen?"

Ozzie takes half a step forward. "They're guests of Miss Kelly. I'm surprised she didn't mention it. Weren't you just in a meeting with her?"

"Oh, of course!" he says pretentiously. "So you're both a part of the live audition we'll be hearing Friday? Well, welcome, I can't wait to see what you've got. My silly fiancée." He laughs and shakes his head. "She didn't specify your names *or* that you were in the building. Good thing she's pretty, right?"

Jarrett whips his head toward me, the worry on his face not *nearly* enough, and Ozzie growls sinisterly, but I'm unsure if that's because Warrick announced the big news to me or insulted Reece?

Either and all ways… *What the fuck?*

The fucking surprise now known as *Reece's fiancé* shifts awkwardly. "I have to run. Nice to have met you both, and I look forward to Friday."

Both Jarrett and Ozzie's leery scrutiny is directed at me. I can feel the burden of their eyes burning into me, but all I see is red—a crazy, enraged, should've-fucking-known-better shade of red.

"I'm gonna step outside," I seethe, not giving a shit if they hear me or not.

Once I'm in the fresh air, alone, rationale starts clawing its way to the surface for a fighting chance and I'm able to think some things through. Something's just not adding up. I've always prided myself on being an excellent judge of character. I said my father was a dick, he is. I backed off Liz and Cannon because in my deepest recesses of realism, I knew he was good for her, he is. I pegged what's-his-*fiancé* as a prick before he'd spoken... and how'd that turn out? So there's no way I could be so fucking far off the mark on Reece—jumping in my brother's face because of my faith in her scruples, moving to be near her and let's not overlook—*I stopped fucking other women!*

I need to get the hell out of here and give reason time to seize control of my temper, which is precariously near out-of-control status, before I say or do things I might regret. I walk quickly to the main street and grab a cab, really starting to hate not driving my own car, and don't look back. I don't want to be followed. I don't want her, or Jarrett, or *anyone* to talk me down or ramble off explanations that I might accidentally believe.

I want to test the extent of my conviction, my faith in this girl who's come barreling into my life and perhaps changed me forever. Because if I pull back the curtain of baser attraction and instant connection only to find I don't *trust* her, I shouldn't be here.

Me: Where are you?

I'm heading back to Reece's place after spending all day wandering around the park, coffee shop, several music stores, and one bar. I need Jarrett to make himself scarce before I get there.

Jarrett: Date with Cheryl. Don't wait up.

Me: Who's Cheryl?

Jarrett: Realtor.

Me: Her name is CHERI.

Jarrett: Fuck, I think you may be right.

Me: Good luck with that, message before you come back tonight. Need some time alone with Reece.

Jarrett: 10-4. You ok?

Me: I know I've got her name right, so I'm doing better than at least one person I know.

Jarrett: Fuck off.

Me: Will do. Take your time.

I know Reece's home from the several texts and voicemails I've checked but not responded to. I'm waiting to talk to her face to face... well, I'm waiting to talk to her until I can look down at her face.

After an afternoon of soul searching, I'm *certain* there's a logical explanation to all this, and I'm ready to hear her out. Reece isn't a liar; I believe that indisputably. I've spent too many nights with her—in person, on the phone, on Skype—talking endlessly. The passion when she kisses me, the way she responds to questions I haven't yet asked, the fact that she remembers everything I say... Reece Kelly's been *mine* for a while now.

I toss money in the tray and jump out of the cab as soon as it's at a slow roll, anxious to settle and reaffirm things with her, maybe even take them to a new level. The trip up to her floor seems to happen in slow motion, and when I hurry around the corner and see her door, the objective thoughts I've spent all day summoning are gone.

"You're fired!" she screams, using that massive presence of hers to block the door. "I tried to be nice, loyal, because you *have* been a major part of the company for so long, but I can see you're incapable of giving me the same respect. It's over, Warrick, the games, the lies... I want you gone tomorrow!"

Walk away, guy. Help me help you. But he's not gonna help me—because he's pushing his way through the door, grabbing her arm, and... did he just snarl "cunt" in her face? Her shriek pierces the air as I grab him by the back of his shirt and chuck him against the opposite wall.

"You grabbed her?" I'm on him, raining blows to his face with each question/lesson I scream. "Push your way in?"

261

Blood sprays from his nose with that punch, and Reece yelps louder.

"You don't fucking touch her, ever!"

I can't stop. Flashes of his hand digging into her arm, her stumbling back as he barged in over her, her look of fear play in my mind and fuel my rage. I keep punching, easily dodging his few feeble attempts, and feel my knuckles tear open.

"Rhett, stop, enough!"

She's trying to tug me off him, and he's moaning, covering his head, no longer fighting back. He's done, not getting up, so I stop, but don't take my eyes off him. He moans some more, clutching one of his sides and rolling onto the other.

"Rhett, Rhett, look at me!"

Reece... the haze of anger, a fury so strong it transported me to the place where only instinct exists, slowly fades, and I see her face clearly. Worried, red, and tear-stained. Her body trembles.

"Hey?" she asks if I'm with her.

"Hey."

"There you are." She blows out a shaky breath, racked with the definite possibility of more tears, and throws her arms around my waist. "Are you okay?"

"What?" I pull her away from me so I can see her face. That was far from what I was expecting her to say.

"Are you okay?" she repeats, running her hands over me, her eyes following their inspection.

Dude's still groaning on the ground, a few neighbors are spying out their doors, and I'm covered in blood… but she's worried about me. She didn't drop to her knees at his side, like in every scene such as this in every movie ever made, to check on him. *She came to me.* It will forever be the official moment when I conceded defeat.

"Reece, I'm fine. Are you?" I do a quick scan of her—everything's seemingly all right—then pull up her sleeve. Five distinct finger marks are already turning from red to an ugly shade of purple, and my anger reignites. I lean around her and warn him as clearly as I can. "You ever come near her again, and I'll kill your sorry ass. I didn't break your legs, so get the fuck up and limp out of here, *now*. Because the longer I look at these marks you put on her, the more tempted I am to go ahead and kill you right now."

He stands weakly, one hand on the wall for support, and spits blood on the ground. Then the pussy pulls out a goddamn hanky and wipes his mouth. "Reece, you know how bad he just screwed up, don't you?" He sneers.

Just when I was starting to think I may have gone too far. But obviously I stopped short, seeing as how he's feeling good enough to issue threats to the woman he just manhandled.

"Don't fucking talk to her!" I fly at him, my finger so far in his face it's touching his nose. "You need to leave. I'm not even kinda kiddin' you, I'm trying not to really hurt you, dumbass. Walk. The. Fuck. Away."

"Get your finger out of my face," he scoffs and straightens his shirt. "Rest assured, I *will* be pressing charges. In fact..." He starts digging for what I assume is his phone.

"Warrick?" Reece stands way too close to him, so I fix that, moving her behind me. She pokes her head around me but stays put. "If you press charges, so will I. You forcibly entered my home, threatened me, and left bruises on my arm. Wanna call the police and compare stories or walk away like some semblance of a man who can take a butt beating when he deserves it?"

Oh, there's that... it's all I can do not to laugh and kiss the hell out of her sassy little mouth.

"Very well." He stands up as straight as he can. "I'll simply speak to your father then."

"You do that," she fires back. "But not in my building, 'cause I'll have you tossed out on your sorry ass. Slink away, Warrick, with whatever dignity you foolishly think you still have left."

"You heard the lady." I step closer to him and point down the hall. "Counting to five, then I'm aiming for your kneecaps. And I'm already on three."

CHAPTER twenty-two

Reece

The fallout from tonight's main event will be monumental, no uncertainty there, and I don't typically condone physical violence… but I'd be lying if I said that wasn't one of the hottest things I've ever seen. My heart should be racing in anticipation of the impending aftermath, the possible lawsuits (I don't trust Warrick to keep his word), or the effect of legal trouble on our upcoming projects. But that's not why my heart's thrumming erratically. Rhett was so *savage…* protecting me.

I should be ashamed of myself, thinking that way.

I'll work on it.

He follows me into the apartment and kicks the door shut, then aims a remorseful frown at me. "How much trouble did I just cause you?"

I laugh nervously. "A lot, but nothing I can't handle. I'm more concerned with the trouble it might cause you. Rhett, Warrick's a weasel. He won't consider what he did to deserve it, and he probably will press charges."

His head dips, and he rubs his forehead, sighing. "I'll handle it. Yours, mine, any backlash. You don't worry about anything. Maybe I went a little overboard, and I'm damn sorry it worries you, but I'm never gonna be the guy who *talks* about taking your hands off a lady!" He raises his head. "He can't put his hands on you or call you names, Teaspoon. No one can."

There they are again—the "you *may* burn in hell because fighting is wrong and shouldn't turn you on, so jump him quick before you go" tingles.

"Sit down. I'll get you some ice for your hand." I head to the kitchen, contemplating sticking my head in the freezer for a cool down. I'm a deranged girl.

"Come back here, I don't need any ice. I need some answers." His tone is somber and full of unresolved anger from more than just the fight. I peek around the corner, and he lifts one expectant brow then beckons me forward by crooking his finger. "Come sit down, Reece."

I walk over hesitantly and sit on the opposite end of the couch, for a whole five seconds before he leans toward me, wraps an arm around my back and the other under my legs, and hauls me right beside him.

"Why was he here?" he asks with an eerie brand of calmness, keeping me in his hold.

I stare at my hands in my lap, suddenly fascinated by my terrible cuticle care. "Basically, Warrick and my father are very manipulative and overbearing, always have been, always been allowed to be. When they think things should go a certain way, they truly believe that if they browbeat me, or whoever, long enough, that person will somehow magically agree and play along. Their current project is conforming me to their plan for the company. Warrick was actually being sugary sweet when he first got here."

"And then?"

"And then I reminded him that he really shouldn't be wandering around in public alone until doctors are absolutely sure he's been prescribed the right medication for his delusions."

He laughs and shakes his head, and when he settles, runs the back of his non-busted hand down my cheek.

"They think you should marry him." It's not a question, nor spoken with any malice.

I nod, and now know why he disappeared today and ignored my calls and texts. "He's not my fiancé, Rhett, never has been. He did not once propose, and I wouldn't have accepted if he had. I swear to you, I've never had *anything* with Warrick. I don't know who told you what, but I'm telling you the truth."

"I know."

"You do? Then why the vanishing act today?"

"'Cause I wanted time to think, rationally, and not act on my quick temper. Which worked out well"—he chuckles—"since I ended up beating his ass anyway. I needed to be sure this, us, is more than blinding physical attraction, that I actually have trust in *you*."

"And?" The word comes out a croaky gulp.

He smirks. "I'm here."

"Don't get so coy so fast, mister. I could be angry at you for not talking to me first, ignoring my calls, being all high and mighty, and debating my trustworthiness. I don't do that to you."

He has the decency to look uneasy. "Are you?"

"I haven't decided. Did Ozzie or Jarrett know why you left today?"

Guilt flashes in his eyes. He seems to carefully deliberate whether to lie to me or betray his brother and a man who could crush his bones to make his bread. "Yes, they both heard Warrick, but"—he holds up a finger—"I didn't say anything except I was stepping outside."

"So why do you think they acted like they were no more sure if you'd been abducted by aliens than they were that maybe they had an inkling of what may have triggered your really long walk?"

"I know exactly why my brother did it. He knew the only way I'd ever be sure about us is if I reached this conclusion myself. Nothing, and almost no one, penetrates my surface, Reece. I don't give away trust, it has to be pried from me. And if I walk away, I never look back. But if I decide to stay, I'll stay as long as I'm wanted. Jarrett knows me, and when to back up and let me find my way. It wasn't that I didn't trust you, not for a second, it was that I didn't really know how much I did. Does that make sense?"

"Yes," I whisper.

"And if I had to guess, I'd say Ozzie wanted to see what I'd do, if I thought enough of his girl or not. They did you a favor, Teaspoon, both of them. I don't deserve you if I don't know your worth."

It's a shame he doesn't do pretty words. I'd really fall hard then.

I steady my breathing and scoot impossibly closer. "Now what?"

"Depends. You okay with all that? 'Cause your argument's valid, and I never don't believe someone who says I'm an ass."

"More than okay. You 'bout done talking?" I pour sexy challenge on it.

He answers in one feral movement that has me flat on my back and pinned beneath him, his mouth claiming mine with a ferocity that rivals the building need inside me. I'm like a three-armed nympho and can't decide where to touch first, exploring every solid, beautiful part I blindly find. Desperate and ignited, I groan into his mouth and grab his firm ass cheeks, pulling his hardness tighter against me.

He sucks down my neck and rips my shirt open in single jerk, then nips and licks across my collarbone and between my breasts. I arch up, pushing it all into his face.

Anything, anywhere he wants to put his mouth, I want to feel it—I ache to feel it. He tugs down both cups of my bra roughly and lifts his head, staring at my exposed, heaving chest. One finger traces around, then over, each nipple, and they peak to pointed hardness under his touch.

"Rhett?" With a slight hitch in my whisper, I move to cover myself, but he thwarts that attempt. Is he taking so long to get a lasting look because he only plans to see them once? That *is* his pattern, and the thought immediately stomps out my flame. "Rhett?"

"Phenomenal, Teaspoon. Only thing not little about you."

I scoff, trying to push him off me. "Thank you." I roll my eyes and again try to hide myself.

"Hey, what'd I say about the pretty words? You make em' up in your head while I make you crazy. If you don't still feel everything I do to you tomorrow, I didn't do it right, and *then* you can get pissy with me. Now, smash those beauties together for me so I can suck on both without coming up for air."

His face's delved in before I've computed his instructions as he blindly captures my hands and guides them to the sides of my breasts. We push them together, and he takes total advantage. First the left, he covers the whole nipple with his mouth, swirling his tongue around it and flicking the tip. After a long suck and nip, he slides his face to the right one and repeats the pattern as his skillful hand works between our bodies on my pants. Since my hands are busy, I can only lift my hips to help him, but he growls his appreciation around my breast and shifts his body weight, managing to get me stripped down to only my panties.

He releases my nipple with a wet pop and looks over me reverently. Wearing a wicked smile to rival the Devil himself, he skims his fingers over my flesh, tracing every curve, dip, and the edges of my panties. He's on his knees, but lowers his upper body, eyes cast up over my tummy and pinned on mine as he hooks his fingers in both sides of the lace. He peels my panties down slowly, taking the time to lay soft, open-mouthed kisses on every exposed inch, 'til the scrap of material's been tossed over his shoulder.

My stomach muscles coil in anticipation as he kisses his way up my completely bare flesh. He laughs lightly along my skin, his eyes on mine so he can feed off my nervous exhilaration. His hands push on the insides of my thighs, spreading my legs wide open, just as he said he'd do. The cool air hits my need and causes an involuntary quiver through my whole body.

"Now what?" he asks in an antagonistic, but feral, timbre, grinning.

Is he seriously asking me a question right now? If so, I sure hope he doesn't expect a coherent answer.

"Tell me, Reece. I can *see* what you want. You're breathing so hard your tits are jiggling, which I like very much by the way. Your skin is flushed everywhere, and you're so wet you're sparkling. But I want to hear you to *say it.*"

"I, uh…" I pant and swallow hard, my eyes clamped shut. "I assume you'll be putting, your um, mouth down there?"

Super savvy, Reece.

His laugh is sharp and short, and my eyes fly open. "Down here?" He trails a fingertip up my thigh, over, and down the middle of my wetness. "This where you mean?" He winks, and a wave of want rolls through my stomach.

"Yes," I whisper with a quick nod.

He scissors his fingers to run them up and down each side of my labia, finally pinching them tightly around my clit. Loud, unprecedented noises escape me, and I squirm, pushing into his touch. I hear his chuckle, my eyes closed again, and try to maneuver my body to place his fingers exactly where I want them, but fail. Tortured, frustrated, and turned on beyond reason, I throw ladylike linguistics to the wind and snarl, "Rhett Foster, you'd better eat my pussy right this damn minute!"

"Good girl," he praises with unrestrained intensity… and his mouth covers me.

"*Holy!*" I wail, my hips jerking up, immediately pinned down for me.

This is *nothing* like I imagined; the human brain isn't equipped to create on this level of wonder. The warmth of his mouth mixes divinely with my wetness for an added zing of heat. His lips massage all the engorged, throbbing flesh while his tongue, his indecently talented tongue, flicks and teases my clit, pushing the tight bud up and around, coaxing it to fully blossom. He hums, the vibrations helping bring my blessed explosion up from my toes.

"Mhmm, here she comes."

His muffled purr is joined by two fingers sliding inside me fast, thrusting in and up to rub my internal walls, and I splinter into countless pieces. A frantic pulsing extends up into my belly so much so that those muscles are contracting too. The euphoria seems to go on forever, a strange but beautiful mix of wanting more so badly it hurts, yet floating through the boneless surrender of every muscle in your body. Rhett's hoarse rumble is intoxicating as he remains where he is—fingering and sucking me—'til I spasm with hypersensitivity.

"No, no more." Huskiness coats my breathless plea and I throw an arm over my eyes, sated and more relaxed than a syringe full of anesthesia could accomplish.

"You falling asleep on me, babe?" He asks with reigned laughter.

Babe? Babe is new.

"No," I answer but don't move.

"Up you go," he says as I'm hoisted up in a bridal hold. "Let's get you to bed."

Now my eyes open, and I look at him in wonderment. "We're not *done*, are we?"

"Your eyes are already closing again, Teaspoon, so I'd say that's a yes. Tell ya what." He gently lays me on my bed and situates the covers over me. "I'm gonna use your shower. When I get back, if you're raring to go and jump me, I'll see what I can do about that. But if not, sweet dreams, Miss One and Done." He kisses my forehead, lips tickling me with his laugh.

"Morning." His breath is warm on my neck, as hot as the sexy sound of his raspy morning voice. "I know you're awake."

"Mhmm." I feign a sleepy hum, my skin flushing with embarrassment as flashes of last night barrel through my mind.

"Jarrett's here now. Got in late."

"Okay?"

"Just warnin' ya."

"Warning me for what?"

He pulls me back against him and brushes my hair off my neck. "Remember the last time I slid up behind ya?"

"Yes," I squeak, tiny explosions going off in rapid sequence in my stomach.

"This is gonna be better." His mouth latches down on my neck as he yanks my leg up and back over his hip. His erection prods at my entrance—wonderful risk you take when you fall asleep without your panties on, I guess. "Turn your head and gimme your mouth."

He kisses me, soft and slow, each languid glide of his tongue relaxing me a little more. I don't know if my breath stinks, if he's already put on a condom, or anything other than... everything quickly fades to a tranquil haziness when Rhett Foster's near me, touching, talking, kissing, or doing *anything* to or with me. I angle myself up and push back into him to let him know just that. His hand caresses my cheek, and he kisses me deeper as his rigid length gradually enters me. I pull back from his mouth, needing to breathe, as the stretch comes with a beautiful sting.

"Look at me." He glides his other hand across my stomach and pushes in only slightly more. "Reece, baby. Look at me. Relax, just feel."

I barely manage out a trembling whisper. "I'm trying. You're—" I stop myself.

"I'm what? Say it. I promise I'm gonna like it."

I do look at him now, and his sexy grin is edged with arrogance, but his dark blue eyes are sincere, filled with the actual gravity of the moment.

"You're a lot to take in." I giggle, purely my nerves making noise.

"And you're magnificent." He covers my mouth with his own once more, and right when I sigh, he thrusts fast and hard, all the way inside me.

I whimper in his mouth, but he swallows it, full lips caressing mine, his hand rubbing my stomach lovingly. His hips curl and roll against me from behind in a way that feels glorious, pushing and pulling himself in and out my body like the tide. His large hand massages one breast, the slick moisture between our bodies building, dampening our skin. I succumb to the rhythm of him thrusting, surrendering as his thickness drags along every spot in me, hypnotized by the primal, almost tormented noises that clamor up, deep and tantalizing, from his chest.

"Reece, goddamn, Reece." He groans, maneuvering my head to suckle up my neck to my ear. "Feel better now? You like me inside you?"

"Yes," I moan, arching to press my ass farther into him.

He releases my breast and takes my hand, guiding it between my legs. "We gotta get you there, babe. You feel too fucking good."

Together, our fingers stroke my clit just right, and within seconds, the speed of his drives into me and his grunts in my ear both pick up. The masculine sound of what I do to him, how *I* make him lose control, coupled with our frantic ministrations between my legs, sends me freefalling over the mindless edge.

"Rhett, oh, I'm—"

"I know, babe, I feel you. *Fuckkk.*" He nuzzles my neck and digs his fingers into my hip, holding me tight against him. "Your pussy, fuck me, keep going, baby. Keep coming."

His thrusts become short, brutal stabs until he stays buried within me and I feel him twitch once, twice, before he lets out a prolonged sigh of contentment. We stay just as we are for long minutes, regaining our breath as our rapid heartbeats settle.

Suddenly he rolls on his back, taking me with him, until I lay on top of him on my back. Two large, comforting hands ease up my sides, across my breasts, and coast back down my arms to lace his fingers through mine.

"You know your shirt's off, right?" I snicker.

"I do now." He tickles my sides. "Quit looking for everything I do differently with you. I already told you, *you* are the exception. And *exceptional.*"

"So I shouldn't wonder if—"

"No need to wonder, I'll tell you. I am definitely, without question or hesitation, going to fuck you a lot more than once."

"Oh, you and those pretty words." I sigh dramatically.

"Get up, brat." He shifts us and swats my butt. "Take a shower with me."

CHAPTER twenty-three

Rhett

Cab's on its way." Jarrett's at the door, one hand on the knob, when I walk into the living room. "Grab your shit. We'll be gone before she's done blow-drying her hair."

"What the hell are you talking about?" He rarely makes sense, but before I've had coffee? I won't even attempt to decipher through his words without some caffeine, so I head straight for the kitchen.

"Dude, we'll grab your precious coffee out somewhere. If you didn't take those damn sleeping pills, you wouldn't need that shit anyway."

I don't bother correcting him. I haven't needed anything to sleep since... nope, telling him that would just add a whole other deep conversation to my morning.

"Rhett, snap out of it and move your ass! And you'd better hope we get our deposits back on those apartments we just *had* to have, Lover Boy, or you're reimbursing me."

Now I'm with him—before the coffee's even done brewing, look at that. "We're not leaving. Since you've obviously been tracking my *recent activities*, I'm assuming you also noticed I took my time in the shower? Also, this crazy thing I'm doing now," I point at the coffeemaker, "is often referred to as 'making myself at home.' Cancel the cab."

"No need, I didn't really call one." He moves away from the door and takes a seat at the kitchen bar. "I was just testing ya."

"I pass?"

"Of course you did! No child left behind, bro, no child left behind." He laughs and slaps out a beat on the countertop. "*I* knew Reece was different for you. Just wanted to make sure *you* knew Reece was different for you."

Says the guy who gave me a shitload of grief about her in the very recent past. But much like I explained to Reece, I was way ahead of his test. I'm gonna let him have glory though.

"I'm well aware, but thanks." I finally get a sip of coffee down as the hair dryer shuts off. "Not one fucking wisecrack to her about whatever you think you know, or heard. You embarrass her in any way, and I'll knock you into next week. *Hear me.*"

"I swear, you are the *only* person alive who's not in a *better* mood after sex. Maybe you're not doing it right?" He laughs.

"He's doing it right." Reece bounces around the corner, face vibrant, blond hair silky around her shoulders. "And he's still here, so apparently, so I am!" She snickers and gives Jarrett a high-five!

"See?" He stares at me but points at Reece. "*That* is an appropriate post-mating mood! Jesus, tie a string around your wrist so you remember that shit. So, Reece *Tea*spoon, you seem happy. Get it? Witherspoon, Teaspoon?" He's way too proud for having just thought of that obvious play.

"We get it," I mutter, still a little shell-shocked by Reece's sassy entrance. I'm drained by all that is my brother, and I don't care much for "Teaspoon" coming out of anyone's mouth but mine. I snag an arm around her tiny waist and tug her up against me, handing her my steaming mug. "Just made it. He's on one this morning, drink up."

She glances at me over her shoulder and smiles. "Thank you."

"Reece, hello, I wasn't done. Tell me, what exactly are your intentions with my brother?" Jarrett grins from teasing her—which I could swear I told him not to do.

"Well," she drawls with a giggle at the end. "Let's talk later. I might need your input, but I don't want him to know." She points back at me.

"Alright." I loudly spoil their fun and spin her to face me. "Maybe we should get some work done today. Whadda ya say, Lucy? Ethel? You both in?"

Every ounce of happiness she'd awoken with, a very nice stroke to my ego, evaporates instantly. Her mouth turns down at the corners, little body rigid against mine, and she's about to chew her nails 'til I stop her hand.

"What is it?" I ask her.

"I, uh, just think maybe it's better if I go in alone today." Her worried mumble's aimed at the ground.

"Why?" Jarrett pops his head out from the freezer, frozen waffle halfway to his mouth. I'll have to explain the parameters of "making yourself at home" later. "I'm ready to jam, get started! Oh, and I may have mmphfmh wedmfy—"

"Jarrett," Reece coos at him, stepping away from me. "We can't understand you with the waffle in your mouth. Why don't you try again while I cook it for you? Rhett, you want some?"

I can't eat now, my stomach's heavy with worry, guilt. "No, I'm good thanks. Jarrett, you first. What was the waffle part at the end there?"

"Cheryl mentioned open mic nights on Thursday at a club she co-owns downtown. I thought we could scope it out for some talent?"

"That's a wonderful idea," Reece says enthusiastically. "But who's Cheryl?"

"Shit! Maybe I'll just call her Teaspoon."

"No, you won't," I inform him. "Try calling her Cheri."

"Oh, *Cheri*," Reece catches up. "Should I even bother asking if you know the *name* of this club?"

"Um, Tempo? I think," he answers.

"There's really a club here by that name, so let's assume you're right." She grins at him. "Popular place, I had no idea it was hers. That'll be fun, I'm in. And here you go. Syrup and butter's in the fridge." She hands him a plate of two fully cooked waffles.

"Downshift, babe." I smile at her. "He wasn't done, could get ugly. Finish the story, Jarrett."

"Like I said, I knew Reece could scout some more awesome talent, so I said we'd be there." He takes a bite, chewing so slowly he might actually be putting the food back *together*. "And after I'd said that, is when she dropped to her knees."

"We're gonna be here all damn day! So while your dick was in her mouth, you agreed to what?" I bark, urging him on with a roll of my hand.

"That'd we do a couple songs to get the night rollin'."

And there it is.

I look at Reece and find her beaming. I shock myself with the realization, that this isn't terrible. It's actually not too damn bad at all, a chance to play, and golden compared to the hundreds of other things I would've guessed he was gonna say.

"I'm good with that if you are." I shrug and tell her. "We'll definitely need to get in the studio and knock out some serious practice sessions in the next two days, but it's doable."

"I'm great with it," she says.

"See, you worry for nothing. You guys gotta learn to trust me. So we need to get to work. Which brings us back to Reece's thing. What's with you going in alone today?" Jarrett asks her.

I watch her subtly squirm, then do the answering as I scrub the back of my neck. "I kicked the shit out of that Warrick guy last night."

"Hold up, the dude yesterday who said he was her fiancé? Ozzie filled me in, and I assumed, when I got here and you weren't on the couch, you'd figured it out too. So why'd you kick his ass? Get ahold of him before you two talked?" He motions between Reece and me.

"Nope, he was in Reece's face, grabbing her arm when I got here." My hands clench in anger, the scene replaying in my mind.

"Sounds justified to me. What's the problem?" This time his question is directed at Reece. I don't intervene, because I need to hear her answer too. I need to know exactly where her head's at this morning.

"It's complicated." Her shoulders droop with her defeated sigh. "Warrick has power because my father gives it to him, and my father has power because I haven't taken it away. I was hoping I wouldn't have to. But they won't go easy on this, and I'll be forced to make some bold decisions. I just think it'll go smoother," she scoffs, "if I tackle today alone. Get it over with and out of the way."

Jarrett says nothing. He already knows it's not an option.

"I'm going with you," I state, no lack of conviction.

"Rhett—" she starts to argue, but I'm already walking down the hall to finish getting dressed.

Ozzie meets us in the lot before the car Reece called for is even parked. I climb out then offer Reece a hand.

"Fun night?" Ozzie sports a sly grin, I think. The man doesn't exactly have an array of expressions to choose from.

Reece is glowing scarlet, giving away the answer to the question he *wasn't* asking, and when Ozzie notices and it registers... whadda ya know. We're back to his expression one of two—lethal scowl.

"I gather you heard about my altercation with Warrick?" I ask pointedly while Reece utters an "oh" beside me. I succeed in caging my laugh, but Jarrett doesn't.

"I did." Ozzie broadens his stance and crosses his arms. "Not that I believe a word of what he's up there whining like a schoolgirl about, but humor me. What happened?"

"Warrick's here?" Reece gasps. "I told him not to come near my building."

"And I told him not to come near you," I seethe, ready to find him and make good on my threat. I give Ozzie the short version of events, long past patience, with Reece adding a few comments in my defense.

Ozzie scratches his jaw in silence and considerable contemplation. "Okay." He jerks his head determinedly. "Might as well head in. Except you." He side-steps to block my path. "You and I will pull up the rear. Have ourselves a chat."

Reece bites her lower lip, so with a comforting smile, I reach to her mouth and stop the torture. "It's fine. We'll be right behind ya."

Jarrett throws an arm over her shoulder and guides her away, leaving me with the man whose wrath is literally emanating from him.

"Did you know I have no family?" he asks, continuing to talk when I would've answered. "No wife, no kids. Spent the better years of my life serving the Crescendo family. First there was Mr. Carter, Reece's grandfather—wonderful man and leader, God rest his soul. Next, Mr. Kelly. But always, *always*, I've seen to my sweetpea, Reece." He glowers at me. "We better start walking, so listen fast. I'm glad to see you came to your senses about that nonsense yesterday and are here with her today. Good man wouldn't send her into this mess alone."

"Never," I manage to get in as we walk quickly to catch up.

"Waiting to see how you handle the thick of things right inside these doors. I don't like you yet, drummer boy, but I been hatin' *them* for years. So you do right today, and right by her *always*, and I'm thinkin' to take your back. But." He stops, and stops me with a tight grip on my arm. "You do one thing to hurt that precious little girl in any way? You'll never even see me coming. Do we understand each other?"

"Perfectly."

"Good talk." He slaps me on the back. "Now that we got that settled, nice job on his face. He puts his hands on her again, you better break 'em."

"Might do that anyway. Might be today."

"Guess we'll see." He opens the door for me. "Showtime."

We walk inside, and only Jarrett awaits us in the lobby.

"Where's Reece?" I ask too loudly, my rattled voice bouncing off the vaulted ceilings.

"Her dad was waiting. She went with him to—"

"Follow me," Ozzie snarls.

I let him lead even though I could easily run smooth over him right now. Ozzie takes us to the room where they're gathered, and the instantaneous relief that overtakes Reece's face strikes a protective cord in me.

She stands and makes her way to us, her hand seeking mine. She clasps down on it firmly, her other hand at Jarrett's back, and ushers us into the room. "Gentlemen, Father, this is Rhett Foster, percussionist, guitarist, vocalist, and songwriter; and his brother Jarrett Foster, guitarist,

286

bassist, vocalist. You may recall the company has purchased two, almost three, songs written by Rhett already. He's also the artist you heard in the demo I provided, as well as part of the live audition you'll hear later this week."

"Mr. Kelly." I step forward with my hand extended, but Reece's father makes no acknowledgement and remains seated. A gimped-up Warrick stands beside his chair with two impressive black eyes and a butterfly bandage across his nose. Why he's still in the room is plaguing me and pissing me the fuck off, but I'm gonna trust Reece to do this her way... for now.

"I'm familiar with your work, Mr. Foster." Her father looks at Warrick. "*All* your work. But I don't think the entire board is, including my daughter. I've been waiting for you to join us, to avoid redundancy. You understand."

My scalp tingles with intuition, and I cast Reece a sidelong glance, curious anxiety riddling her face. I'm not exactly sure what he's insinuating, but I know it won't be good. The man's fingers are steepled arrogantly under his chin, and the evil plotting in his tone is unmistakable.

"Tell me, Mr. Foster, have you been completely honest with my daughter, or did you plan to prey on her wealth and naivety so well that once ghosts arose, she'd be too *blinded by love* to care?" he sneers.

Jarrett steps up behind me, letting me know he's there. Reece opens her mouth—I'm sure to stop this—but I squeeze her hand. When she looks at me, her eyes ask, I answer, and though she doesn't like it, she nods.

I try to reason with the man calmly, *for her*. "Mr. Kelly, with all due respect, I'd ask you to refrain from speaking ill of your daughter. And perhaps this issue you seem to have would be best discussed between you, Reece and myself, privately?"

"Oh no, young man. You seek to procure your spot in the Crescendo family by whatever means necessary, so I'd say the whole family is entitled to hear exactly who you really are. Reece, you brought this impulsive, dangerous decision to our door, so I'll let you do the honors." He holds a manila envelope out to her.

After another questioning peek at me that I again answer silently, she takes it from him. "Father, nothing in here should affect Rhett's role at the label. You heard his demo and agreed he's a true talent. Why are you doing this? Because he throttled Warrick?"

Throttled? Good word, babe. Much more concise and powerful than "beat his sorry ass like the sniveling punk he is."

"His depraved attack on Warrick was as unfortunate as it was unwarranted, but it did serve in bringing some very pertinent information to light," her father answers dispassionately.

At least my father is a zealous asshole; this guy's glacial, dictating and toying with people's lives as though stating the time. He's also got me by the balls, although he's incapable of understanding exactly how or why. His last statement just told me what's in the envelope, and I'm not the least bit regretful. I'm also completely unconcerned with what it means to my career and this label.

288

But I'm scared shitless of how Reece will react.

It's always been my experience that no matter where it is you're going, the trip there and the trip back are exactly the same distance.

I no longer believe that.

I don't ever want to go back to the man I was before Reece barged into my life, taking me by continual surprise and reminding me a little more with every smile, laugh, and retort… that I wasn't born to be miserable. I was born to look for, find, and embrace the good in the sporadic, once-in-a-lifetime people God tosses right in my path.

Exactly like she did with me.

CHAPTER
twenty-four

Reece

I don't care what's in this envelope. Rhett is a moody, broody, fresh and fruity man with all of his own uniqueness… and I have a sneaking suspicion, he may be all mine.

"Daddy?" I hear myself say it, and now I know what desperation for approval and compassion sounds like. "Rhett didn't attack Warrick—he rescued me." I push up my shirt sleeve. "See these? Warrick put these bruises on *your* child! He threatened me, called me names, and tried to force his way into my home, all because I refuse to be bullied into some crazy, concocted relationship! Why don't you care about *that*? I am your daughter!" I feel tears dripping down my cheeks and Rhett's strong arm barricade me against him, but nothing snares my senses as keenly as my father's vicious laugh.

"Enough with the theatrics, Reece. You're acting like a child. There's no need for emotions when you can deal in facts, black and white. Open the envelope, and let's end this mockery once and for all."

Once and for all, he's extinguished any hope I had left of ever having a decent relationship with my father. The man is a sociopath, he inherently lacks the ability to feel.

But I have nothing but hope in Rhett, and if he doesn't want me to open the envelope, I won't. Nor will I ever mention it again.

"Do you want me to open it?" I whisper to Rhett, taking his hand.

"Oh, for God's sakes! He was locked away in a boys' home for mental evaluation. He lost control and attacked his own father, just like he did me!" Warrick screams. "He's an animal!"

Rhett's body stiffens, his deep breaths thunder in my ear, his hand in mine now clammy.

"Should you choose to continue with this lovestruck circus of yours, Reece, that story may just find its way to the press. We certainly can't have vicious criminals amongst our family," my father adds.

"You can't do that! He was a minor. That record's been sealed for almost a decade. Come to think of it, you crooked fucking bastards, how do you even have it?" Jarett explodes and crawls—literally *crawls*—over the conference table headed for Warrick, who squeals like a little girl and runs... right into Ozzie's chest.

"I've had enough of you." He lifts Warrick off his feet by his shirt and tosses him away like trash. "You"—he glares at my father—"and all your hypocritical, idle threats. Reece, you tried to do right, sweetpea, and I'm proud of you, but you're done now. All the flashy lights and fancy noise around this company, people expecting a good time. But you get a look, and all those lights and noises are just a very sad car wreck. It ends today. Everybody in this room knows who owns this company, and that's Reece Nicolette Kelly, and there's not a damn thing any of you can do about it. All these threats you're throwing around? Do you really think Mr. Carter didn't teach me anything, ensure I'd be prepared to watch over his granddaughter? I've been your driver, servant, confidante, and watchman for way too long. I've got more dirt on the two of you than a grave digger. So do not test me. I'll sing like a bird."

That's the most I've ever heard Ozzie say at once, and damn if he wasn't saving it all up to ensure that when he dropped it, it'd go off like an atom bomb.

My father speaks to him condescendingly, his nose actually tipped up in the air. "A disgruntled employee with no proof. How worrisome. Please, Oswalt, don't waste our time."

Ozzie grins and pulls his phone out of his pocket. *He's been waiting a long time for this.* He brings up his digital photo album and starts scrolling. From this angle, I can't see exactly what he's showing them, but my father and Warrick sure can. Their wide eyes, bobbing Adam's apples, and pasty white faces broadcast their fear.

"After this, we can all listen to the recordings, if the 'whole family' wants a real party," Ozzie says.

I decide to kill two birds with one boulder—one long overdue and the other just for fun. "We covered the burden of proof portion of your bluff, Father. Let's take care of the 'disgruntled employee' part now, shall we? Mr. Waterman?"

Our CFO hasn't spoken this entire time, but he's engaged now, a grin splitting his face. "Yes, Ms. Kelly." He opens some folders, pulls out a few papers, and double-clicks his pen. "Mr. Riley?"

"Ozzie," I mutter out the side of my mouth, "that's you."

"You're right." He laughs. "Nobody ever calls me Mr. Riley. Yes?" he asks Mr. Waterman.

"Do you happen to have a dollar bill on you, sir? And while you look—Mr. Rhodes, wake up please. You're needed for this!" Our CFO slaps the table, startling the sleeping man across from him.

We might need to find a new attorney. Mr. Rhodes was, indeed, *asleep*.

He comes to, clearing his throat and straightening his suit. "Uh, of course, of course. What are we doing?"

"Mr. Riley? That dollar?" Mr. Waterman asks.

I squeeze Rhett's hand, anxious little butterflies about to carry me away. I've been waiting for this day, the exact moment, to put into motion the plan I've dreamed of for years.

Ozzie's skeptical, his brows bowed into one suspicious line as he hands over the bill.

"And now, sir, if you'll sign at the three red flags, you'll become Crescendo Records' new COO and a forty-nine percent shareholder. Not that Mr. Rhodes warrants much credence, but he did draw up of these contracts, as delegated specifically by Ms. Kelly." Mr. Waterman explains. "I assure you, I double-checked them, and everything's in legal order."

Rhett's mouth brushes my ear. "You are the exception, the prettiest damn remedy in the whole world, and the most astonishing person I have ever fallen into."

"See, you know the pretty words." I blush fiercely, loving his beautiful mouth as much as his dirty one.

"By the way"—he tilts my face up to meet his eyes, and the sensual glint there conquers me once and for all—"I'm so down with being a bird."

"*Really*, a bird, you say?" I tease.

"Fuck me." He groans, raw and exposed. "But yes, hell yes."

My father jumps to his feet, red-faced and screaming, "Enough! Reece, this is ludicrous. You are merely proving my point with these shenanigans. You can't sell half of everything I've worked for to the chauffeur for a dollar! I'll never allow it! This company belongs to our family!"

"Please quit tossing the word family around. You have no idea what it means," I counter with a cool lift of my chin. "And I can do whatever I want. Grandpa ensured that."

"You wait until your mother—"

"Notices?" A sardonic laugh escapes me. "Mother will hardly care what happens here—you trained her not to, remember? As long as the money keeps rolling in, she'll be no more concerned than she's ever been. And the money *will* keep rolling in, *if* you cooperate." My anger falls flat, and I allow my vulnerability to come through. "Dad, I don't hate you. I have no intention of taking what you have, in fact, earned. Any portion of royalties up to this point will be paid to you fairly. I just can't work with you moving forward."

"Insanity," he grumbles, looking around the room for support and finding none, except from Warrick, who's of no consequence. "You'll ruin everything your grandfather spent his life building."

"Maybe." I shrug. "Thankfully, he had more faith that I could handle it than you do. I think between me, Ozzie, and Mr. Waterman, we'll be just fine, but I appreciate your concern. Retire peacefully, please. Play some golf, spend some time with Mom, and I'll see that you're taken care of. Cause any trouble for Crescendo or Rhett, and I'll fight you tooth and nail. That's all I can offer. I hope you take it."

He doesn't respond, staring at me with… an odd mix of anger and shock. He didn't think I had it in me.

Surprise!

"Oz?" I grab his attention—no, scratch that, it seems I already had it—his thoughtful, dare I say *glistening*, gaze fixed on me. "You got it from here?"

"Always, sweetpea." He takes a second to mouth "I love you," then he points at Rhett and very much aloud gnarls, "I'm still looking for a reason to kill you."

I roll my eyes and laugh. "Get to operating, Chief. Start with house cleaning and changing all the security." I look one last time at my father. "Bye, Dad. Maybe I'll see you on the holidays? I hope so. Come on, Jarrett, we'll practice tomorrow."

"Where we going?" Rhett asks.

"I don't know. Where you taking me?"

Where else would three musicians, buzzing from an empowering morning, go besides the Grammy Museum?

I've been before of course, but the boys haven't, and watching them holds my interest much more than the exhibits. Jarrett has a child-like exuberance, spinning in circles, talking loud and fast. Then there's Rhett. He takes it all in with silent, considering appreciation—especially the historical drum sets.

"That's the kit Ringo Starr played on the Ed Sullivan show," he says almost to himself. "Liz would be foaming at the mouth if she saw this."

"She likes the Beatles, huh?" I ask.

He laughs. "Yeah, lil' bit."

"And you?"

"Nothing not to like about the Beatles."

"But?" I ask.

"But there's others I like more."

"Which are?" Every bit of information I pry, and I do mean pry, out of him is another little treasure that belongs only to me.

He shifts to fully face me, his steel-blue eyes searing into mine. "Guess."

This is a test. *Where the hell is my number two pencil?* It's important, *imperative*, to him that I nail this; his need for affirmation that our connection isn't an illusion is suffocating. If he'd have asked me to guess a genre, or maybe even a drummer, I might've stood a chance. But a whole band?

Jarrett comes to my rescue, hand on my shoulder. "Dude, give her a fighting chance. How about any one in your top five?"

"Deal." Rhett's bottomless stare still bores into me. "I've got five in my head. *Pick one of them, Reece*," he *says* to anyone else listening, but to me, he's begging.

The tiny hairs on my nape perk, and my nervous gulp gets stuck. Okay, take what I know about Rhett and informed musical respect, carry the one... I can do this. He'd appreciate a passionate songwriter, a great drummer, a folksy feel (like the Civil Wars). He'd choose a band that needs every member to complete the magic, not a one-pony show. And he'd definitely prefer a group that never broke up, but… there just aren't a whole lot of those to choose from.

His gaze drops to my mouth. He's waiting, hanging on for the words that will either deflate or vindicate him and everything he's almost afraid to believe about us. No pressure.

I close my eyes and summon every instinct I've always relied on. A one in five chance are good odds, right? After a fragile prayer, I whisper, "Fleetwood Mac."

"Hot damn!" Jarrett whoops and claps me on the shoulder harder than I think he realizes. "Okay, I'm gonna get outta here and catch y'all *much* later, 'cause I'm pretty sure my brother's about to fuck ya right here. Nice job, Reece."

Gradually I open my lids and look at Rhett. The sexy smirk of impressed admiration I find sends my stomach into spasms.

He holds out his hand, palm up, and I slide my clammy one into it. "You get me, so you know what happens next," he says.

The juncture between my thighs begins to ache beautifully, and it's a struggle to breathe. "Uh huh."

He grabs the back of my neck and hauls me to his mouth, kissing me with feral abandon. Just as my legs threaten to give out, he leans away. "You ready?" He breathes heavily. I nod and his mouth curls into a predatory promise. "Oh, I don't think you are, but I'll get you there."

CHAPTER
twenty-five

Rhett

"The second thing, boy, is the clincher, and it's a tricky one." He laughs, a brittle, dusty sound that pains me too. *"'Cause if you're a gentleman, it won't happen 'til after you've sworn to always take care of her. But it reminds you she's the one, so keep working to keep it. When you're sound asleep, bone tired, and you wake up for no reason at all... turn your head. If she's left the bed and you can't sleep without her beside you, thank the Lord right then and there. He got you where you're supposed to be, with her. Then you get up, go find her, and show her exactly how much she means to you."*

I wake with a start, a sheen of sweat on my skin, the dream of my grandfather's words vivid. Beside me is an empty space. *She left the bed.*

My first thought is... what the hell is with these sappy reflections? But obviously my grandfather was
300

plagued with the same affliction, and I'm not a bit ashamed to resemble him in any way. Then the Rhett I recognize kicks in, and my next thought's of dragging her back to this bed and starting my morning right. Not sure she'll be agreeable though; wherever she is, she's got to be sore.

Last night was the single most gratifying experience of my life. The second the name of my favorite band—not the fourth, fifth, but *the* band—left her lips, something in me snapped, and I'd never wanted a woman more. But with Reece, I want every part of her to be *mine, only* mine.

I'd fucked her, rough and sloppy—sweaty bodies slapping against each other, her screaming my name pushing me to go faster, deeper 'til we both howled in volatile release. Then I'd taken her gently, learning each inch of her silky flesh, her soft kisses endless as I slid inside her slowly. Her sweet pussy, swollen and snug, had gripped me mercilessly as she'd whimpered a bit with each thrust, yet demanded in a hoarse whisper that I never stop.

Goddamn.

Maybe I should never stop fucking her.

I hear her talking as I get closer to the kitchen, and I stop. While I'm more than okay with the glowing review she's giving my performance, it better not be to my brother.

"So more than once, never with a shirt on, and he's still here. Those are all good signs, right?"

I brace myself, because if it's Jarrett who answers, I'm not gonna be happy. And why the hell is she still worrying about those things? Have I not made it clear, on a man-card-threatening level, how I feel about her?

Obviously not. That shit changes now.

No one answers her aloud, so I walk around the corner, pleased to find she's alone and talking on the phone. I sidle up behind her and curl my arms around her waist, chuckling as she startles with a squeal.

"Landry, I gotta go. Rhett's up and just scared me to death."

She's quiet, listening, as I brush her hair aside and kiss down her nape. She hasn't showered and her skin smells like sex with me, and that has me pushing my rock-hard dick into her back.

"Hang up," I growl, sliding one hand inside her panties. She's wet for me. "Now." I thrust a finger inside her.

"Gott-a go," she pants, flinging the phone onto the counter.

"Good morning." I add another finger.

She moans her reply, rocking against my hand.

"You wanna come, don't you?"

"Yes." She rolls her hips faster.

"Not gonna happen." I deny her my hand and flip her around to face me. I chuckle before I can stop myself, because she is *not* happy about being deprived and her adorable scowl is aimed at me.

"What was that for?"

"Got your attention. Seems we still need to get a few things straight, Teaspoon. Obviously you're not picking up on my tongue-clicking, and I'm too fuck-tired for any interpretive dance." I grab her hips and hoist her up on the counter, pushing her legs apart and stepping between them. "Tell me, Reece, who's your man?"

Her cheeks flame bright pink, and she tugs on her bottom lip with her teeth. "Well, I wish it, if he'd—"

"He would. Say it." I run my hands up the tops of her thighs.

"But it's only... I mean—"

"He still would. Say it." I pull her forward and step closer, my dick hard and coaxing between her legs. "Say it."

"You," she mutters.

I grab her chin and demand her gaze. "You're goddamn right I'm your fucking man. Have been, will be, looking like always. You already knew this, so stop second-guessing. You need affirmation, come find me." I lean in, rubbing harder against her. "I'll give it to you. We clear?"

"Yep." Her lazy smile illuminates her beautiful face, and I take the languid, soul-stroking kiss that only Reece can give.

"Keep 'em closed." She snickers, trying to cover my eyes even though she can't reach them.

I laugh. "They're closed, babe. Don't hurt yourself."

It's Wednesday evening, and the three of us—her, Jarrett, and me—got a lot of work done today, so I feel pretty good about where we're at for the show tomorrow night. I'm tired and ready to go home to eat, shower, and sleep inside Reece, but with the excitement in her voice, I'd never deny her a full-blown reaction to the surprise she has planned.

"Okay, open!" she squeals.

Especially when this is the surprise. "Who put it together?" I ask, staring at *my* drums set up right here in the studio.

"Ozzie and the new helper he hired, his nephew Theo. Do you like it? I was iffy on how you'd feel about other people setting them up without you, but—"

"I love it. Thank you, Tea." I walk closer, half to make sure they put my babies together correctly but more just craving the feel of sitting behind my own heads. My sticks are even lying on top of the bass. I pick them up and roll them through my fingers. Been too long.

She sashays over, the little skirt that has been driving me crazy all day swishing over her thighs. "Why don't you play me something?"

"Might not sound like much with just the drums, but how can I say no when you ask me like that? Come 'ere." I widen my legs and pat the stool between them.

"You can't play with me sitting there."

"I can, and I will. Now come here."

She scoots between my legs and looks over her shoulder at me, still doubtful.

"Who's here besides us?" I ask.

"No one."

"Nice to hear." I wink. "Because if you name the song, we're gonna christen my drums *my way*." I dip my head to lick one long stroke up her jawline to her ear. "You, bent over them."

"Have you—"

"No, Teaspoon. Just you." I grit out the answer to her unfinished question in a purposeful, seductive timbre.

"Then how do you know it's your way?"

I shake my head with a stifled laugh. Always with the questions, this girl. "Got a hunch. Get the song, and we'll see if I'm right."

"And if I get it wrong?" she asks, fidgeting.

"Then I'm gonna lay you on your back, spread you open on my bass, and take you that way." I nip her lobe, and she moans softly. "Ready?"

I count it off, easily reaching around her, and beat out "Clocks" by Coldplay. Not quite as good with just the percussion, but recognizable I'd say. As if it matters—I can't lose.

She glances over her shoulder, jade eyes smoldering, and licks her lips. "'Clocks,' Coldplay."

The sticks go flying over my shoulder. "Stand up," I grunt, flipping open the button on my fly as she does. I lay her down on her stomach, just how I want her—cheek flat on the head and ass up, reaching for me. "Grab over the edge, far as you can."

I kick the stool out of the way, drop to my knees, and lick up the back of her leg while my hand coasts up the other. What her legs lack in length, they make up for in silky softness... and the slight tremble that runs through them every time I touch her. I flip her cute lil' skirt up onto her back, and a rumble barrels up my chest at the sight of her little white panties. I barely get the lace pulled to the side before I'm sliding my tongue through her sweetness then spearing it inside her.

"Rhett," she moans, squirming against my face, begging for more.

"Mmm," I hum, knowing she loves the vibration. I replace my tongue with two fingers, working her as I rise to get my jeans and boxers down with the other hand. But some things... you really do need both hands. "Hold on, babe. I'm hurrying."

She grumbles at the loss but shimmies her panties off eagerly and lays back down just as I had her as I take care of business. Gloved now and hungry, I tap the inside of her ankle with my foot, and she broadens her stance, popping her ass up higher. I can't resist grabbing each firm, tiny cheek and massaging roughly. *Yeah, this is definitely my way.* I rub the head of my dick over and around her clit, pressing in, teasing her, thriving on her desperate whimpers

"Rhett, please," she begs and wiggles impatiently.

"Please what?"

"*Now*, please!" She tries to push back, to take me in herself, and she's so damn wet, if I wasn't holding my cock, she'd succeed.

"Lean *way* over for me." I help push her up, wanting her ass as high as possible; it's perfect. Her toes can't possibly be touching the ground now, just the drums holding her up, and it's the sexiest fucking thing I've ever seen. My girl, my drums... my pussy.

"Like that?" she pants.

"*Just* like that. Good girl." I groan, driving into her halfway, then play with her ass cheeks some more, opening her up to thrust all the way in. "There she is."

I lay across her back, sucking and biting her neck while plunging through her gripping muscles again and again, but raise slightly as my gluttonous girl pushes up on her hands for leverage and bucks against me in counter rhythm, crying out for more.

"Harder," she growls, banging her hand on the drum as she meets me thrust for every brutal thrust. "Fuck it, Rhett, fuck my pussy like you love it!" somebody who *feels* like my Teaspoon, *smells* like my Teaspoon, but most certainly does not *sound* like my Teaspoon screams.

Goddamn, that's hot, and the slow roll of release starts up my legs and spine 'til I'm ready to explode inside her tight heat. I find her clit and torment it, my other hand yanking her into me by the hip. "Get there, babe." I flick her trigger faster and feel her start to pulse, in and out, short, tight little grips around me. "Yeah, there it is, there it fucking is."

With one long, loud cry, she thrashes her head from side to side, propelling herself on and off my dick frantically, and I can't hold on another second. I roar as we come together, then collapse onto her back, catching my breath along with her.

"So how do you like my drums?" I ask when I have the air to do so.

In raspy, nervous honesty that enslaves more than scares, she whispers, "I think *I love* your drums."

CHAPTER twenty-six

Reece

Our first official gig as Fostered Fusion is tonight, and I surpassed "hot mess" straight into "scorching shambles" hours ago. We're only doing two songs, which we've rehearsed plenty, and I have the utmost confidence in the boys. I'm only concerned about whether or not *I* can really do this. I got so comfortable in the background, with my chance never coming—even though I was heiress to a record company , yeah, makes total sense—and my father all but convincing me I wasn't good enough, that I think it may have actually crept in and got stuck in my subconscious.

And tonight, I perform with Rhett, whose opinion matters to me as much as my own. The man who, last night, in a passionate haze, I basically told I think I love him. Because I was too terrified to tell him I was positive.

I want to show *us both* that I can do this.

While the guys head over to Tempo for a quick sound check, I run home to change and get ready. I settle on a not-too-short cobalt halter dress, silver jewelry, and my hair down in soft ringlets. My silver stilettos top off the ensemble—tall enough to give me some height but not jeopardize my ability to stay upright. I wipe the cold sweat off my palms one last time, grab my stuff, and head out the door, smacking into a brick wall with an "oomph."

"Easy, sweetpea. You okay?" Ozzie holds my shoulders and looks at me, no real worry in his twinkling eyes. "Reece, you listen to me good. You were born to perform. Why, this old man almost cries every time you do—it's that amazing. Get him out your head."

"Who?" I ask, despite knowing exactly who he means.

"Your father. Why I have good mind to…" He wipes a hand over his mouth. "He can't hurt you anymore, baby girl. I doubt he'll be stupid enough to ever try again, but if he does, you got two men who love you and will never let it happen."

"*Two* men?"

He slips my hand over his arm, leading us toward the elevator. "One is me, and you know the other is that Rhett character you insist on keeping around." He laughs lightly. "That boy is in love with you. Maybe he doesn't realize it, or maybe he does and just hasn't figured out how to say it, but as a grumpy man who trusts few myself, I know what I see, and that boy's a goner."

"I pray you're right."

"I know you do—it's written all over your face too. And I'm always right. Now you just go and put on a great show tonight, and everything else will fall into the space it's supposed to, when it's supposed to."

"'K," I say halfheartedly. "You staying for the show?"

"Of course I am. Gotta make sure our company only has the best groups, don't I?" He chuckles as we share a conspiratorial smile.

"Damn, Reece, you clean up nice," Jarrett says and lets out a slow whistle, prompting Rhett to spin around and watch my approach.

In this moment, an unbreakable bond is forged between us, the spark of attraction sizzling up ours spine and transforming into destiny.

His eyes rove over me with a primal, yet so tender appreciation, then find mine and silently scream to me that he feels it too. With a jerk of his chin, he asks me to come to him, and of course I do. When I'm standing right in front of him, his sexy grin curls slowly and grabs my hips, dipping his head to rest our foreheads together. "You're exquisite," he murmurs in a timbre so deep, I drown.

"I love when you use the pretty words," I say in a hushed breath.

"Only for you, Reece. Only you."

"Hey, Teaspoon, and your friend *Teacup*? Y'all wanna save the word-sex for later please? We're up in, like, ten!" Jarrett yells.

I really try not to snicker at Rhett's snarl. *Teacup—I may have to reuse that sometime.*

"Guess this is it. You ready?" I ask Rhett.

"Almost." He pulls his drumsticks out of his back pocket and presses them gently against my lips. "Kiss 'em."

Not that I've watched any porn recently, or would ever have the nerve to actually do so, but he's opened the secret compartment within me where "Sex Kitten Reece" has apparently been hiding, and for a fleeting second, I imagine how cool it'd be to lick his sticks like a couple of lollipops and drive him absolutely crazy.

"Don't test me, Teaspoon. We gotta go on, and you don't really want to get fucked in front of all these people," he cautions in a husky rumble.

My eyes flash up to his. "Wh-what?"

"I know exactly what you were just thinking, babe. You do it, and I'm carrying you off into a corner and coming in. So keep your wicked lil' tongue put away and kiss 'em, or hold on tight. Lady's choice."

"Kiss the damn things, Reece, PG-style! Cheryl's walking to the mic to intro us," Jarrett says, peeking out the curtain.

"*Cheri!*" Rhett and I remind him together.

"Just for the record"—I look at Rhett—"I have no idea what you're talking about. I wasn't thinking anything, other than... hit it hard," I tease and kiss his drumsticks, suppressing a laugh.

"You remember you said that," he grunts and takes my hand, giving it a reassuring squeeze. "Let's go kill this."

We take the small stage right behind Jarrett, and Rhett lets go of my hand to climb behind the drums. Reality comes crashing down on me, and my stomach flips over, pulse roaring in my ears. Each step means one more highly probable chance of falling on my face, but I finally make it to front and center.

I'm onstage, whipping my own reins.

"How's everybody doing tonight?" Jarrett asks the crowd, picking up my terrified slack. When the noise dies down, he buys me more time. "We're Fostered Fusion. Thanks for being here. This first song was written by my brother, Rhett, on the drums back there, and it's called 'Timeless.'"

I love this song. I love the harmony we wrote in to blend mine and Rhett's voices, and I love knowing he's right behind me. With that comforting realization, my mouth opens and the words start to flow out. I'm sharp though, so I fall a half-step back from the mic, letting Rhett's smooth, rich alto commandeer. I smile, because even as I sing, pitchy and on auto-pilot, my thoughts wander elsewhere.

I'm off, he's on. I'm fairly optimistic and pretty happy most of the time, he's… not. But we're both dreamers, and apparently, have finally found our perfect counterpart.

Jarrett breaks into his guitar solo, and I glance over my shoulder at Rhett. Damn, he's beautiful. He winks at me, and when I turn back around, I sing his lyrics on point—for him.

The crowd loves it—how could they not? It's a phenomenal song. The lighting changes, and I see Ozzie, beaming, from a front-row table… beside Landry! She blows me a kiss and screams at the top of her lungs.

This time, I talk. "Thank you. We've got one more for you tonight. Jarrett, gimme that guitar and sing with your brother. Ladies, lemme hear ya clappin,' I think you're gonna like this."

I sling the strap over my head, toss a saucy grin over my shoulder, and hang on tight… 'cause when the Foster boys do a cover of "Lover, Lover," it's more than a performance—it's the sexiest damn thing a lady has ever heard, seen, or felt… in every female part she possesses.

The women in the audience agree, and don't let me down. They're up on their feet, dancing and clapping along, almost instantly, trying to shake it half as well as Jarrett does.

The raucous applause when we're finished lasts long after we leave the stage. One step into the wing, Rhett grabs me, swinging me around in circles as he kisses me to my core. I think if people could fly, this is what it would feel like.

As soon as Rhett puts me down, Jarrett wraps me in a hug just as exuberant, sans the flight. "That was fucking awesome! I didn't realize how much I missed it. Thank you, Reece, so much."

"Are you kidding? Thank *you*, both of you! I've never felt anything like that in my life." I'm *shrieking*, Rhett chuckling at my high-pitched euphoria.

"Oh my God!"

Never mind—*that* is shrieking.

Landry comes charging at me, hugging me with the strength of five grown men. "I am so proud of you! And you two?" She eyes the boys appreciatively. "I knew you were good, but damn. I'm almost positive I just witnessed at least three women actually orgasm."

"Young lady, I did not just hear that." Ozzie frowns at her as he strolls up. "Sweetpea?" He holds open his massive arms, and I spring into them. "You, my wonderful girl, were magnificent. I couldn't be more proud of you or love you any more if I tried."

"Thank you. I love you too." I sniffle into his barrel chest. "So whadda ya say? Good enough for our label?"

He laughs. "Too good. Fine job, Jarrett. And Rhett, congratulations. You've earned another day of me letting you live."

"I appreciate that. Now can I have my woman back?" Rhett responds.

Ozzie makes a low, scary sound but turns me loose. "Only because this old man's going home. Great job, all of you."

"Night, Ozzie." I wave, tears barely contained.

"Alright!" Landry claps. "First round's on me!"

We make our way through the crowd, thankful for all the compliments we receive as we pass, and find a table off to the side. I slowly sip a margarita as we check out the other performers, wondering if we'll see that one undiscovered diamond in the rough.

Sure enough... two acts after the thought and a soloist takes the stage, causing me to sit up straighter with her first note, ears perked. Rhett's keen too, shooting me a look from the corner of his eye. Even Jarrett detaches from Landry's mouth long enough to pay attention.

It's an original song, and she's strumming it flawlessly, but when she starts muting her chords into a gritty beat and gives just her voice and lyrics the spotlight, her performance goes from good to pure art.

"I want her," I gush.

"Fuck, me too," Jarrett purrs.

"Hey!" Landry pops him upside the head.

I shush them both, not wanting to miss a second of this. She's young, about my age I'd guess, and eccentrically raw, a natural gravel in her voice a person can't fabricate. Her skirt looks as though she wove it from hemp, and her red hair is braided in two parts hanging over her shoulders. She's fascinating.

"Thank you," she says to the crowd and leaves the stage.

"I'll be right back." I jump from my chair and take off through the crowded room in a dead sprint.

CHAPTER
twenty-seven

Rhett

I follow Reece backstage but keep my distance in the shadows, giving her room to thrive. Her musical instincts are excellent, and I have not a single reservation that she'll run Crescendo Records as the brilliant, passionate, honest spitfire I see every time I look at her. I can't wait to have the privilege of watching it happen.

With no break in conversation or so much as a glance my way, she motions me over with a crook of her finger. Looks as if I need to hone my shadowing skills. A more pleasing thought—maybe she'll always be able to sense when I'm near.

Reece introduces us when I come to stand at her side. "Rhett, this is Jovie. Rhett's a member of Fostered Fusion."

"Nice to meet you, Jovie. Great job out there tonight. You write that song?" I ask.

"I did," she purrs, stepping into me. "I watched your set. You were amazing."

Music's far more her forte than subtlety, and I'm uncomfortably baffled as to what the appropriate response is here. Do I defend Reece's honor and announce that I'm hers? Let her handle it woman to woman? I haven't the foggiest, so I do what I assume most guys would do—I avoid eye contact and say absolutely nothing.

While I'm busy doing that, they engage in a private conversation, right in front of me, consisting of female-type vernacular that evidently can only be accomplished with hand flicking, laughing, nodding, and several appearances of those "duck lips" women do. Then Jovie says she can't wait to see us at the studio on Monday and walks away with a friendly wave and smile.

I don't think I lost consciousness, but damn if I have a fucking clue what just happened.

"Teaspoon, what the hell was that? You do realize that girl wanted me, right?"

She snickers and burrows into my side, wrapping her arm around my waist. "*No, are you sure?*"

I pull her away and gently grip her shoulders. "I'm sure. Women get ugly, babe. Maybe you should let this one go, I don't want any problems. Not that *I'd* be the problem, I would never, I just mean—" I stop talking because she's stopped listening, too busy laughing... at me? "What's so funny?"

"You are. Of course I know she wanted you. I'm not deaf or blind. Neither is she. But now she's crystal clear that it's not an option. And thanks to that adorable fumble-bumble speech you just gave, I'm reassured it's *really* not." She reaches up and strokes my cheek, her laughing eyes now somber. "I can't fault women for hoping. You're pretty hard to miss, and that's without them even knowing the best parts. Because those? Those you choose to give only to me."

Her words hardly finished, my mouth crashes down over hers in urgent hunger. Her lips part for me, and my tongue delves inside for a taste of what's mine as she runs her tiny hands up my chest, fisting my shirt and making those sounds she has to know drive me insane.

Some bumbling idiot bumps into my side, forcing us apart, and I remember where we are—and how ready I am to be somewhere else, alone with her. "Just to avoid any possible confusion in the future, I should probably tell you now—I won't be as reasonable if guys come on to you like that."

"After a while, that jealousy thing you're workin' will probably get on my nerves and we'll need to reconvene. But for now, it's hot and okay." She laughs. "Don't tell any feminists I said that."

We spend the next day getting Jarrett and I moved into our new apartments. I don't give a shit where my stuff goes, but Reece doesn't share my lack of concern. After holding the furniture delivery guys captive for almost two hours—I tipped them very well—she's now been in the kitchen, deciding what goes where, for just as long.

I, however, am in the living room, sitting on the couch she insisted they move one inch to the left, then right, at least four times. I'm having a beer and watching a documentary on the post-Civil War economy... because my cable doesn't get turned on until Monday and this is the only channel I can get, but more so because "Reece Homemaker" is fucking scary.

"Rhett," she calls from the kitchen, and I cringe, "would you rather your silverware drawer be the one closest to the dishwasher for easy unloading or under the plate cupboard so you can grab both at the same time?"

Apparently my easy agreement to her previous ten questions backfired. Instead of politely—'cause it's nice of her to help—sending the message that I don't fucking know what things like a "banana tree" are nor do I care where they go, my capitulation seems to have encouraged her to ask more questions. "How 'bout you take a break and come in here for a second?"

She does, blowing her hair out of the green eyes that bulge out at me expectantly. "I don't really have time for a break if I'm gonna get this done before we have to meet Jarrett and Landry for dinner."

I reach out and grab her hand, pulling her to me, then into my lap. "Teaspoon, it's very sweet of you to do all this. Thank you." I tuck some of her unruly hair behind her ear. "But stop. Don't know how you could've possibly forgotten, but I have a dick."

"What?" she blurts.

"Let me finish. I have a dick, which means not only do I not give a rat's ass where shit goes, but my girlfriend, who has a tight, warm little pussy, lives within throwing distance. Someone could break in here and steal, or rearrange," I gasp sarcastically, "every single thing, and I'd never even notice, 'cause guess where I'm gonna be?"

"*Girlfriend?*" It comes out a puff of air.

I have to laugh; of course that's all she heard. "You know that. So I'm assuming it's a *nice to hear* thing?"

She nods.

"Okay, well, I think it'd be nice to hear you say you're done with all that"—I nod toward the kitchen—"and what you'd really like is to fuck your man senseless before we have to meet them for dinner."

"I still think you guys should've named the group after me," Landry pours on another guilt trip from across the table. "After all, I'm the reason Reece was at On Tap that fateful night this all started. And it was also *me* who got her to come back for Rhett's birthday!"

She's not wrong. Landry's actually turned out to be... not half as bad as I originally suspected. As much as I frown upon the flaky stunts she pulls on Reece all too often, a couple of them lent destiny a hand.

"Think we're all set on the name, but I agree, I owe you a thank you. *Thank you,* Landry." I give her a genuine smile, and Reece's hand finds my leg under the table and squeezes her agreement.

"You're welcome." Landry lifts her chin proudly. "Oh, I know! Instead of the band name, you can repay me by doing a show at Goldsbury! Thatcher would totally agree—he asks me how you guys are doing all the time— JC too. Oh *please*, it'd be perfect."

"Sounds kickass to me." Jarrett looks at Reece as he says it. I'm unsure if it's because he sees her as "the boss" or simply because he respects her opinion—maybe a little of both.

"Um, yeah..." Reece stammers, quickly reaching for a drink of her water. "It's definitely something we should talk about. We'll let you know." She offers Landry a weak smile.

"Rhett?" Oh *now* Jarrett asks for my input, or rather, my backing.

I glare at him pointedly—no way am I touching that with a ten-foot pole. Reece obviously has an issue that I don't even have a guess on, and I'm not about to outnumber her publicly. Both my heads know better than that shit. "Like Reece said, we'll talk about it."

Our waitress mercifully times her arrival with our orders, and the subject's forgotten for now. Between Landry and Jarrett's penchant for yammering and some actual eating, there's no blatant silence, but Reece is sullen and only just politely participatory for the remainder of the meal. When we finish and say our good-byes—a tearful parting for the girls since Landry flies out early in the morning—I lead Reece to my car. *Yes*, I finally drove my own car tonight.

"Clue me in, Teaspoon, 'cause I got nothing," I say right before I shut her door and walk around to get in, giving her a few seconds notice that I noticed.

My door's unlocked when I get to it, and I notice that too—always will.

"We should do the Goldsbury. It's a great idea," she blurts the second I'm in the car. "If Jovie works out, maybe we could bring her too."

I admit I don't have the exact read on what she doesn't want to say quite yet, but I damn sure know how to coax it out of her. I don't respond to the bullshit cover she just rambled, but rather, dive right in to the coaxing. "That man?" I point at a couple walking past us to their car. "He's got a lot to learn about the woman beside him, but knowing when she's stewing over something and saying everything but what she really wants to? He's got that part down pat."

She doesn't respond right away, then finally does so with a snicker, "looks like we're on our own."

She nods toward the windshield, and I glance... well, shit. People storying only works when the *people* don't drive out of the parking lot. *Thanks man, good lookin' out.* I'll just sit here with mine, cranky and tongue-tied, while you go bed down with yours.

No sense sitting here any longer now, I start the car, and start thinking that relationships are a pain in the ass, when she sighs and reaches for my hand.

"I'd like to think that overall, I'm pretty easy to be involved with. Would you agree?" she asks.

She's lucky she threw in the "overall," hedging her bet, or my answer would be based on the last hour... and piss her off. "Generally speaking, yes, but you're definitely well-versed in some African tongue-clicking of your own." I glance from the road to her and grin. "And I don't even have your yellow sorted out yet, forget the other colors."

"Oh please," she huffs. "I'm a teeny bit out of sorts for one whole hour, and you're gonna try to say I'm as confusing as you? Ha! It may take me a little while sometimes, but I put stuff out there."

"Yeah? So you're ready to ask me about the thing with my dad? 'Cause it's been a little while, and you

325

haven't." I lift one brow, knowing she's staring at me as I stare at the road.

"What does that have to do with anything?"

Nothing, really. And I know the sensible thing to do is fight current fights, not old ones, but I've wondered about her not asking for a while now, and here's the opportunity to bring it up. "It's the perfect example, the very epitome of this entire conversation. A huge 'something you're not ready to put out there,' so I'm left guessing at what you're thinking or if you're even thinking about it at all." *Not as ill-timed as I thought; actually, now that I've said it, it is fitting.* "Use your words, Reece, even the ugly ones."

"That's a terrible example," she says with hushed significance. "I didn't not ask you about that because I was afraid to bring it up or because my words would be ugly, but because…"

"Because why?"

"You just turned the wrong way, captain." She fails to hide the tinge of laughter.

"Why didn't you say something sooner?"

"Uh, *because we're busy fighting?*"

In. Fucking. Furiating. "Reece, tell me where to go," I grate my staid warning.

She sighs and points. "Get in the left lane and turn around at that next light. I'll tell you when to exit."

I move into the left lane but turn instead into a parking lot… and park. "Look at me."

She does, without any dramatization. Unexpected but appreciated.

"Because *why*, Reece?"

She doesn't miss a beat, attune to exactly where I'm picking the conversation back up. "Because you were standing right there and heard yourself what I was told. I won't lie and say I haven't wondered about it, but I refuse to give them the power to affect you and me. They wanted to drive a wedge between us, make me doubt you. I *don't* doubt you, not for a second, and I trust that if you ever want me to know anything else about what happened, or why, you'll tell me."

"Just like that, huh?"

"I hear that's how it usually happens. Just like that." She snaps her fingers. "Anything else you wanna get off your chest?"

I want to ask her about what started all this in the first place—the cause of her sudden shift in mood tonight. But instead, I decide to return the blind faith she just explained—if she wants me to know, she'll tell me. So, resolved to that plan, I shake my head, thinking it's best not to speak quite yet. This round trip from fighting, which according to her we were doing, back to "us" is the least concerning part of the new, crazy feelings going on inside me, and I need a minute... or several.

"Great, then can we get out of here? You didn't exactly pick the safest spot to pull over, and I'm not in the right mood for a carjacking."

"Why didn't you say something about that sooner?" I snap to, starting the car and peeling out of the lot.

"Because we were busy making up." Her voice is soft and sentimental, which is sweet and doesn't go unnoticed, but...

"Oh, Tea." I laugh. "I'll show you how we really do that when we get home." If we're gonna do the whole "couples fight" thing, which we most definitely are since half of our couple is a woman, then we are even more certainly revamping our make-up procedure. "Which hinges on you sharing directions with me this time."

"Take the next exit, then you're on the freeway. I thought men never asked for directions?" she sasses.

"Depending on the destination, your man does. When we're going home and post-fight fucking is on the agenda, I'm asking."

CHAPTER twenty-eight

Reece

Three weeks later...

"Really, Reece, you brought the redhead? You're supposed to be my best friend and... and I don't even know you anymore!"

I have to be on stage in twenty minutes, and Landry's chosen now to drag me into the bathroom and shriek in my face about...

"What are we talking about?" I ask in a fabricated calm.

"That girl you brought, the one on stage, singing, with red hair?" Her voice scales up yet another octave as she flaps her arms around like a lunatic.

I dodging the potentially lethal limbs. "Jovie? What's the problem? She's great."

And she is—the first official artist signed to Crescendo *by me*. Jovie showed up that following Monday, right on time, with a binder full of original, heartfelt pieces, a hungry sparkle in her eyes, and a willingness to work as hard as needed. I couldn't put a contract in front of her fast enough. And she's real; I only had to tell her once that Rhett is mine, and she's acted nothing but accordingly.

"The problem? You have to ask? Tell me she's not fucking Jarrett! I saw the way he looked at her that night, and that's when I *was* there! Lord knows what they've been doing since then while I'm not! What is it about goddamned redheads?"

Ah, now I'm caught up.

"Landry"—I duck and weave, latching onto her shoulders to settle her wild arms—"I can't do this right now. I gotta go on stage, but let me give you something to think about, and when I'm done, if you still want to talk about this, we will. Deal?"

Her face wrinkles in sour skepticism. "What?"

"I don't think she and Jarrett are having sex. We've all been really focused on getting ready for tonight."

That's the understatement of the year. From the second I told the boys I was definitely on board to do a show in Vegas, they insisted on two practices a day. Rhett didn't have to tell me that performing at his old stomping grounds, in front of Thatcher and JC, was beyond important to him. Tonight's show needs to be flawless.

"But even if they were, why would it matter? Do you and Jarrett have some arrangement or commitment I'm unaware of?" I ask her.

She puffs up, crossing her arms defensively. "Well, no, not exactly."

"And can you look me in the face and honestly say you haven't messed around with anyone else?" I challenge her with a loving smile.

"I get it, sheesh—whose side are you on?"

"Always yours." I hold my arms open for a hug. "I'm sure Jarrett will enjoy his time with you while he's here. Just don't be mean to Jovie, okay? No scaring off the talent." I laugh, giving her one last squeeze.

"Fine, but she's not hanging out with us at *our* after party! I'm drawing the line there."

I release her and step back. "Yes, she is. I brought her here and have no intention of making her feel like an outcast. And fair warning, I'm not hanging out for very long afterwards, Lan. Sorry, but I've got post-show plans of my own."

Do I ever. Rhett never asked me what had *started* our fight that night several weeks ago; luckily he got distracted by getting us home and showing me the proper way to make-up. The rest of the weekend. Ever since, I *look* for reasons to squabble so he'll remind me of such procedure. But most importantly, it bought me time—to come to my senses.

My initial reaction when Landry had suggested a show in Vegas was a resounding hell no! The thought of returning to my boyfriend's old "sin den" and seeing women he'd been with in the ways he's only with me now... no woman would knowingly put herself through that, right?

Wrong.

You only run from that which you're afraid of, and I'm not afraid that Rhett doesn't love me. Maybe he hasn't actually said it yet, but he tells me every day in his smiles, looks, secrets, time. In everything he chooses to share with me, he tells me. So I tossed my "insecure panties" right out the window and strapped on my sneaky, confident girlfriend pair. He'll never know I had doubts that night... or what hit him on this one.

"Reece, hello?" Landry waves her hand in front of my face, bringing me out of my fog. "I asked you a question."

"Crap, we gotta go. Come on!" I grab her hand and rush back toward the stage.

"But you didn't answer me," she whines. "What're these big plans that you're ditching me for? I never get to see you!"

"I'll tell you later, promise." I let go of her hand and wave as I head backstage, and despite her frustration, she blows me a kiss.

Rhett's pacing, twirling a drumstick through his fingers in double-time as I hurry up to him. "You sure you're done? You weren't gone very long," he grumps sarcastically.

"I wasn't pooping," I blurt, fire springing to my cheeks.

"Well, okay, as long as you weren't pooping." He laughs, tapping the end of my nose. "Ozzie called, made me promise to tell you he said he loves you and good luck. Oh, and for me to break a leg, preferably both of them."

I snicker and shake my head; even staying behind to run the company, my Ozzie thought of me—and found a way to harass Rhett (who secretly likes it, makes me feel important if he can keep Ozzie riled up). I love their banter. It's their macho way of bonding, which they do more of every day, and it means the world to me to watch the two most important men in my life slowly accept one another.

"Where's Jarrett?" I ask, looking around and coming up short.

He magically appears, a beaming Liz in tow. "Right here! Look who I found!"

"What the hell?" I don't think Rhett realizes he said that out loud, wide-eyes on Liz. "What're you doing here?"

"Ask your girlfriend." She grins my way then hugs Rhett. "Cannon's in the front row with his sister. Told me to tell you good luck."

Rhett stares at me, his steely blue eyes brimming with gravity. "You?"

I nod and flash him a wink. I knew it'd mean the world to him to have Liz here tonight, so I snuck into his phone while he showered and made it happen. As an amazing man once said—I'm just full of surprises.

"Thank you," he murmurs to me. "And you"—he looks at Liz—"thanks for coming. No Con-man this time either?"

She laughs. "No, you're gonna have to come to him. He refuses to leave the girls."

"I'll see what I can do." He glances at me then Jarrett, who's already bobbing his head in agreement. "You got room for three, Mrs. Blackwell?"

"You know it." She pats his chest. "I'm gonna go grab my seat. Show me something, boys!" She somehow finds my hand, and her squeeze brings my eyes to hers. "*You*, show their asses up."

"I heard that!" Jarrett yells at her retreating back.

"The hell you did," she calls over her shoulder. "Everybody knows you can't hear a damn thing!"

We give the Goldsbury crowd a phenomenal show if I do say so myself—which I do. As Jarrett strums the final notes on "Lone Worth," our closer of the nine-song set, I glance down to front center and see Liz brush away a tear, Cannon leaning in to kiss the top of her head. Landry and JC are at their table, smiling just as wide as they have the entire performance. I'm gonna pretend I didn't somehow notice where Sommerlyn disappeared to, or with whom.

I thank the crowd and step back, showcasing the guys. I'm ready to head off stage when his voice freezes me in place. I turn and watch him climb from behind the drums, his hair and shirt wet with sweat, biceps hyper-flexed and glistening from all that banging.

"One more, Tea," he growls into his head mic, eyes searing into mine.

I barely register movement to my side—I assume it's Jarrett setting me on a stool? But I can't look away from Rhett to confirm. I'm entranced as he moves behind the keyboards. Apparently I'm not the only one with surprises up my sleeve.

"Anybody mind if I play one more?" he asks the crowd, receiving a booming response of whistles and cheers. When the roar dies down, he winks at me, the sexiest of all his smirks he's saved til' now on his face. "You always seem to listen better if I sing it, so *hear me*, Teaspoon."

Using only his rich, sensuous voice and the keys, he never breaks our locked gazes as he sings "Never Stop," the slow, wedding version, by SafetySuit. When he learned to play piano, I know not. I'm also a little fuzzy on where we are or my own name, but I know this song... and what he's telling me with it.

He loves me.

I'll never get used to him either.

Liz *finally* yawns. I was counting on her to tucker out long ago, and I'm so anxious, I'm squirming in my seat. Landry, incredibly concerned I wouldn't stick around, wandered off with Jarrett at least an hour ago, and JC very kindly offered to "make sure Jovie found her room all right" about that same time. No one's made mention of where anyone else is, and I'm certainly not bringing it up. So the four of us—me, Rhett, Liz, and Cannon—are the last ones standing.

"Thank you again for inviting us, Reece. I knew it'd be great, but I gotta say"—Liz grins at Rhett—"that finale? Wouldn't have believed it if I hadn't seen it with my own two eyes. I'm happy you're happy, Rhett. You sure held out long enough, waiting for the best." She shifts her thoughtful regard to me. "You succeeded."

Arm around my shoulders, he pulls me in closer and lays a soft kiss on my temple. "Don't give her a big head, Liz. She won't be able to carry it around on her little body."

"Cute, but you can drop the act. We're all on to you after that song." Liz rolls her eyes and stands. "If you wanna get laid with me awake, let's go," she tells her husband.

Cannon jumps up so fast his chair topples over, and we all laugh.

"Breakfast in the morning," she yells while being carried away.

"Man's so desperate to get some, he forgot to care where his sister is. Thank God—I'm not dealing with other people's bullshit tonight. I need a shower, bed, and you." Rhett stands and offers me his hand. "Where are we sleeping?"

"I thought you'd never ask," I purr, knees trembling. I'm about to reveal my final surprise, my solution to any lingering doubts I had about coming back here. I pull the key card from between my cleavage and slip it into his palm. The final, *lasting* memory of any "trips" will be of *us*.

"Tonight, Mr. Foster, you and I are visiting Hawaii."

Arabian Nights Suite

Thatcher King

"I could go another round."

"I have to get back to work, but you're more than welcome to stay and rest. Room is yours for the night." It's the least I can do; she could probably use the rest after all the things she just let me do to her. This one? Wild and insatiable, a defiant edge to her voice as she demanded more from me with an unmistakable glint of rebellion in her eyes. She was fucking to forget something or someone.

"Turn around and look at me," she demands, the unique determination in her tone so different from the petulance I expected that I'm compelled to grant her request. "I thought you were the man in charge?" She gives me a daring grin, her tousled curls cascading around her shoulders, lips swollen, impeccable body bare.

"Your point?" I continue dressing, denying my baser urge to take her again. If things were different, I'd let her talk me into spending some more time in her.

"You're the boss. You don't *have* to get back to work, and we both know it. Don't talk to me like of your bimbos, Mr. King. Walk over here like a man, call me by my name, and kiss me long and hard. That's how you properly thank a lady who knew exactly what she was doing and gave it as good as she got."

Oh, she's cunning, trying to set herself apart with the cool indifference act, a classic bait-and-switch. It's unfortunate she doesn't mean a word of it. A good chase might actually entertain me for a while. But she was an excellent fuck, and this game she's trying to play is far more enjoyable than tears and shameless begging. So I'll indulge her, briefly.

I cross the room and stop at the edge of the bed, bending to wrap a hand around the back of her long, slender nape. "I had a wonderful time, Sommerlyn. Enjoy the room and let my staff know if you require anything else."

I cover her mouth with hard finality. Her response is swift and violent, her moans delicious as I delve my tongue in to command hers. Coming up on her knees, she presses for more—more friction for her nipples against my chest, more depth to our mouths colliding… more.

I take one last taste and step back, chest heaving in cadence with hers. "Safe trip home, gorgeous."

"We'll see." She bounces her shoulders in carefree dismissal. "Hang on." She walks on her knees to bridge the gap I created. "Your tie's crooked, *Boss*."

Coming next in the Finally Found novels…

Thatcher King's story!

S.E.Hall, lover of all things anticipation and romance, is the author of The Evolve Series: Emerge, Embrace, Entangled, Entice and Baby Mama Drama, as well as the stand-alone novel Pretty Instinct. Her co-written works included The Provocative Professions Collection: Stirred Up, Packaged and Handled, One Naughty Night and full-length novel Matched with Angela Graham as well as Conspire, a romantic suspense with Erin Noelle.

S.E. resides in Arkansas with her husband of 18 years and 3 daughters of the home. When not writing or reading, she can be found "enthusiastically cheering" on one of her girls' softball games.

Newsletter: http://eepurl.com/7E-nP

Facebook: https://www.facebook.com/S.E.HallAuthorEmerge

Amazon: http://www.amazon.com/S.E.-Hall/e/B00D0AB9TI/

Twitter: https://twitter.com/Emergeauthor

Tumblr: http://sehallauthor.tumblr.com/

S.E. Hall

EVOLVE SERIES

Emerge

Embrace

Entangled

Entice

Sawyer Beckett's Baby Mama Drama Guide For Dummies

FINALLY FOUND NOVELS

Pretty Instinct

Pretty Remedy

CO-WRITTEN BESTSELLERS

WITH ANGELA GRAHAM

Matched

Stirred Up

Packaged

Handled

Pretty Remedy

Handled 2

One Naughty Night

WITH ERIN NOELLE

Conspire

 *playlist*

Pretty Remedy Playlist

Red Nose–Sage The Gemini

Over The Rainbow–Israel Kamakawiwo'ole

The Fear–Ben Howard

Dark Horse–Katy Perry

In The Air Tonight–Phil Collins

Fancy–Iggy Azalea

Black–Pearl Jam

I've Got This Friend–The Civil Wars

Broken–Seether

The Blower's Daughter–Damien Rice

Clocks–Coldplay

Lover, Lover–Jerrod Niemann

Never Stop–SafetySuit

acknowledgements

This part never gets any easier; it's almost as hard as the blurb. I'm so scared that once I start on specific names, I will forget someone... and I don't ever want to do that. So many people are important to me, people who help in little, big, and sideways every single day. If I named them all, the acknowledgements would be longer than the book.

So let me just say—if your name isn't in here, it doesn't mean I don't acknowledge and appreciate everything you do for me. I hope I tell you "thank you" so many times you get sick of hearing it and let you know what you mean to me.

Julie Fleming- this world lost you tonight. You will be greatly missed, every single day. Your warmth, love, kind heart and thoughtfulness touched so many. I will never forget the many special things you did for me, and your Elite family, to let us know we were loved. Your precious husband and children will be prayed for daily and asked how we can help ease their pain; we promise. XOXO Mama and Elite

Jeff—I wouldn't eat or have clean clothes, the utilities wouldn't get paid, and who knows where the kids would be if it weren't for you... so I think it's safe to say: I couldn't pursue my dream of writing without you. You provide more than support. You carry me over your shoulder, walking barefoot over shards of glass covered in snow uphill both ways, through life. I love you.

S.E. Hall

Girls—Thank you for loving me for the mom I am. No, I'm not like her mom or that mom, or… any mom you know really. But I love you, I'd die for you, and everything I do is for you.

My family—It's been a rough year. The next one may hold a few suckholes too, but I know I have you, so I'm gonna keep on keepin' on. Thank you. I love you all.

Amy Lynn—I love you, little sister. I didn't tell you that enough until recently. I'm proud of you and am here for you, anything you need. As long as I have breath, you are not alone—and I will help you fix it. (As long as you keep typing. Just kidding.)

Lyndsey Gene, Amber Jean, and Rachelle Jones—THANK YOU for helping me knock this one out! Your love of crooked lines, hand edits, and my meltdowns mean the world to me. I couldn't have done it without you. I love you all! xoxox

Angela Graham—I'm better for knowing you—a better writer, friend, and person. Knowing I have you in my corner, a phone call away, is a comfort for which I'll never be able to repay you. I love you very much; you're my best friend. I love writing with you, talking about anything and everything… and you always know what to say. I sincerely wouldn't have made it these last few months without you; you're now my "say what I need to hear" phone call, the one on my side no matter what.

Hilary Storm, Erin Noelle, and Ashley Suzanne—you're so special to me, so different, but each an intricate part of what makes me whole. I love you all and am so very thankful to call you friends. Hilary always gives it to me straight up, followed immediately by "let's make it happen, what can I do?" Erin is always kind, soft, and shining the sun on it, whatever it is. Smoopy keeps my heart pure. And Bat Ashley—my go-to for "how do we laugh about this shit?" The one who says random funny stuff (that only I understand) until I forget to cry. I love you, girl, always.

346

Toski Covey—To this day, you believe in me. You "get me," and I love you for it. I always feel better after one of our calls... and then I stop and realize, we just covered, like, seventy-eight topics in an hour. That's awesome. You're my short lil' oink human, TCo, I love you. Thank you for ALL you've done for me. I wouldn't be the same, my books wouldn't be the same, without you.

Sommer Stein—I love you, sis. You're amazing, always putting up with my bat-shit crazy, disorganized self with love and a beautiful vision no one else could emulate. Thank you. xo

Jill Sava—Jillsy, I don't have enough or the right words. Basically, I adore you and I think you're one of the most amazing people I have ever had the honor to know. I draw inspiration from you every single day, and I sleep better knowing "Jill's got this shit." You're... the exception to all I thought I knew. I love you. Thank you.

Cyndi Shortcake—Thank you for all your help, your sweet lil' voice, your seldom seen but funny as hell when it is big bad angry voice, and for being my friend. I love you very much!

Carrie "Cookie" Horton—I love you, Cookie! Your help has been so appreciated, thank you! You're a good lady, and I'm lucky as hell to have you! You've been in my life for a while now, and I'm beyond blessed every single one of those days. xoxo

Angela Doughty (Cupcake), Tabby Coots (TabbyCat), Bethany Castaneda (SheSaw), Kellie Montgomery (MonkeyButt) and Michelle Shock (you down with a nickname if I give you one? LOL)—Ladies, you are one fine ass army of awesomeness!!!! Each of you are there to help me with anything I need, anytime, and never ask for anything in return. I love you girls so much and want to make sure you know I appreciate it and I thank you! xo

ELITE—I know, and I swear I'm about to cry because I didn't list every single one of you by name. But I know your names, and where you live, and your birthdays, and your kids' names, and I love you, all of you. NO ONE ROCKS LIKE ELITE ROCKS!!!!! This group—you love each other, you're kind, you lift one another up… I couldn't be more blessed by each and every one of you. THANK YOU xoxoxo Mama

Rhett's Beta Readers: Michelle Grad (my heat-seeking missile), Linda Cotter, Jennifer Flory, Van Wyk, Toski Covey, Carrie Horton, Cyndi Lane, Jill Sava, Lacy Daniel, Kelly Adamo, Angela Doughty, and Kailie Sarkissian… thank you, ladies, for helping bring Rhett to life, telling me what I needed to hear, and supporting me. I appreciate you all so much! xo

Tracie Short and Sandra Macom—my Darlin' Duo. I love you both so much. If I don't hear from you for more than a few days, I feel like a limb is missing. Here's to Tits, smoke benches, MY TREAT AT SUBWAY DAMMIT, and that .10 ticket!!!!! xoxoxxo

My Angel, Nicole Kelsey—You take my breath away. I literally think you are an angel amongst us. I didn't know humans really had the capacity to be THAT selfless, kind, and compassionate. If I could be anyone else, it'd be you.

Ena Burnette—I love you, girl! Thank you for all your love and support these years! xoxo

Author Love—Thank you, ladies! xo ONE LOVE!

Brenda Wright—I'm sorry. LOL—I owe you about a thousand of those. (Please see the part above about being disorganized.) Thank you, girl!

Cassie C, Madeleine F, Monkeybutt, Jill S and Katherine H— Thank you for overlooking the scattered mess I am and making the words… pretty.

Erin Roth—Always has my back. Thank you girl! xo

And to the readers, bloggers, and other authors who continue to support my books, lend an ear, and share the love... THANK YOU!

S.E. HALL

ANGELA GRAHAM

The Meet Your Mate Mixer is, not surprisingly, a clever name for a let's-see-who'll-get-sloshed-and-hook-up-first-to-boost-ratings free-for-all. It's made up of sixteen very attractive, single-for-the-most-part young people with a beach sunset in the background, bump-n'-grind music pumping, and a table filled with free alcohol as far as the eye can see.

Oakley's off to the side with a few of the other guys, and judging by his animated facial expressions and Heisman moves that he's telling them all about himself, one great play at a time.

So far, Jasmine and I have stuck together. We're sitting on one of the white velvet couches—totally appropriate, and often found on a beach—each nursing our first drink.

"Should we dance, or try to mingle?" she asks, sounding as unsure as my answer will be.

"I guess we could." I scan the room for the least-intimidating-looking targets with whom to socialize. "How about them?" I point to a group of three girls—one I know to be Callie Cole, an Olympic gymnast.

"Good choice." Jasmine smiles with a nod, and up we go.

While I make my way across the tent, I steal an indirect glance at Oakley, who's no more aware of my whereabouts than he is of nuclear physics. The Russian supermodel whose name I'm not sure of has joined his group, though, seemingly fascinated with his football stories.

Jasmine nudges my shoulder, smiling when she sees where my focus has traveled. "He's just a proud man showing off. Don't overthink it, Harlow."

I force a small smile of agreement and decide once and for all that she and I will be great friends.

"Hi, ladies," Jasmine announces for us as we arrive upon the trio. "Mind if we meet and greet with you?"

"Of course not! I'm Callie, and this is—"

"I'm Anya McCall," a cute little brunette chirps, her eyes the color of sapphires and shining brightly with an excitement I can't begin to describe. I say "little" because "frail" seems insulting, but I think a strong gust of wind might literally knock her over.

"Anya? That's different," the third girl in the group says with an evil snicker. "Has anyone been *Anya* tonight? I bet you'll have something *inya* before the week is through."

The vulgar crack is more appalling than funny, which is probably why no one else laughs.

"Emma. Your name's Emma!" A deep growl comes from behind her, the body attached to the sinister sound soon revealed.

I can tell instantly that they're related. His hair's a darker brown, leaning more toward black than her blondish highlights, but their eyes are that identical deep blue and they have the same chin. And not that he's smiling, but their mouths are shaped similarly. The biggest differences are that likely even a tsunami couldn't knock him over, and there's absolutely no excitement emitting from him.

Anya or Emma—I'm unsure at this point—rolls her eyes with an exasperated huff before droning out the guy's introduction. "This is my older brother, Cruz, motocross extraordinaire, X Games champ, and royal pain in my ass."

"I know who you are," the same girl cracking pathetic jokes purrs, slinking closer to him. "You're the Motorbike God. I love to watch." Her fingers trail up his chest, and my gag reflex kicks in. "It's so dangerous, so…sexy. Like you. I'm Rachel Gardner, by the way, stand-up comedian. But some things I take *very* seriously."

"I can see how you wouldn't get a lot of practice at subtlety, being a comic," Callie quips, straight-faced. Better than Jasmine and I, who almost choke on our drinks. Now *that* was funny. I'd say—not out loud, of course—that they should switch jobs, but Rachel's not exactly built like a gymnast.

"At least I'm current. How many years ago did you actually place in something, again?" Rachel digs, the ugliest sneer curling her mouth.

"I'm Harlow McWright," I blurt out, my hate for confrontation propelling me, and all eyes cut my way. "I'm not good at much…famous for nothing.

Oakley," I say, pointing at him, "brought me as his plus one. We've known each other since high school."

Cruz looks over his shoulder in Oakley's direction, then pins a scrutinizing stare on me but says nothing. It's odd, but in a broody, hot way that definitely works for him.

And just as quickly, he's focused back on his sister. "Seriously, Em, just tell people your damn first name and leave out the middle part. It's *not* cute, and I don't think you want me to go to jail for killing someone, right?."

"Shoo," she tells him while literally shooing him with a wave of her hand. Surprisingly, he complies and stalks back to his chair, with Rachel right on his heels. *Yes, please, take her with you.* She's a nasty piece of work.

This leaves me, Jasmine, Callie, and whom I believe should be called Emma for everyone's safety quickly easing into friendly conversation and grabbing flutes of champagne when the waiter passes by. Emma must have a special taste for something else, considering she's handed a red plastic cup.

"I forgot how intense your brother can be," Callie says with a laugh, revealing they already know each other.

"Oh, that's right, you did that Medal Challenge thing with him. Girl, that was one weekend and how many other contestants?" Emma replies, scrunching her nose but smiling. "Try spending twenty-one years as his little sister!"

"Touché." Callie tips back her glass and empties it.

All the drinking leads to a laughter-filled dance with all the classics, the sprinkler, shopping cart, lawnmower, and epic funky chicken. It's the most fun I've had in years.

"Y'all ready for a break?" Emma yells over the beats, fanning her extremely flushed cheeks. "I gotta sit down."

Before she can take one full step toward a chair, Cruz catches her elbow, guiding her to a table. She looks exhausted, and is the first to chug the ice water that's offered by a young woman—an intern, I assume—who scurries quickly back to her spot beside the producer. He's a scary, serious man wearing an earpiece and watching us closely.

I recall his name is Adam, flushing at the memory of being introduced briefly before filming began and assuming he was security. That mistake was cleared up instantly, to my humiliation. To my credit, though, it was an easy blunder considering his broad shoulders and muscular form, not to mention the permanent scowl that makes the Secret Service seem playful. I guess I pictured a producer looking different, or being...older.

Adam's in his mid-thirties, tops, with hair as black as midnight and trimmed perfectly. He's the only person on the crew wearing black slacks and a dress shirt, rolled to his elbows and open at the top, his dark tie hanging loose. The way he carries himself is in the air surrounding him, all business and to the point, without cracking a smile even when he explained security would be in white polos and khakis. But despite his dressy producer duds and serious demeanor, there's something wild about him.

And considering we're at the beach, it's an odd sight...but it somehow suits him well.

"Hey, there you are!"

A tipsy Callie snares my attention then stalls, her mouth falling open when she notices the couple dry humping at the table. How they're not the first thing we *all* spotted, I'm not sure. "Ladies, this is my plus one, my best friend, Dana."

We say hello but Dana barely acknowledges us, enraptured by the guy she's literally riding. She's wearing a long, flowing green gown that's covering his lap but does little to hide what I nauseatingly suspect is actually happening under it.

"Maybe we should give them some privacy," I suggest, which is insane since there are cameras everywhere. What I *meant* was, "I'd rather do anything but watch. Anyone care to join me in leaving?"

Callie's not having it, which I could've guessed just from what little I know about her already. "Dana, who's your *friend*?" she asks with a loud bite.

"Oh!" Dana snickers and pries her lips from his, her hips still gyrating. "This is Dalton. He's Nadia's trainer."

"Nadia's the whore—I mean, the *model* hanging on your man," Jasmine leans over and whispers in my ear. My head's filled with too many champagne bubbles and I've already been ignored for almost two hours by said man, so I simply give a curt, uncaring nod.

It's those same bubbles I'm blaming for my next totally uncharacteristic outburst. "I thought you were the guy on *Criminal Minds*!" I more than yell at Dalton. I swear I did—the hot, badass one. *Morgan, is it?*

"Oh my God, me too!" Dana squeals, leaning further into him, if that's possible. "But then I saw you up close, baby, and you're way hotter than Shemar Moore."

His eyes slam shut and a deep inhale hisses through his bared, gritted teeth. He grips Dana's swiveling hips and holds her still, confirming his dick is, in fact, engaged, and no doubt wishing we'd get the hell out of here. I'm wishing so too.

I've never witnessed sex before. Even if they are hiding it, there's a camera not ten feet away—and equipped with zoom, I'm guessing. Surely the viewers will just think she's wiggling around to get comfortable. Yep, bet her mom will buy that too when she watches.

Dalton's head falls back and he moans, "Damn, like a dream come true."

"I know, baby, I know," she answers, her eyes open and a huge, pleased smile on her face. "It's like you and I were meant to meet here. We practically have the same brain."

"Or split a small one," Cruz grumbles, vigilant at his post beside Emma.

A smirk crosses my lips, and I get one in return when I glance his way—his first not-murderous expression of the night.

"We sure do. You're just my type." Dalton's head snaps up and he grabs the back of hers, pulling her closer for a sloppy kiss.

"I was thinking the same thing, Smoopy," Dana croons against his mouth, her back arching.

"Are they—" Emma starts to ask, as though unaware she's speaking aloud. *Yes, it's that shocking.*

"Aaand we're done here!" Cruz barks.

Dalton's lips fall to Dana's chest that I have a feeling won't remain covered for much longer. I finally whip around to spare myself the view, wobbly on my feet.

"Easy there," Cruz whispers, his hands steadying me at my waist.

I'm drunk; he and I both know. In fact, everyone does—except my boyfriend, who's still reliving game plays.

"Thanks," I mumble as he releases me. I lean back to catch his eyes—the ones that move from me across the lawn, narrowing when they land on Oakley. I expect Cruz to call out for him to come get his mess of a girlfriend, but instead, he turns abruptly to his sister.

"Come on, Em, time to head to bed. I'll walk you ladies up too." He glares into me. "Since you have no *escorts*. It's late, and liquor's flowing. Let's go."

Emma's pouting but she stands, as does Callie with a yawn, while Jasmine questions me silently.

"I'd, uh...better wait for Oakley. He wouldn't—"

"Quarterback!" Cruz shouts in his direction.

"He's a lineman," I cut in, but Cruz just shakes his head and continues.

"Seeing these ladies back to the house!"

Oakley manages to raise a hand in "Thanks, bro" acknowledgment. I refuse to look at anyone, painfully aware tears will spring to my eyes if I see puzzled disappointment in theirs.

The five of us head up to the house without a word—that is, until Emma can no longer hold in what the rest of us are still mulling over in our hazy brains.

"So, I'm not crazy—they were having sex, right?"

Cruz rumbles a "Jesus" as we all do our best to continue an unglamorous walk/stumble, holding onto each other and him through fits of laughter.

Get Matched Now!

Made in the USA
Columbia, SC
08 April 2018